Penguin

FAT, FIFTY & F***ED!

Dedicated with much love to the gorgeous Wilma Schinella, my inspiration, muse, main squeeze, partner-in-crime, editor-in-residence, travelling companion par excellence, and general all-round extraordinary human being.

ACKNOWLEDGEMENTS

Many thanks to Morris Gleitzman, who read an early draft and enthusiastically encouraged me to keep going; Australian Voices in Print, and Irina Dunn at the NSW Writers Centre, who announced their 2003 Popular Fiction Competition at exactly the right moment; agent and competition judge Selwa Anthony, who read all the entries and decided mine had something extra; Bob Sessions, Publishing Director at Penguin, who agreed with Selwa; publisher Clare Forster, who guided me along a new path with humour and grace; designer Nikki Townsend, whose cover you couldn't miss at a mile; and again, SuperAgent Selwa Anthony, who has been there every step of the way, with Selena Hanet-Hutchins just a half-step behind her.

FAT, FIFTY & F***ED!

GEOFFREY McGEACHIN

PENGUIN BOOKS

PENGUIN BOOKS

Published by the Penguin Group
Penguin Group (Australia)
250 Camberwell Road, Camberwell, Victoria 3124, Australia
(a division of Pearson Australia Group Pty Ltd)
Penguin Group (USA)
375 Hudson Street, New York, New York 10014, USA
Penguin Group (Canada)
10 Alcorn Avenue, Toronto, Ontario, Canada M4V 3B2
(a division of Pearson Canada Inc.)
Penguin Books Ltd
80 Strand, London WC2R 0RL, England
Penguin Ireland
25 St Stephen's Green, Dublin 2, Ireland
(a division of Penguin Books Ltd)
Penguin Group (India)
11, Community Centre, Panchsheel Park, New Delhi – 110 017, India
Penguin Group (NZ)
Cnr Airborne and Rosedale Roads, Albany, Auckland, New Zealand
(a division of Pearson New Zealand Ltd)
Penguin Group (South Africa) (Pty) Ltd
24 Sturdee Avenue, Rosebank, Johannesburg 2196, South Africa

Penguin Books Ltd, Registered Offices: 80 Strand, London, WC2R 0RL, England

First published by Penguin Group (Australia),
a division of Pearson Australia Group Pty Ltd, 2004

10 9 8 7 6 5 4 3 2

Text copyright © Geoffrey McGeachin 2004

The moral right of the author has been asserted

All rights reserved. Without limiting the rights under copyright reserved above, no part of this publication may be reproduced, stored in or introduced into a retrieval system, or transmitted, in any form or by any means (electronic, mechanical, photocopying, recording or otherwise), without the prior written permission of both the copyright owner and the above publisher of this book.

Design by Nikki Townsend © Penguin Group (Australia)
Cover illustrations by Andrew Hopgood
Typeset in Berkeley Oldstyle 11.5pt by Post Pre-Press Group, Brisbane, Queensland
Printed and bound in Australia by McPherson's Printing Group, Maryborough, Victoria

National Library of Australia
Cataloguing-in-Publication data:

McGeachin, Geoffrey.
   Fat, fifty and f***ed!
   ISBN 0 14 300257 0.
   1. Midlife crisis – Fiction. 2. Men – Fiction. I. Title.

A823.4

www.penguin.com.au

one

A three-quarter moon sat low in the night sky, its pale glow illuminating the lumpy puddles of vomit dotting the deserted forecourt of Burrinjuruk's two-star Truck-on-Inn hotel/motel. It was just on four in the morning and the biggest party in the small town's long history had finally fallen on its face. Security spotlighting flared around open-topped 44-gallon fuel drums overflowing with greasy paper plates, chop bones, crushed beer cans and flattened wine casks. Buttressed by glistening piles of empty stubbies and longnecks, the drums cast elongated shadows out across the silent roadway. The sound of a tinny guitar and drunken singing from an upstairs room indicated that some die-hard revellers were determined to party on downhill into the rapidly oncoming dawn.

In a parking area behind the motel, the passenger door of a cherry-red Kenworth semitrailer swung open and a thin, dark-haired, forty-something woman lowered herself tentatively to the ground. She stood for a moment, swaying on her stilettos, then established balance. With the flat of her hand she attempted to smooth the creases out of her cocktail dress but quickly realised it was a lost cause. She glanced at the gold Lady Rolex on her wrist and swore. Moving slowly, with the studied inelegance of someone trying to persuade themselves they're not too drunk to drive, the woman tottered across the uneven asphalt towards a row of parked cars. She took the crumpled silk knickers protruding from her handbag and tossed them in the general direction of one of the overflowing bins. They missed.

Her car, a newish, metallic-silver Volvo Estate, stood out among the collection of dented and aging hatchbacks, utes and panel vans that crowded the car park. She backed out too quickly and the Volvo's rear bumper nudged one of the temporary wooden barricades set up for the party. She swore again. Luckily for her, the motel had an extra-wide driveway to accommodate the giant, long-haul meat trucks that were its main customers. The Volvo found the approximate centre of the exit ramp and pulled slowly out onto the empty roadway, beneath a neon sign flashing the message: GAS-GRUB-GROG-24/7.

Five kilometres further down the road, Col Curtis twisted in his seat and scratched awkwardly at his left shoulder. He glanced across at the speed radar. Dashboard-mounted, the unit's digital display indicated it was currently in standby mode. Curtis's white, police-issue Land Cruiser was tucked discreetly into Burrinjuruk's only major side street, next to the bank. Sergeant Colin Curtis was in a very good mood. Drunks and speeders hadn't been a problem tonight, which was absolutely fine by him. He knew most of his local troublemakers would have passed out at the motel by now, and the recently opened bypass was already taking nearly all the heavy through traffic away from his patch. Things had certainly changed since he first arrived in town.

For many years Burrinjuruk, nestled at the bottom of a steep hill, had been a notorious late-night speed trap. Interstate truckies, operating on amphetamines, low profit margins and impossibly tight schedules, loathed the township. From midnight to dawn, with all sensible civilians tucked up in bed, the truckies considered the deserted roadways their own and they had hated Burrinjuruk's former resident cop with a passion. Curtis's predecessor was an officious bastard and it was his technique, as much as the speeding tickets and demerit points, that riled them. Hand raised and waving his radar gun, he would leap dramatically from the shadows out onto the highway, posing heroically under the town's single streetlight. One dark night, an unknown driver used his rig to turn the officer into a thirty-metre, red, pink and brown smear on the bitumen. There were no skidmarks on the roadway, nor any other evidence of swerving, braking or evasive action by the truck.

The following morning, a service station forty k's down the highway reported a forced entry. Nothing was missing, but a high-pressure water cleaning gun had been used and neatly replaced. Forensic police from Albury carefully collected some bits and pieces from the service-station drain to add to what had been scraped off the highway in Burrinjuruk.

The funeral was not well attended and was marred by derisive, staccato airhorn blasts from passing trucks. As the deceased officer's replacement, Colin Curtis had represented the state's police force at the service.

Sergeant Colin Curtis liked his new job, and the truckies liked his attitude. They slowed down a little and he eased up a lot, but only from midnight to dawn. During daylight hours the road rules were rigidly enforced. Burrinjuruk, a quiet town and a one-man station, turned out to be an ideal posting for Curtis. A house and his sergeant's stripes came with the job. There was no way he would have been promoted in the city, even with his record. You had to go along to get along in the big smoke, and there were some things he just wouldn't do. This little town was better than most city precincts for an older officer, and anyway, he had really hated all those years of being Constable Colin Curtis.

Though technically off duty from ten, Curtis spent most nights like this, in uniform, in the Land Cruiser, parked next to the bank. He was just reaching for his thermos of coffee when headlights appeared over the crest of the hill.

The radar beeped a moment later. Curtis glanced over at the display. Forty. He shook his head. As good as any breathalyser reading at this time of night. Drunks either drove too slow, to avoid attracting attention, or too fast, hoping to get home before the accident happened. The car rolled past and Curtis frowned. There was only one Volvo like that in the whole shire. He looked at his watch. Ten past four. She was really rubbing his nose in it this time. Let it go, he decided after a moment. Poor old Martin was going to have enough on his plate this morning without having to bail out the wife on a DUI.

The Volvo disappeared into the night. Curtis twisted in his seat as the itching started up again. Sitting up high, he rubbed the troublesome shoulderblade against the headrest. He liked the itching, even after thirty-odd years. It usually kept him awake all night, which was exactly the way he liked it. When you're awake you can't dream.

two

On the other side of town Martin Carter was also awake. He lay in bed willing his mind to go blank, with the same spectacular lack of success he'd had over the past six hours. A possum landed on the corrugated-iron roof of the house with a familiar dull thud. Martin remembered the possum trap up in the rafters of the garage, above the old two-stroke Victa. Christ, bloody lawnmowers. He was wondering how many hours of his life he'd frittered away walking mindlessly up and down behind that damned lawnmower, when he heard the Volvo's engine cut out, followed by the crunch of gravel under the tyres as she freewheeled up to the garage. Very considerate. A light touch of a finger on the bedside alarm clock and the time was projected onto the ceiling. Four-fifteen. Thank God for the Innovations mail-order catalogue. Infidelity could now be made easily visible and timed right down to the minute.

On the bedside table, next to the alarm, was a framed family photograph. Him and her. And the boy and girl. Younger then, teenagers now. Hers. Everyone in the picture looked unhappy. No way he'd fit into those trousers now, he knew. Misery might love company but it was also totally crazy about lunch. That drive-through burger joint in the new highway service area just out of town had been the final nail in his sartorial coffin.

Martin listened to careful footsteps in the hallway and then the bedroom door opened and closed. She flicked on the light in the ensuite and saw that he was awake. They looked at each other blankly, both their faces empty of emotion.

'It's late, after one-thirty,' she said flatly. 'There was a lot of cleaning up to do after the party. I'm going to take a shower. Go back to sleep.'

Water started running and he waited for the rustle of the plastic shower curtain before getting out of bed. The bathroom door was slightly ajar, and after pulling on his robe he glanced in. Her dress lay in a crumpled heap on the floor. Jesus, what that dress cost and now look at it! The mirror on the medicine cabinet was already steaming up but he could still see her reflection in it. Red scratch marks were clearly visible on her neck and shoulders. He watched impassively until the mirror fogged over completely and then walked out into the hallway.

Light was coming from under a door. The boy's bedroom. He turned the handle. The boy, sitting in pyjamas at his computer desk, looked back from the monitor towards Martin in the doorway. On the screen was an image of a scrawny, naked girl having complicated and athletic sex with several men. Martin and the boy stared at each other, their faces expressionless.

'Keeps fuckin' dropping out,' the boy said. 'It's a really shit connection. Seriously pissing me off.'

Martin stepped back into the hallway, closing the door quietly behind him. Light came from under a second door. He knocked gently and waited, then knocked again. He opened the door to the room of a teenage girl. The bed was still neatly made. Not by her, though. Lazy little cow. From the open window he could see the purple panel van parked under a gum tree. Tuesday night, so it was the turn of the apprentice plumber from nearby Cardenvale. The van's windows were heavily steamed up, even though it was a mild night. Just before he closed the door, Martin saw the family portrait on her pinboard. It was the same photograph as in the master bedroom, except in this one his head had been neatly cut out with scissors.

In the kitchen Martin put instant-coffee granules into a mug and waited for the electric kettle to boil. He swallowed his pills dry. A small white one for lowering his blood pressure, plus a blue one – a diuretic – to help the first do its job. Both blister packs were now empty. He'd refilled the prescription yesterday but had left the pills in his desk drawer at the bank. He made a mental note to remember to bring them home tonight. There was also the cholesterol-lowering drug that he teamed whenever possible with thickly buttered toast and raspberry jam. Stupid, perhaps, yet somehow perversely satisfying. Today, however, he just took his coffee out to the verandah to wait for the sunrise.

The house was a typical bush homestead, a single-storey, tin-roofed weatherboard with a wide verandah running around three sides. Built back in the late 1940s for a soldier/settler, the house and the three acres it stood on would be all his in just fifteen more years. At least that had been the plan. Low-interest staff loan. One of the perks. The bank paid him, he paid the bank. It was a sort of money-go-round. He remembered how he used to justify himself at all those dinner parties in the early days. Banking wasn't as boring as most people thought, he would say, and besides, it was secure, permanent, a job for life. Long-service leave, gold watch, superannuation, lawn bowls. That was a bloody laugh, he decided as he sipped his coffee, and the laugh was on him.

The plastic chairs on the verandah were damp with dew, so he walked across to the garage to get a rag. Inside there were still piles of fliers from the Don't Close Our Bank committee, and some SAVE THE MEATWORKS placards left over from that final, pointless rally. At least the local printer had done well out of the death throes of the town.

Something rustled in the rafters. Martin looked up. Rat

or possum? Snake, maybe, after a rat. Amid the jumble of plastic conduit and copper plumbing pipes left by some former owner, he could see the wooden butt of the rifle. An army-surplus Lee Enfield .303, it had been up in the rafters when Martin moved in. Probably belonged to the original owner of the house, he'd guessed. He knew he should have handed it in during one of the amnesties, but this was the bush and things were a bit more casual. And anyway, you never knew when you might have to blow the head off some pest. They'd used those old Lee Enfields in the school cadets, he remembered, him and Starkie.

God, high school. That was a long time ago. The good old days. Were they? Funny, but he really couldn't recall.

Martin stared up at the butt of the rifle for a long time. There were cartridges for the weapon in an old shoebox somewhere on one of the shelves, he remembered. Would they still be any good? He wondered if the steel of the muzzle would feel cold against his forehead. A quick push down on the trigger, loud noise, all his problems solved. And he wouldn't have to clean up the mess for once. Did you actually hear the bang? An interesting question.

*

Martin showered and dressed without disturbing his wife. He seriously doubted whether a rifle going off in the garage would have disturbed her either. His total elimination from her life really wouldn't disturb her all that much, he realised. They were already well on their way to that particular situation anyway.

The girl came into the kitchen as he was rinsing his mug in the sink. The boy was hunched over a bowl, noisily shovelling cereal into his mouth.

'Oohh, check it out, the almost new suit,' the girl said. 'Well, I suppose today is kinda like a funeral.'

She was sixteen now and actually very pretty. Martin was always intrigued by the way that sneering, whining voice could make her appear so ugly.

She smiled brightly at him. 'At least now we can get out of this shithole of a town,' she said.

The boy glanced up. His cold smile was a challenge. 'Yeah,' he said, 'maybe go some place with decent broadband access.'

Martin picked up his car keys and briefcase from the hall table and glanced at the closed bedroom door. He studied his reflection in the mirror over the table. Not too jowly, considering, and at least he still had most of his hair, even if it was greying rapidly at the temples. The empty look in his eyes was what scared him the most. He shook his head slowly. What in hell happened to you, Martin Carter? he asked himself.

As he carefully backed the Commodore out past his wife's badly parked Volvo, Martin noticed someone had thrown up over the rear offside panel. Beer, charred steak and stomach acid were probably not that good for the shiny Scandinavian paintwork, he thought, but decided against stopping to hose it off. Must have been some party. Retrenched slaughtermen, some with redundancy cheques for over fifty thousand dollars in their pockets; long-distance truckies out for a good time; an ocean of beer – and his good lady wife.

The drive into town took barely five minutes. For the first year he had walked it as part of an exercise regimen, but then he'd stopped caring. She'd commented that it wasn't really fitting anyway, whatever the hell that meant. Martin looked at the dashboard clock: 8.50. God, not even nine o'clock and it was already a shit of a day. He didn't really expect things were going to improve.

three

Burrinjuruk had begun its life as a stopping place for overland cattle drovers needing to graze and water their stock. Later the town served the same rest and refuelling function for truckdrivers using the highway to deliver live cattle to the meatworks, or to pick up the resulting output, chilled, frozen or vacuum-packed for export.

With the new bypass in place and the impending closure of the meatworks due to a business rationalisation by its owner, Burrinjuruk had begun to die. Boarded-up shops and empty homes were more the rule than the exception along the once thriving main street. At least parking isn't a problem any more, Martin thought as he pulled the Commodore up in front of the bank. On a whim he rolled the car forward into the only posted no-standing area in the whole town. Bugger it, he decided, who cares?

A small group stood waiting for him outside the locked bank. Daryl, Fran and Esme. His staff.

So very young, he mused, and now so very redundant.

Esme had a tea-towel-covered cane basket over one arm, and he suddenly remembered there had been talk of a party-come-wake. In the basket would no doubt be Esme's banana cake and a couple of bottles of cheap sparkling wine.

Who would name a child Esme in this day and age? he wondered. What chance did a twenty-year-old have with a sixty-year-old's name?

As he stepped out of the car, Martin heard the *whoop whoop whoop* of the siren on the police Land Cruiser. It rolled up beside him. Colin Curtis switched off the engine and leaned out of the window, smiling.

'Hate to give you a ticket on the last day, mate.'

Martin shrugged. 'Not my problem, Col. It's the bank's car again from four, so do your worst. They can afford it, and it'll help you fill your quota.'

Colin shook his head and gave him an offended look. 'Those malicious rumours of a traffic-infringement quota are a totally unfounded and highly defamatory urban myth,' he said in mock seriousness. Then, smiling broadly, he raised his eyebrows.

Martin smiled back. Colin could always manage to get a laugh out of him.

The policeman glanced over at the group waiting outside

the bank. 'You reckon you'll need a hand today, Martin?' he asked. 'That's a hell of a lot of cash for you girls to handle.'

'Ouch. I'm crushed,' Martin said with a sigh. 'But with Fran and Esme as my first line of defence, I doubt your manly presence will be required.'

Colin laughed. 'Okay then, but it's your funeral.'

That was the second time he'd heard that word this morning, Martin realised.

'So what's the day look like?' Colin went on.

'The SecuraGard van is scheduled to drop off at ten, and the first of my John Smiths should stagger in about noon with their cheques and their fake IDs. They'll all be way too fragile from last night's booze-up to cause us any grief.'

Col nodded. 'Tell me about it,' he said. 'Derek over at the motel reckons he'll need to hire a front-end loader to clean up all the empties in the car park. That's after he spends the morning hosing away the chuck. Seems the serious piss-artists were parking tigers all over the shop from an hour after kick-off. Must've been all that pre-game practice.'

'Sounds about right,' Martin smiled. 'Projectile vomiting as a party trick. Joys of alcohol, eh?'

The policeman shrugged. 'Now, if you're sure you won't need any muscle . . .' He let the sentence hang in the air.

'Thanks anyway, Col. Our biggest problem today will be the ones who can't remember their assumed names. You reckon it was compulsory to be on the run from the law to get a job up at the meatworks?'

The only reason Martin's branch had remained open as long as it had was the slaughtermen's insistence on being paid weekly, in cash. They all seemed to have a morbid fear of tax-file numbers and any kind of bank account that required identification.

Curtis put up both hands. 'Don't want to know about it, mate. First thing you learn on these one-copper postings is you gotta go with the flow.' He scratched his chin. 'It is kinda hard to ignore a Korean carcass-boner named John Brown, but,' he said.

Martin nodded in agreement. 'No other major dramas last night?'

The sergeant looked at Martin and briefly considered saying something about the Volvo, but decided against it. 'Nope. Pretty quiet night all round. It was a good thing they got their final pay by cheque instead of cash yesterday. They couldn't drink it at the party and it stopped some silly bugger trying to pinch it. A cashed-up drunk is always a tempting target.'

'Even some of those psychotic Neanderthals from the killing floor,' Martin said.

'Beats me why any bugger would even think about messing with a bloke who can carve a mooing Poll Hereford into a pub-raffle meat tray in three minutes flat,' Colin said. 'Not something I'd like to get in the middle of, that's for sure. And I'm allowed to carry a pistol.'

He glanced up at the sky and then at his watch. 'Well,

I think it's about time I hit the highway with my trusty radar gun and issued a few urban myths.'

The Land Cruiser's already-warm engine started easily. Curtis slipped on a pair of mirror-lens, aviator-style sunglasses and leaned back out the window. 'Okay Martin, you remember what to do if the ammo dump explodes?'

Martin smiled. It was a regular piece of banter between the two men. 'I'll fire three shots in the air to wake you up?'

Colin grinned, waved and gunned the Land Cruiser away from the kerb with a squeal of tyres on bitumen.

*

Martin walked slowly up to the front doors of the Burrinjuruk branch of the Federal Austwide Sansho Banking Corporation and offered a subdued 'Good morning' to the waiting group. The bank, a single-storey 1930s sandstone building, while not totally shabby, was showing obvious signs of neglect. Paint was flaking from the verandah posts and windowsills, and on the sign above the door a graffitied 'd' and 'e' had turned 'Sansho' into 'Sandshoe'. He unlocked the doors and Daryl, Fran and Esme followed him inside, Daryl heading straight for the alarm panel to punch in the security override code. As Esme walked past, Martin lifted the checked tea towel covering her basket and whistled softly.

'Some cheeky domestic champagne and your world-famous banana cake, eh?' he said.

Esme blushed. Esme blushed on a regular basis.

Fran chimed in, 'My sister's bringing us a couple of roasted chickens and potato salad and coleslaw after two.'

Fran and her 'sister' were an object of some conjecture in the district. Fran was a placid blue-eyed blonde while the sister was olive-skinned and dark-haired with a fiery temper. They owned a struggling market garden and poultry farm outside town and neither woman had ever been seen out with a man. Colin reckoned all the talk was just sour grapes because the 'sister' had won the open-entry woodchop at the district agricultural show three years running. But she certainly knew how to cook a chook. Her potato salad was pretty damn good too, Martin remembered as he relocked the front door.

'I'll pick up a slab on my lunch break,' offered Daryl.

The typical Aussie bachelor's contribution to a bring-a-plate do, Martin thought. 'Mate,' he said, 'if you can find a case of beer within fifty k's of this town after last night's little shindig, I'll pay.'

He glanced around the main banking chamber. Over the previous few weeks it had been slowly stripped back to the bare essentials in preparation for today's final shut-down. He shook his head. 'Okay, let's get set up and try to look like we care.' He turned to Daryl. 'Better put a couple of buckets out front, Dazza, and have the mop and some Pine-o-Cleen standing by just in case. Most of our John Smiths are going to be in pretty shabby shape when they finally manage to surface.'

Daryl nodded and the staff moved off to prepare for the day. Martin walked into the manager's office, which was just to the right of the tellers' windows. He came back out again almost immediately, holding up a curling fax.

'It's officially official, boys and girls,' he said.

The three tellers looked up from their cages.

'The money to cover the meatworks pay cheques arrives at ten this morning and we pay out from eleven. Final pays plus all entitlements plus redundancies. Paid out in cash, as per their negotiated agreement. Which is, of course, why we're still here.' Martin smiled sadly. 'You guys really should have been in their union.'

He quickly scanned the rest of the fax. 'The Burrinjuruk branch of the Federal Austwide Sandshoe Banking Corporation closes forever at four this afternoon,' he read. The group managed a smile at Martin's acknowledgement of the graffiti. 'Final cheques for bank staff, including allowances, holiday pay, sick pay and redundancy, to be posted to your home address in five to seven working days.'

Nobody spoke.

'Of course,' Martin continued, 'after four this afternoon, there won't be a bloody bank within two hundred k's to cash them at.' He screwed up the fax and tossed it into one of the plastic buckets near Daryl's cage. 'They also want the bank pistol and any security videotapes. Anyone seen the gun recently?'

Daryl, Fran and Esme shook their heads.

Martin shrugged. 'Better think about getting that grog on ice, Esme,' he said. 'I reckon we'll all be needing it later.'

*

The bank's single security camera covered the main banking chamber and ran through a VCR/TV mounted on the wall of Martin's office. He pressed the eject button on the unit and a cassette slid out. The title was unfamiliar but the 'XXX' on the spine suggested it was almost certainly not a training video on bank procedure. Martin knew for a fact that sexy Swedish au pairs were a bit thin on the ground in Burrinjuruk. He put in a blank tape, pressed RECORD and walked back into the chamber, tossing the XXX cassette over the wire cage to Daryl.

'That must be yours, Casanova,' he said.

Esme glanced at Daryl and blushed for the second time that morning. Interesting, Martin thought, and shouted back over his shoulder as he re-entered his office, 'All unofficial copies of the bank keys should probably be slipped discreetly under my door in the next fifteen minutes.'

It took Martin ten minutes to track down the bank's .32 calibre automatic pistol, which he finally discovered neatly wrapped in a tea towel inside a biscuit tin at the back of his filing cabinet. The loose cartridges rattling around the bottom were covered with tiny white flecks of desiccated coconut, reminders of the time the tin had contained Iced Vo Vos.

During his search for the gun, half a dozen keys had been slipped under his door. Martin wondered if there was anyone in Burrinjuruk who didn't have a key to the bank. Maybe head office had been right in refusing his regular requests to install an ATM for after-hours banking. In this town, who needed it?

Around nine-thirty Fran brought him a mug of lukewarm instant coffee, which he sipped at his desk. The security monitor now showed the three tellers getting their cages ready for the expected rush. Martin picked up the pistol and examined it, trying to remember exactly where the release for the magazine was located. The brass clip suddenly fell out of the bottom of the handgrip and landed on his desk. He picked it up. It was empty. Martin looked at the family photograph on his desk. He stood up and took off his jacket and tie and unbuttoned the collar of his shirt. Sitting down again, he began loading the cartridges into the clip, carefully blowing the flecks of coconut off them first. He pushed the loaded clip firmly into the base of the automatic and it locked into place with a solid metallic click.

Martin studied the photograph on his desk for a long time, absently stroking the metal of the pistol. He put his thumb over the muzzle. It was cold. He turned the pistol around and looked down the barrel. Hooking his thumb backwards around the trigger, he placed the muzzle against his forehead, between his eyes. He made a clicking noise with his tongue. What have I got to lose? he asked himself.

At ten past ten, Daryl unlocked the bank's main door in response to a confident and rhythmic knocking. A pair of uniformed security guards stood behind a two-wheeled trolley stacked with canvas bags. The hinged metal bars that secured the tops of the bags were padlocked and sealed and the guards were armed with revolvers. The older of the two smiled pleasantly at Daryl.

'Good morning, young sir. Anyone here order a shitload of cash money?'

'You're late, Frank,' Daryl said, swinging back both doors.

Frank shrugged. 'Some dick left a Commodore in the no-standing zone where we usually unload.'

At ten-fifteen, Martin walked out of his office. He had been watching on the security monitor as Daryl and Frank checked the delivery, and Daryl had just signed the receipt on Frank's clipboard. The younger guard, new to Martin, was leaning on the counter, smiling and chatting to Fran.

You're really backing the wrong horse there, mate, thought Martin. 'Everything okay, Frank?' he asked. 'All signed for?'

The guard nodded. 'She's all yours, Martin. You're in the money.'

'I guess I am, Frank,' Martin agreed. Then he pointed the bank's pistol at the group.

'And now, ladies and gentlemen, I'm terribly sorry, but this is a stick-up.'

four

A broad grin spread over Daryl's face. 'Jeez, Mr Carter, you're a dag,' he chuckled. 'I thought we were planning to have the party after we closed.'

Frank and Martin looked into each other's eyes. There was a long pause, then Frank nodded and slowly raised his hands.

'Okay,' he said, 'if that's how it is, Martin.'

'That's how it is, Frank,' Martin said. 'I'm sorry.'

After a moment of confused silence, Daryl also raised his hands. Behind Frank, the young guard was looking uncertainly at Martin, one hand wavering near his pistol. Even standing with his back to him, Frank sensed his indecision.

'Let's not do anything fuckin' stupid, eh Wayne!' he growled. 'They signed for it, so it's not our problem. The bank and the insurance company can sort it out.'

Wayne hesitated.

'Come on, it's only money, mate,' Frank said lightly.

Wayne raised his hands, but the look on his face said he wasn't very happy about it.

'Do we have to put our hands up too, Mr Carter?' It was Esme speaking from behind the counter.

Martin turned. Fran and Esme were standing together in Fran's cage, looking perplexed. Esme had a half-inflated balloon in her hand. Martin glanced at Wayne, back at the women, then back at Wayne. 'Um, yes. And you'd better come out here and join us,' he ordered. All the head-turning was starting to make him dizzy.

'Should we put our hands up now or after we come out?' Fran asked.

'Er, now, I guess.'

Esme raised her hands and let the balloon go. It shot up, spluttering around the roof before landing on a blade of the ceiling fan.

'Want me to take Wayne's gun, Mr Carter?' Daryl suggested eagerly. His eyes held a look of respect Martin hadn't seen in his five years as manager. Wayne glared at him.

'Does this mean the party's off?' Fran wanted to know. 'It's just that my sister's going to be cooking all morning . . .'

Jesus, Martin thought, this was starting to get very complicated. 'You two can put your hands down now,' he said to the women, 'but no sudden moves, all right?'

They nodded solemnly and Martin turned his attention back to the guards.

Esme slowly took another balloon out of her cardigan pocket. She looked at Fran, who gave a small shake of her head.

Warily, Martin took the pistols from the two guards and then herded the group into the bank's secure-document storage area, which doubled as the staff lunchroom. The room had barred windows with opaque, wire-reinforced glass and a steel security door. Off to one side were separate male and female toilets which also had barred windows fitted with the same shatterproof glass. Martin motioned his captives towards the laminex-topped table in the middle of the room.

'You should be comfortable here for a while. There's plenty of tea and coffee.'

'And biscuits,' offered Esme brightly. 'I refilled the jar yesterday. Assorted Creams. Arnott's.'

'Good one, Esme,' Daryl said. 'Dibs on the Orange Slice.'

Backing out of the room, Martin noticed the wall-mounted telephone and jerked it roughly away from the plaster by its cable. The phone reminded him of something else.

'Better hand over your mobiles too,' he ordered.

Daryl and Frank gave up their phones immediately. Fran said hers was in the cash drawer in her cage. Esme didn't own one; her mother held grave fears over the possibility of her only child developing a brain tumour from the radiation. Martin pointed his pistol at Wayne.

'Give it up, Wayne,' Frank said.

The young guard pulled a tiny phone from his shirt pocket and sullenly tossed it to Martin.

'Wayne's got a really little one,' said Frank, and Esme blushed.

Martin locked the door on the group and dropped the guns and phones into one of the buckets Daryl had organised. Noticing Esme's picnic basket, he unlocked the door again and pushed the hamper inside with his foot. As he relocked the door he heard a low whistle and Frank's voice.

'The fully catered bank heist,' the guard said. 'My all-time favourite.'

Alone in the middle of the bank, Martin looked at the cash bags still stacked on the trolley. He looked at the pistol in his hand and then at the clock. Ten-twenty. He looked at the bags again.

'The next step is usually the getaway.'

Martin spun round, pointing the gun towards the source of the voice. Colin Curtis was leaning nonchalantly in the open doorway, arms folded. He shook his head.

'I don't think you really want to use that, mate,' he said, indicating Martin's pistol with a nod of his head. 'I reckon a dead cop in the middle of the main street will really mess up what little chance we've got in this year's Tidy Towns competition.'

Martin motioned with the pistol for Colin to come in and close the door behind him. Colin complied, then raised his hands.

'Looks like you're having a bit of a bad day, Martin,' he said. 'Want to talk about it?'

Martin shook his head. 'What's to talk about?' he asked. 'Apart from the fact that I'm fat, fifty and my life's fucked, everything's just peachy.'

'Come on, mate, cheer up. Don't be so hard on yourself.' Colin paused. 'You're not really all that fat.'

Martin lowered the pistol slightly. 'Isn't it a bit risky taking the piss out of someone who's holding a gun? Do they teach you that in hostage-negotiating class?'

Colin shrugged. 'I slept through that one. Anyway, I know you're not going to shoot me.'

'Really?' said Martin. 'What's stopping me?'

'Well,' Colin mused, 'you're basically a decent human being, for a bank manager. And you've still got the safety on.'

Martin looked down at the pistol.

'It's that little switch by your thumb,' Colin explained.

Martin tilted the pistol to one side.

'Remember, mate,' Colin said, 'I showed you when we renewed your licence last year. Push it down if you decide you really want to shoot me. But I'm happy to keep my hands up, so let's leave it on safe for the moment, eh? Right now I'm probably as nervous as you are.'

The two men looked at each other for what seemed like a very long time.

'When did you turn fifty?' Colin finally asked.

'Yesterday.'

'Bugger,' Colin said, shaking his head. 'I knew it was around now sometime. Didn't get the cake and candles then?'

'The family managed to forget. Not totally unexpected, the way things have been going at home lately.'

'No need to go off the deep end though, mate,' Colin said. 'I forgot too.' He paused. 'Of course,' he said slowly, 'I am standing here at gunpoint with my hands in the air.'

'You're a mate, Col. I'm supposed to subtly remind you a few days in advance.'

'You must have been a bit too subtle then.'

'We both had a pretty busy week coming up,' Martin said, 'so I thought, The hell with it, why should I make a fuss?'

'Good point,' Colin agreed. 'But like I said a moment ago, I am standing here at gunpoint with my hands in the air. When you don't make a fuss, you really go all out, don't you, mate?'

Colin indicated the security camera with his head. 'Is that thing recording right now?'

'Yes, why?'

'Does it record sound?'

Martin shook his head. 'Just the picture.'

'Got another camera in your office?'

Martin shook his head again, confused by this line of questioning. Colin turned slightly so that his back was towards the camera and lowered his voice.

'Okay then, Martin, here's the plan. In a minute I'm going to rush you and you'll whack me on the side of the head. I'll go down, apparently out cold, and you drag me into your office, out of sight of the camera.'

Martin was mystified. He raised the pistol warily. 'Why would we do that?'

Colin gave him an exasperated look. 'So we can talk in private, figure things out.'

Martin, still wary, eyed Colin suspiciously.

'You should really go with me on this, mate,' Colin urged. He waited, then: 'You said it yourself, Martin. You're fat, fifty and fucked. Totally fucked. Think about it. At this moment in time you have exactly nothing left to lose.'

*

The surveillance monitor in Martin's office showed the two men facing each other, talking. Suddenly Colin lunged forward and after a brief struggle he was on the floor. Martin grabbed him by his ankles and dragged him clumsily towards the office. Both men disappeared out of view of the camera.

When they reached the middle of his office, Martin dropped Colin's feet. On hearing the door close, Colin sat up and rubbed his left temple.

'When I said whack me in the head, I meant pretend to whack me in the head,' he groaned. 'Jesus, that bloody hurts.'

'Sorry, I got a bit over-excited,' Martin said.

Colin blinked several times and shook his head. 'And if you have to drag someone, Martin, do it by the arms,' he added. 'It stops their bloody scone banging on the floor every second step.'

'Right, I'll try to remember that,' Martin said earnestly. He carefully removed Colin's pistol from its holster and put it on the desk. The dull black police automatic was a lot bigger and heavier than the bank's pistol, he noticed.

Colin climbed slowly to his feet and sat in a chair. He squinted. 'I think I'm going to need some aspirin,' he said. He looked up at the wall clock and then back at Martin. 'Now, do you have any sort of a plan, mate?'

Martin stared at him blankly.

'Anything?' Colin repeated. 'In about forty minutes' time you're going to have a bunch of grumpy, hungover, borderline-psychotic slaughtermen in here looking to cash some pretty awesome pay cheques. And I'm sorry to have to tell you this, but your little mid-life crisis isn't going to mean dick to them.'

Martin slumped into his chair on the other side of the desk and groaned softly. 'Jesus, just look at my life, will you? I did everything the way I was supposed to and now it's all gone to hell. It's all over for me, let's face it.

God, what have I done? I must be out of my mind.'

Colin watched him intently. 'So I guess that means this is all somewhat spontaneous?' he suggested finally.

Martin nodded weakly. There was another long silence.

'Okay,' Colin said, 'as I see it, right now we have two options.'

Martin eyed him warily.

'One,' Colin continued, 'we pretend it was all a big practical joke you and I cooked up to celebrate the closing of the bank. We should be able to sell it to the staff and the armoured-car bods by the time they finish off Esme's grog. Nobody else needs to know.'

'And our second choice?' asked Martin.

'You go on the run with the money after tying me up. When they finally catch up with you, you'll probably get ten years non-parole, if you're very, very lucky. Or,' he went on, 'you can go out in a blazing roadside gunfight, the legendary Mid-Life-Crisis Carter, bank manager turned bank robber.'

Martin said nothing for a long time. 'You know, I really don't understand anything any more,' he said at last. 'I just don't get it. When I was twenty it all made sense. Sort of. There was a path and you followed it. You worked hard, were polite to the boss, kept your mouth shut, and everything turned out fine in the end.' He shook his head. 'I put in the hours, paid my taxes, saved up a deposit and bought a house. I was loyal to the bank, did what they asked, went where they sent me, and now they've screwed me. And everything I ever did and everything I believed in means absolutely nothing.'

Colin listened without comment.

'Politicians lie outright, rort the system, bully people, spread fear and division, demonise the weak, and nobody seems to care. The education system teaches kids bugger all. They can't spell or add up, and if they get a job they don't see why they should turn up at nine o'clock if something more interesting happens to come along.'

'You left out that all cops are bent,' Colin put in.

Martin smiled. 'I thought we'd take that as read.' He stood up. 'I think I'm going with option two.'

'Hey mate, come on, I was only joking,' Colin snapped.

'I'm not,' Martin said firmly. 'It's option two.' He flipped the pistol's safety to off.

Colin put his hands back up, shaking his head sadly. 'This is not smart, Martin, not smart at all. But you've got the gun, so I suppose it's your call. Mind if I show you something first, though?'

Martin nodded in agreement but Colin suddenly appeared distracted, glancing somewhere off past Martin's shoulder. Momentarily confused, Martin looked away and Colin deftly swept the pistol from his grip. Just as suddenly the weapon was in the sergeant's hand. Martin was struck by how big that muzzle seemed when you were staring straight into it.

'I actually did pay attention in that class,' Colin said, switching the pistol to safe. He handed the weapon to

Martin, butt first, and put his arms back in the air. 'I think you're being a dickhead, Martin, but if you're really serious about this, take the Land Cruiser. In for a penny, in for a pound, I guess. She's got a full tank of fuel, plus there's a jerry can in the back.'

Martin looked at him in astonishment.

'There's also a mobile phone and charger in the glove compartment,' Colin added. 'Some boofhead left it on a table in the milkbar and it hasn't been blocked yet. You remember my number if you need to talk about anything?'

Martin nodded mutely.

'So you intend taking the money?' Colin asked.

'I guess so,' Martin said after a moment's thought. 'Otherwise it makes it kind of a wasted morning, doesn't it? You can put your hands down if you like, Col.'

'No, it's okay. You really have to follow procedure in this sort of thing.'

'I'm sorry it turned out like this,' Martin said. 'Won't you get a lot of grief for letting this happen?'

Colin shrugged. 'I like this town,' he said, 'it suits me. Foiling a million-dollar robbery will only get me promoted back to the big smoke. I've done that, and who needs it?' He smiled. 'But thanks for your concern anyway, mate. I'll try to bear any professional embarrassment manfully.'

Colin indicated his trouser pocket. 'May I?' he asked, and after a nod from Martin pulled out a set of keys and tossed them across the desk. 'You know, maybe you should take my uniform as well,' he suggested. 'Add to the picture of a dedicated lawman relentlessly pursuing miscreants and evil-doers.'

Martin held up a brass key on the ring. 'The front door of my bank?' he asked.

'And why should I be the only person in town without one?' Colin replied indignantly, unbuttoning his shirt.

'Jesus Christ,' Martin gasped as Colin peeled off his pale blue police-issue shirt. 'What the hell happened to you?'

The sergeant's upper torso and back was pockmarked with ugly, jagged scars. Colin looked at them as if seeing them for the first time. 'Jumping Jack,' he said simply.

'What?' Martin said, staring at the mass of scar tissue.

'Anti-personnel mine,' Colin explained. 'Pops up to about waist height before it goes off. I was the lucky one. The bloke standing between me and the mine wasn't. I can still walk. Some bits of scrap iron still floating around in there though.'

'Vietnam?' Martin asked.

'Sure as hell wasn't the Kmart parking lot.' Colin scratched at one of the scars. 'Nasty little thing, the Jumping Jack. Meant to maim. Kill a bloke and that's one down. Wound him and two have to carry him out, so that's three out of action. I did get a free ride in a Yank medevac chopper, though.'

'You've never mentioned it,' Martin said. 'Being over there. How come?'

'What's to talk about? Got called up, went, got blown up, and now I'm here – a sworn officer of the law currently aiding and abetting a major criminal enterprise.' He pulled off his boots. 'Don't think these'll fit you,' he said. 'Sorry.'

'Did you ever come across a Jack Stark?' Martin asked suddenly.

Colin stopped in the middle of unbuckling his belt. He gave Martin an odd look.

'Over there, I mean,' Martin said. 'Vietnam.'

'I know where you meant, Martin,' Colin said quietly. 'That's a pretty strange question, straight out of the blue.'

'It's a pretty strange day, Col.'

'You can say that again.'

'So you knew him then?' Martin asked.

'Crazy Jack Stark? Well, I never actually met him but we all heard about him. Very odd bloke. What's your connection to the mad major?'

'He was my best mate in high school,' Martin said.

'Really?' Colin looked at him with curiosity.

'Small world, eh?' Martin said. 'We were both in the ballot. Jack got called up, like you. I missed out and went to work for the bank. I wrote to him a few times after he went over there, and then we lost touch.'

'It happens,' Colin said. 'Too busy killing and eating the godless communists, I suppose.'

'I didn't even know he was a major,' Martin said. 'So what happened to him?'

'Not sure, really,' Colin said. 'Battlefield commission, which was unusual for a nasho. Must have been bloody good at his job. Rapid promotion up the chain to major, then he apparently went troppo and got cashiered over something hush-hush.'

'Cashiered?'

'They gave him the elbow, eighty-sixed him,' Colin explained. 'Dishonourable discharge, which is a bit grim. Luckily they don't still rip off your bloody epaulettes and break your sabre over one knee.'

'Jesus,' Martin said, 'what happened after that?'

Colin shrugged. 'He sank without trace for a long time. Apparently he went bush. Holed up somewhere in FNQ.'

'Far North Queensland?'

'Yep, the land that time forgot – home of the macadamia and other assorted nuts. Current rumour has him living in a fortified bunker on top of a mountain up past Cooktown. They reckon Casa del Stark has killer guard dogs, landmines, booby traps, and two nubile young blonde nymphomaniac twins eager to service his every depraved whim.'

'You're kidding, right?' Martin was agog.

'Dunno for sure, but that's what's on the grapevine. Should suit him down to the ground, from what I've heard. Gun nut, survivalist, one-world government and conspiracy theorist, world-wide-web whacko. We're rooted and it's all the fault of the Jews, capitalists, homos, blacks, immigrants, double-parkers and unwed mothers. Apparently he's even got a paranoid website operating – www.starkravingnuts.com would seem appropriate.'

Martin began unbuttoning his shirt. 'Maybe I should think about heading north then,' he said, 'somewhere up past Cooktown.'

Colin held up his hands. 'Don't really need to know, mate,' he said. 'Second thing a copper learns on these country postings is that ignorance is bliss.' He smiled. 'And by the way, Martin, happy birthday for yesterday.'

five

It took Martin barely ten minutes to transfer the cash bags to the police Land Cruiser, which he had backed up to the side door of the bank. On a whim he'd tossed the bank's pistol and the revolvers he'd taken from Frank and Wayne onto the passenger seat. Colin's police-issue automatic now nestled in the holster on Martin's belt. The security van was out of sight, parked under a tree behind the bank. Colin's shirt was too tight and was beginning to itch. The trousers were loose in the crutch and the legs were way too long. Martin had pinned them up with the office stapler. Colin had been spot on about the boots not fitting, so Martin was still wearing his own brown suede shoes.

Using Fran's computer, Martin had typed out a sign for the front door, and while waiting for it to print, he took one last look around the empty bank. The triple-X porn video was still sitting on Daryl's counter. Martin picked it up and headed back to his office.

'Finally come to your senses, did you?' Colin asked.

'Just forgot my pills.' Martin retrieved the blood-pressure and cholesterol pills from his desk drawer, slipped them into his shirt pocket and smiled. 'Plus I wouldn't want you getting bored . . .'

*

At exactly 10.45 a.m. the police Land Cruiser pulled away from the bank and headed towards the highway. Out of sight of the town, Martin turned right onto a gravel road. As he turned the airconditioning up to full, he noticed a CD poking out of the player. He pushed the disc in and a high-pitched, ululating noise filled the cab. Jesus, that didn't take them long, he thought, looking in the side mirror for the red and blue flashing lights. The roadway behind him was empty, and it took him a few seconds to realise that the sound was coming from the Land Cruiser's speakers. He stabbed at the eject button and the noise stopped.

'Shit!' he spluttered, looking at the disc. It was a Celine Dion compilation and, according to the label, featured the theme song from *Titanic*.

I hope that's not an omen, Martin said to himself.

*

The Burrinjuruk branch of the Federal Austwide San(d)-sho(e) Banking Corporation was locked and shuttered. The sign pinned to the front door read: CLOSED UNTIL 2 P.M. DUE TO COMPUTER PROBLEMS.

In the locked storage room Frank was talking to an enthralled group seated around the laminex-topped table. 'The great thing about stress-related workers' compensation claims,' he explained, 'especially armed-robbery ones, is they're so hard to disprove. We can make an absolute fortune if we all get our stories straight.'

Even Wayne seemed interested. Frank held out a paper plate. 'Any more of that delicious banana cake, Esme?'

Esme cut a slice and put it carefully on the plate. Daryl topped up the champagne in Frank's paper cup.

The main banking chamber was empty and still. From behind the door of the manager's office came the unmistakable moans and gasps of a woman in the throes of orgasm. Inside the office Sergeant Colin Curtis sat in the manager's chair with his feet up on the desk. He was in his underwear and tightly bound with Christmas packaging tape. On the security monitor directly in front of him, Daryl's porn film was playing. The sound was turned up very loud. Sergeant Curtis was not a happy man. His hands, strapped to his sides, pulled at the packing tape securing him in position.

'You're a real bastard, Martin Carter,' he muttered.

*

It was now around two in the afternoon and the police vehicle was parked off a dirt road in the shade of a tall eucalypt.

'Dickhead! Dickhead! Dickhead! Dickhead! Dickhead!' Martin pounded his forehead against the steering wheel of the Land Cruiser as he cursed quietly.

He stopped the thumping but kept his hands tightly clenched on the wheel. In slow motion, wide screen and glorious Technicolor, he ran and reran the morning's events in his mind.

The robbery was bad enough, but Far North Queensland and Jack Stark? What the hell had he been thinking? Over eighteen hundred kilometres across two states with every damn cop on every road on the lookout for him? And if by some incredible fluke he got past them and actually managed to find Jack Stark's mountain-top fortress, what then? An old high-school friend from thirty-some years back who was now quite possibly a total psycho? Jesus, this was some smooth plan, Martin Carter!

And now, to cap it all, he had to piss. Urgently. The butt of Colin's police-issue Glock had been sticking into his right kidney for the past three hours, which was probably part of the problem. How did cops manage to drive with a gun on their hip? No wonder they always seemed grumpy.

Climbing down from the vehicle, Martin walked behind the eucalypt, keeping a wary eye out for snakes. He glanced around before unzipping his trousers. Pissing in public was always a problem for him. Well, not exactly in public, but in public toilets. If he couldn't hold on for more than three hours, how was he going to manage ten years in prison? Did toilet blocks in maximum security feature individual stalls with locks? he wondered.

A deep groan of pleasure accompanied the easing of the pressure in his bladder, and he played the stream of liquid back and forth across the base of the tree. Glancing up, Martin looked directly into the rheumy yellow eyes of a huge goanna sprawled out along a branch. No need to worry about snakes around here, he decided. The big monitor lizard would have made a meal of any tigers or king browns or red-bellied blacks within a couple of kilometres of his treetop residence. The goanna blinked lazily and flicked its long forked tongue, sampling the air. Martin looked down and quickly zipped up. He backed away from the tree warily. Best not to tempt fate. A hungry goanna might take any opportunity for a quick lunch. Or a light snack, if a man was to be brutally honest.

Martin's stomach rumbled at the thought of food. No breakfast, no lunch and a bout of armed robbery could really build an appetite. If he gave himself up, at least he'd probably get lunch. Or maybe he could call the police from a roadhouse. He could have a hamburger while he waited for them to come and pick him up. Breakfast would most definitely be off by now. And who would pay for the hamburger? If the police paid, would they tip enough? He wouldn't want to look cheap in front of the waitress. This life-of-crime business was turning out to be very complex. Martin's hands were shaking. He couldn't think straight, and suddenly he realised that thinking straight was very, very important.

A quick search revealed nothing edible in the Land Cruiser. Colin usually got his lunch at the milkbar in Burrinjuruk, Martin remembered, or at that damned burger joint out on the highway. Martin started the engine and pulled back onto the road. He would get some food, settle down somewhere quiet and try to figure things out. The highway was a better bet for food than the dirt roads he had favoured so far, even if it was a bit riskier. They would have discovered the robbery by now, and perhaps a police patrol would save him the trouble of making a decision about what to do next.

*

The battered roadside sign read: DONUTS WITH JIM. 2K'S AHEAD. Martin glanced down at his police uniform. Shouldn't look too out of place at a donut stand, he decided. And right now, a coffee and some donuts with a bloke named Jim had a very desirable air of normality about it.

It was closer to six kilometres before a dilapidated caravan appeared in a dusty rest area just off the roadway. It was propped up on piles of crumbling bricks and old railway sleepers. Weeds grew up through the perished tyres, and several battered LP gas cylinders rested against one end. A very old and shabby Chrysler ute was parked under the only tree. From the few remaining patches of paint among the rust, Martin guessed that it had once been blue.

He rolled the Land Cruiser into the parking area, switched off the engine and climbed out. There was silence except for the occasional raucous squawking of sulphur-crested cockatoos and the throb of a small motor somewhere in the distance. Electricity generator for the caravan, he guessed, and then he saw the heavy-duty yellow extension cable running through the long grass. And something else, round and white. A satellite dish? Out here? Was he hallucinating on an adrenalin overdose from the robbery? Maybe some food would neutralise it. God, he hoped so.

A sign on the van's roof announced: HOT COFFEE – PIES – DONUTS WITH JIM, and the serving window was open. Martin looked carefully at the sign. There was a logo in the form of a smiling donut. The donut was wearing a very snappy bow tie.

In front of the caravan a skinny man in his late twenties was sitting in a folding aluminium chair, a thin silver laptop resting on his knees. Apart from the laptop and a pair of wraparound sunglasses, he was totally naked.

That's that then, Martin decided, I am definitely out of my mind. The thought that he really was crazy somehow had a calming effect. He would just have some lunch and a cold drink and then wait to see what happened next. He no longer had to worry about making decisions. He hoped that the food in this hallucination was going to be good.

He smiled pleasantly at the naked man. 'G'day,' he said. 'Nice tan.'

The man nodded but didn't speak.

'Sign back there said two k's but it's well over five,' Martin continued.

The man nodded again and looked Martin up and down. 'Odometer's packed up in the ute,' he said finally, 'so I just guess at the k's when I put the signs out. You gunna arrest me for falsifying distances, officer?'

'Not unless you've done anything else I should know about,' Martin said.

The man considered this. 'I sometimes wave at passing traffic,' he offered.

'No crime in that as far as I know.' Martin hoped he sounded like a real police officer.

'Guess that would depend on what I wave,' said the naked man evenly.

Martin laughed out loud. He was beginning to enjoy this hallucination. 'You must be Jim then.'

The man shook his head.

'Jim about?' Martin asked.

'There ain't no Jim. Jim doesn't exist. Jim is just a cunning marketing ploy.'

Martin looked at him blankly.

'Sign on the highway used to say Donuts with Jam,' the man explained, 'and business was dying in the bum. One day last year, this old chook pulled in looking for Jim. She was half blind, cataracts probably, shouldn't really have been driving. Misread the sign. Decided it was some friendly, country-style offer, so she stopped in for lunch with Jim.'

'Sounds fair enough,' Martin said.

'She could sure pack it away. Had seconds on the chicken and chips and bought a dozen donuts to go. So I thought, Bugger it, why not? and changed the signs from Jam to Jim.'

Martin looked around the empty rest stop. 'Paid off big time, I see. I had trouble finding somewhere to park.'

'We get pretty busy after the opera lets out.' The man put his laptop down and stood up. 'So what can I do ya for, ossifer?'

'You get many goannas around here?' Martin asked.

'Dunno,' the man said. 'Guess so. Why?'

'Forget it. Can I get something to eat?'

'Sure, you bet. Name your poison,' he said. 'Just a figure of speech of course,' he added.

Martin looked at the blackboard menu. 'What do you recommend for lunch?'

The man scratched his chin. 'Well, if it was up to me I'd say try Paul Bocuse's joint in Lyon. You can do it in three hours from Paris on the TGV. Truffle soup is always spectacular, followed by a Bresse chicken roasted over the fire in the main dining room. And there's a cheese selection that would make you bloody weep.'

Martin patted his shirt pocket. 'Bugger,' he said, 'I forgot my passport.'

'You're over twenty-one and you've got a pistol, so you should be able to give a couple of my pies a run for their money. They're probably still warmish. I can nuke 'em if you're game.'

'Sounds okay,' Martin said.

'It's your alimentary canal,' replied the man as he walked to the caravan.

Martin called after him as he climbed the three steps to the door. 'Hey, you got a name?'

The man turned. 'Yep,' he said.

There was a long pause.

'Can I get some chips with the pies?' Martin asked finally.

'*Pommes frites*? *Bien sûr*. Anything else? A cheeky yet elegant, cool-climate pinot noir, perhaps? Lightly chilled?'

'Just tomato sauce, thanks, and a Coke if you've got one cold. I'm driving.'

'Gotcha,' said the man, disappearing into the caravan. Martin reached for his wallet but his back pocket was empty. 'Damn,' he muttered. Colin's trousers! His wallet was back on the desk at the bank.

The man leaned out the serving window. 'Problem?'

'Left my wallet back at the office, er, station,' Martin explained.

The man shrugged. 'Don't worry about it. It's cool.'

Martin glanced over at the Land Cruiser. 'I've got some cash in my truck,' he said.

'Nah, really, it's okay. We usually give free lunches to cops in uniform.'

'Just like McDonald's,' Martin said.

The man considered this. 'I guess you could say we're very like McDonald's in many respects. Apart from the international-franchise aspect, the consistent food quality, and the customer-focused service. Plus that whole business-success side of things.'

'And the uniforms,' Martin suggested.

'Touché,' said the man, stepping out of the van. He was wearing a frilly pink plastic apron. 'Couple of minutes for the nosh,' he said.

'Nice.' Martin indicated the apron.

'Thanks. I've found it pays to wear the approved workplace safety gear when standing over a deep-fryer. You always been a cop then?' the man asked, tossing Martin a can of soft drink.

Martin shook his head as he tugged at the ring-pull. 'It's a fairly recent thing. Why?'

'Well, that's a pretty crap uniform you got there. Just thought someone your age would have gold braid and medals and shit.'

'Late starter. What about you? Always been a . . .?' Martin searched for the word.

'Donut dolly?' suggested the man. He laughed and shook his head. 'Telecommunications and security software's really my line. Started my own company in my bedroom when

I was still in high school. First car was a Ferrari. One day my accountant told me if I sold all my shares right then I'd have 290 million Yankee dollars to play with.'

'What happened?' Martin asked, looking around the dusty parking lot.

'Didn't sell them, did I? I took off to a schmick resort in Bali with no CNN and a blonde with big knockers to celebrate my youthful success. Tech stocks went tits up while I was head down and somewhat incommunicado.'

'Whoops,' Martin said.

'You got that right,' the man said. 'So I reviewed my life choices and went with option two.'

'Which was?' Martin asked.

'Go with the flow, live simply for a while and see where life takes you,' the man explained.

'Better than a long drive off a short pier in a fast car, I guess.'

The man seemed perplexed. 'Why would I want to do that?'

Martin backtracked. 'I just thought, in that kind of situation, doing all your dough – no pun intended – option one would be bailing out, suicide.'

'Fuck that for a game of soldiers,' snorted the man. 'I've still got bulk cash offshore in the Cook Islands and the Bahamas. I'm not stupid, pal. Never put all your eggs in one basket, even if you own the basket. Option one was doing a runner – maybe to Brazil like Ronnie Biggs, or to Majorca *à la* Skasey, but I like it here. It's home.'

'So all that time you were making millions, your fallback position was to be a donut dolly on a dirt road west of Woop Woop?' Martin asked.

'It got a wee bit tricky,' the man said slowly. 'A lot of rich and powerful people got burned when we went under. Some pretty scary people too. And the tax office is a bit dark on me as well. Missed a few payments, rather big ones as it happened. I'm just doing my penance out here till they all forget about me.'

'Not really the kind of stuff you should be telling a cop, is it?'

The man looked Martin up and down and laughed. 'Yeah, right.'

There was a ping from the caravan. 'Luncheon is served,' the man announced. And, after a theatrical pause: 'Officer.'

Martin took a long swig from the can. The soft drink was icy and tingling. He felt that he could taste every individual bubble on his tongue. Maybe he wasn't actually hallucinating. Maybe the adrenalin overload was just sharpening his senses.

Lunch was on the van counter on a plastic plate. The shoestring chips were golden and the meat pies looked and smelled delicious.

'Homemade?' Martin asked.

The man nodded. 'Sure are, if your home's in a giant industrial bakery outside Gosford.'

When Martin bit into the first pie a fat globule of gravy

spurted out onto his shirt front. The man shook his head and handed him a paper napkin.

'Forgot your wallet and now this,' he said. 'Not really working out to be your day, is it?'

Martin dabbed at the spill. 'Mate,' he said, 'you don't know the half of it.'

six

Slowly and cautiously Martin worked the Land Cruiser up the steep gravel track. A sheer cliff fell away on the left, and it was a very long way to the bottom. One thing about living in a country town for five years, he mused, was you learned the proper way to handle a four-wheel drive off-road. To his right was a dense mountain-gum forest, and tangled underbrush rubbed and scratched against the driver's door. Martin was trying his best to keep as far away from the cliff edge as possible. If I go over that I'll die a rich man, he thought, glancing in the rear-view mirror at the canvas sacks in the back. He inched the vehicle carefully over the next crest and then stopped.

Further down the track, a black motorcycle with a sidecar was parked in a tiny clearing off to one side. There was no sign of the rider. Martin pulled hard on the handbrake before switching off the engine in the Land Cruiser. Climbing out of the cabin, he glanced about and then walked slowly over to the motorcycle. Martin didn't know much about motorcycles but this looked to be a vintage model, nothing like those fancy touring bikes that sometimes cruised through Burrinjuruk. The leather seat was big and flat, like something you'd see on an old tractor, and the handlebars were long, arching back along either side of the teardrop-shaped petrol tank. A crudely airbrushed illustration featuring several naked women of Aryan appearance and very exaggerated proportions in the chest region covered the top of the petrol tank. The machine also had some kind of stick-shift gear lever, like a sports car, which Martin found a bit odd.

Two helmets and a battered leather jacket lay on the seat of the long, boat-shaped sidecar. One of the helmets was a black, World War II German army-style coalscuttle with a swastika on the side. It was surprisingly light when Martin picked it up – he guessed it was a fibreglass reproduction. A smaller and newer-looking leather jacket was lying on the ground a couple of metres from the bike. Martin looked around warily. The jacket on the ground wasn't a good sign. There was something here giving him a very bad feeling. That something was telling him to get right back in the Land Cruiser and drive on. He told himself not to be silly, but he nevertheless reached down to the holster and unsnapped the restraining band looped over the butt of Colin's pistol. You should just drive on, he told himself, what's happening here is none of your business.

There was a sound of scuffling in the bushes to his right, and a man and woman suddenly staggered out into the sunlight. The woman was tall and slim, blonde, maybe forty, he thought, wearing leather pants and motorcycle boots. She was very attractive, Martin decided. No, she was actually bloody gorgeous, he concluded. Her plaid shirt was torn at the front and he could see part of a lacy white bra. A fat and rather nasty-looking bikie was holding her by the hair with one hand. In the other he had a shortened pool cue. The man was about the same age as himself, Martin guessed. He had a shaved head and his jeans, denim shirt and sleeveless denim jacket were filthy. Blood was running from several scratches on his face and he didn't appear to be very happy to have company.

'Nothin' to worry about here, officer,' the bikie said. 'Me and the missus are just havin' a bit of a domestic.'

Martin didn't know a lot about bikies' molls but he was pretty sure this woman didn't fit the bill.

'Nothin' he needs to get involved in, eh luv?' The bikie jerked on the woman's hair and she winced, and gave Martin a look. Her eyes were dark brown. Dark brown eyes with blonde hair – a nice combination, Martin thought. What wasn't so nice was the look in her eyes. Part desperation and part cold fury.

So he was right about something bad happening here. Too late to walk away now, he realised.

Suddenly the woman broke free and Martin saw the man raise the pool cue and heard him snarl, 'Bitch.' He was almost surprised to find Colin's pistol in his hand, the weapon pointing directly at the bikie. He wondered if he should say something commanding and authoritative, but nothing came to mind. The gun was enough, though, and the bikie stepped away from the woman, dropped the pool cue and slowly raised his hands.

'It's cool,' he said, smiling at Martin and showing a jagged row of mossy, decaying teeth.

'Sit on the sidecar and don't do anything stupid,' Martin ordered, motioning with the pistol in the direction of the motorcycle. He looked towards the woman, who was rearranging her clothes. 'You okay?' he asked her.

She nodded. 'You have excellent timing, officer,' she said.

Martin was taken with the husky warmth of her voice. He was hoping she would say something else when there was a gentle whistle from the direction of the motorcycle. The woman's eyes flicked towards the bikie and she froze. 'Oh, shit,' she said softly.

Martin spun around and stared straight into the double barrels of a sawn-off shotgun. 'Told you not to get involved,' the bikie grinned.

Martin raised his pistol. The bikie shook his head. 'No

way, copper. You might get lucky and hit me with that peashooter, but I'll bloody definitely get you with this, so why don't you just put it fuckin' down, eh?'

Martin was trying to remember if the pistol's safety catch was off. And where exactly was it on a Glock? Did a Glock have a safety catch? He really didn't want to look down at this particular moment. 'We could talk about this,' he suggested. 'Negotiate something. I've got money.'

The bikie's smile brightened. 'Money's good. How much we talkin'?'

Martin indicated the Land Cruiser behind him with his thumb. 'There's about a million in cash in my truck,' he said.

The bikie looked impressed. 'Jesus, a million cash? You must be one of them big-city coppers. In plain brown envelopes, is it, Sarge?' he sneered.

Martin wasn't quite sure the uniform was doing its job. Out of the corner of his eye he caught a movement. The bikie jerked suddenly as a shadow flashed over his face, and a moment later the pool cue slammed savagely across his mouth. Martin heard the crunch of shattering teeth, then the heavy *baboom-baboom* of a double shotgun blast, followed by the violent jerking of Colin's pistol as it discharged.

So the safety was off after all, Martin noted calmly to himself, and then was mildly bemused by his calmness. There was a smell in the air that reminded him vaguely of double bungers on cracker night when he was a kid.

Except for a ringing in his ears and a horrible gurgling sound coming from behind him, it was suddenly very quiet. The bikie was spreadeagled, face up, on the ground near the motorcycle. A dark red stain covered the front of his shirt. The woman, holding the splintered pool cue and swaying slightly, stood over him. She was breathing heavily, gasping for air. At last she took a long, slow breath and seemed to steady herself. Kneeling down by the man's side, she put her fingers to his throat and checked for a pulse. She looked at Martin and shook her head.

The gurgling noise behind him continued and he looked around. Steaming, lime-green coolant was spewing out of the Land Cruiser's shattered radiator and soaking rapidly into the gravel roadway. Martin sighed. Every time he thought things couldn't possibly get worse, they did.

He turned back to the woman. 'Why did you have to go and do that? I was going to make a deal.'

'Oh, come on,' she said, 'get real. The moment you mentioned that money in your truck, we were both dead.'

'He wouldn't have shot a police officer,' Martin argued.

She looked at him evenly. 'Yeah, right,' she said. 'Brown suede shoes, a shirt two sizes too small, and trouser-cuff alterations by stapler. He might have been a few sandwiches short of a picnic but even he wasn't that dumb.'

Martin glanced down at his shambolic uniform.

'That gravy stain on your chest is the only thing that makes you look anything like a real cop,' she added.

Martin looked at the figure on the ground. He looked at his pistol, and back at the dark red stain on the front of the bikie's denim shirt. 'I killed him?' he asked.

'Could have been a dead heat,' the woman said, 'if you'll pardon the gruesome pun. I think I might have snapped his neck.' She shook her head slowly. 'Some fucking birthday this turned out to be.' She tossed the splintered pool cue into the sidecar.

'Many happy returns,' Martin offered.

'Thanks, but no thanks.' She turned and vomited into the bushes.

Martin was instantly on his knees, the contents of his own stomach mixing with the green radiator coolant on the gravel track. Funny, he thought, no matter what you've been eating, when you throw up there's always some diced carrot in it. He felt a tightness in his chest and a roaring in his ears, and a fuzzy hollow blackness began closing in around him.

*

The next thing he was conscious of was sitting in the shade of the Land Cruiser, propped up against a front tyre. The woman stood next to him.

'Here.' She handed him the canvas water bag from the bullbar, which the shotgun blast had luckily missed. 'Better rinse your mouth and have a drink.'

He swilled and spat, then took a long drink of the tepid, brackish-tasting water. The bikie lay on his back in the sunlight. Martin looked over at the body. 'I guess he's still dead then?' he said.

'What a team, eh?' the woman said. 'When we put 'em down they stay down.'

Martin put his head between his knees. 'Jesus Christ, what happened?' he groaned.

'You blacked out,' she said. 'I was worried there for a minute. Me and two dead blokes on top of a mountain – kind of thing that can get a girl an interesting reputation.' She leaned against the side of the vehicle, her arms folded. 'Okay, you have any sort of a plan, Inspector Gadget?'

Martin looked up. 'Not really, I've been sort of making it up as I go today. I'm new at this. I'm actually a bank manager.' He glanced at his watch. 'Used to be a bank manager,' he added.

The woman peered into the back of the Land Cruiser. 'And you had your fingers in the till, did you?'

'It was a spur-of-the-moment thing,' Martin said. 'I just had a really bad morning.'

'A million dollars cash, eh? And a man without a plan. My day just keeps getting better and better.'

She looked at him keenly. She looked at the dead bikie, the motorcycle and the cliff edge. Then she looked back at Martin and he knew she had come to a decision.

'Okay, sunshine, on your feet. Let's see what we can do about sorting this mess out.'

seven

Forty-five minutes later, Martin – now wearing the bikie's boots and jeans and an old sweatshirt of Colin's that he'd found in the Land Cruiser – was stuffing a third garbage bag full of cash into the sidecar. The woman had carefully slit open the side seams of the canvas money bags with her Swiss Army Knife – the professional model that Martin had always wanted. She had been very particular about not marking or scratching the padlocked metal bars sealing the tops of the bags, which, once empty, had been returned to the back of the police vehicle.

The bikie's denim jeans were worse than Colin's trousers, Martin had discovered. They stank as well as itched. He fidgeted and scratched as he gathered up the collection of guns from the passenger seat – the bank's pistol and the guards' revolvers. Heading back to the motorcycle, he was distracted by the woman bending over to pick up the empty cartridge case from his Glock. Her butt in those leather pants was a sight to behold. He stumbled in the bikie's thick-soled boots and the guns fell out of his hands. As he bent to pick up the pistols, he heard a low wolf whistle from behind.

'Nice arsenal,' she said when he turned around.

Martin tried to read her expression. Her face was neutral but there was something about her eyes that bewildered him. And he liked it, which confused him even more. I'm really out of my depth here, he thought, and then wondered why he had thought it. Out of his depth? He'd robbed his own bank and now he'd killed a man. Out of his depth was a serious understatement. He stashed the guns under the seat of the sidecar.

'Let's get this over with,' the woman said. She was standing over the body of the bikie, who was still lying where he had fallen but was now wearing Colin's shirt and trousers. It had taken them nearly twenty minutes to strip the body of its rank clothing and dress it in the police uniform. 'Okay, you get the shoulders and I'll get his feet. I hope you've had your Weet-Bix.'

It took the two of them another fifteen minutes to drag the body across to the Land Cruiser and manhandle it into a sitting position in the driver's seat.

'Guess we just found out why they call it dead weight,' the woman panted as they finally wrestled him into place.

She patted a bulge in the dead man's shirt pocket and pulled out Martin's pills. 'These yours?' she asked.

Martin nodded. She looked at the labels and handed the packets to him. 'You know, a man with your kind of money really should be taking better care of himself,' she smiled.

'I'll keep that in mind,' Martin said. Then, as the woman slid Colin's pistol into the holster at the bikie's waist, 'Lucky for us the safety catch was off.'

'Glocks don't have a regular safety. They've got something called safe action. You just have to pull the trigger, but you have to pull it pretty hard and in exactly the right way.'

'Lucky for me I got it right then.'

'Lucky for both of us.' She smiled again.

'Should we put his seatbelt on?' Martin asked, looking at the dead bikie slumped in the driver's seat.

'I'm afraid at this point in time a traffic accident is the least of his worries.' She looked at Martin for a moment, then pulled the seatbelt around the bikie's body. 'However, since he's now playing the part of a hypertensive, stitched-up bank manager, we'll put on the belt. You would, wouldn't you?' she asked.

This whole thing was even stranger than the donut van, Martin decided. He sat on the sidecar and watched as the woman placed a large rock under a front tyre of the Land Cruiser. After putting the gear stick in neutral, she leaned over to release the handbrake. The vehicle lurched forward slightly, coming to rest against the rock. She walked round to the open rear doors and, working carefully, poured petrol from the jerry can over the empty canvas bags.

'You wanna throw me the pool cue?' she asked, turning back to Martin.

He tossed it to her. She smiled her thanks and began wrapping the bikie's bloody shirt around the splintered wooden shaft. When it was tightly tied she dribbled some petrol from the jerry can over the fabric. Something seemed to occur to her and she walked over to Martin.

'Open your mouth,' she said.

Martin looked warily at the pool cue in her hand.

'Hey, c'mon,' she said, 'I'm not going to make you eat it, I just want to check out your teeth.'

Martin opened his mouth and she peered in. 'My goodness,' she said, 'amalgam city. The fifties really were the glory days of Australian dentistry. No dentures, though, which is lucky for us.'

Back at the Land Cruiser she prised open the bikie's shattered mouth and forced it over the rim of the steering wheel. She slammed the driver's door and then reopened it, removing one of Martin's suede shoes from the corpse and turning the ignition to on.

Martin looked at her questioningly.

'Leaving the ignition off is always a dead giveaway when you stage a car accident,' she said. 'Just remembered in time.'

Martin smiled and nodded in agreement, though he really had no idea what she was talking about.

'You wanna stick that empty jerry can back in the rack for me?' she asked.

Martin did as she requested.

The woman carefully surveyed the vehicle, then turned and studied Martin intently. She looked at his hands. 'Bugger,' she said softly.

Martin looked down.

'You very attached to that ring?' she asked.

He shook his head and pulled the gold wedding band from his finger. Probably about time anyway, he thought to himself, since his wife had stopped wearing hers a couple of years ago. He tossed the ring to her and watched as she put it on the bikie's left hand. After further careful study of the vehicle and its occupant, she finally seemed satisfied.

''kay,' she said, 'now all we need is a light. Got a match?'

Martin reluctantly felt inside the bikie's grimy pants pockets and produced a battered Zippo lighter. She picked up the pool cue and held it out to him. Martin lit it, jumping back as the petrol-soaked shirt flared up.

'Grab the rock,' she ordered.

Martin stared at her, unsure of what she meant.

'Grab the rock from under the front tyre,' she yelled.

He pulled the rock clear and the vehicle rolled towards the cliff edge. The woman threw the burning pool cue into the open rear door and the Land Cruiser burst into flames with a savage *whoomp* and toppled lazily over the edge. Tumbling through the air – almost in slow motion, it appeared to Martin – the blazing mass left a smoky trail before it smashed into the ground far below. A moment later, the burning wreckage was suddenly engulfed in a gigantic fireball.

'Jesus!' Martin gasped, stepping back involuntarily as a wave of heat reached him.

'Fuel tank ruptured when she hit,' explained the woman. 'Bastard got himself a Viking's funeral, which is a hell of lot more than he deserved.'

*

Martin watched the plume of black smoke climbing slowly into the clear sky. The woman held up his left shoe and sadly shook her head.

'Didn't your wife ever tell you brown suede doesn't go with anything?' she asked. She casually tossed the shoe over the cliff, in the direction of the burning Land Cruiser. 'An extra clue to your untimely demise in a tragic single-vehicle accident,' she explained to his questioning look. 'They need to find something not burned up down there that's personal and identifiable as yours.'

Martin nodded mutely.

'The smashed teeth and the fire will mess up any chance of forensics matching the dental records for a while,' she continued. 'It should look like he smashed his face into the steering wheel on impact. That covers up the damage I did to his not-so-pearly whites with the pool cue.'

He could only stare at her in amazement.

'And since the bullet from the Glock went straight through him, it won't show up in a post-mortem X-ray and start alarm bells ringing,' she said. 'Plus those padlocked moneybag seals in the back will make it look like all that cash went up in smoke.'

Martin felt himself sweating, but when he put his hand to his forehead it was dry. He looked at his hand. Every line and mark on his palm and the whorls of his fingerprints stood out in startling clarity.

'It's lucky for us that you and shit-for-brains down there are both pretty porky,' the woman said. 'They'll need to run a DNA match to be a hundred per cent certain it's not you. Which will buy us a little more time. It's not like it is on television,' she continued. 'DNA testing actually takes longer than a three-minute ad break.'

Martin looked at the billowing column of smoke and slowly shook his head. He'd just shot someone who had been about to shoot him and now he was helping a complete stranger incinerate the body in a faked car crash. And apparently DNA testing didn't really happen in the ad breaks. Plus he was pretty porky. 'What the hell is happening to my life?' he said quietly. 'I think I'm going out of my mind.'

She put a hand on his shoulder and he stiffened. It had been a long time since a woman had touched him.

'Don't worry about it,' she said gently. 'It's probably just an adrenalin rush, mixed in with a fair bit of shock.'

'You reckon?'

'It's understandable. Take some really deep breaths and try to calm down. None of this is your fault,' she said firmly, 'it's just fate. Someone was going to get killed on this mountain today. Luckily it didn't wind up being either of us.'

Martin looked at her hand on his shoulder. She had long, elegant fingers. She took her hand away. He immediately wanted her to put it back. She smiled at him.

'And on a brighter note,' she said, 'congratulations. You are now one very rich dead man, Mr . . . .?'

'Carter,' he said. 'Martin Carter.'

She held out her hand. He took it and the same tingle shot through his body. Her grip was firm, the skin soft, even silky.

'I'm Faith Chance. Pleased to meet you. Can you handle a motorbike, Martin Carter?'

'Sorry. Led a bit of a sheltered life, I guess.'

She laughed. It was a nice husky laugh. 'Well, you seem to be making up for it today. Looks like I'm driving then.'

She picked up the newer leather jacket from the ground and slipped it on. 'There's no windscreen on the sidecar, so you'll have to wear this disgusting object,' she said, holding up the bikie's tattered jacket. 'But at least you've got all that lovely money to keep your tootsies warm.'

On the back of the jacket were marks where a fabric logo had been roughly unstitched. Someone had crudely lettered a new one in white paint.

'Hells Angles? I know you shouldn't speak ill of the dead,' Faith said, passing over the jacket, 'but God, what a dope.' She pulled on a pair of leather gloves she'd taken from one of the helmets. They were clean, so Martin guessed they were hers, along with the helmet. He put his right arm into the sleeve of the foul jacket and shuddered.

'C'mon, Mr Carter,' Faith laughed, 'be a man.' She slipped the helmet over her head.

As he squeezed into the cramped seat of the sidecar, Faith handed him the German coalscuttle helmet. He put it on. It was way too big. 'I must look like a dick in this,' he said.

Faith swung her leg over the motorcycle and settled into the seat. She looked down and studied him for a moment. 'I could say no to be polite,' she said seriously, 'but I always say you shouldn't start a relationship on a lie.'

Martin decided she was the strangest person he had ever met. But on the other hand she was most definitely good-looking, which was the only positive thing about his day so far. 'So you're okay on a Harley then?' he asked.

'It's not a Harley, and yes, I know what I'm doing, so don't worry. Anyway, with all your weight in that sidecar for ballast, we don't really have to worry about tipping over.'

Martin wondered if he should be offended, but she was smiling warmly and there was that look in her eye again.

'Should still be warm,' Faith said after checking the bike's gauges, 'so let's prime this baby and give it a burl.' She adjusted some controls, then stood up and pushed down twice, slowly, on a foot pedal on the right-hand side. 'Electric starters are for girls,' she said, kicking down hard on the pedal this time. The engine coughed once, rattled and stopped. She leaned down to fiddle with something on the left side of the machine.

'How do you know all that stuff?' Martin asked. 'I mean, what to do with the ... you know, the clues and things? Faking the accident? And the teeth? And the safety on the Glock?'

'Easy,' she replied, smiling, 'it's my job.' She kicked down hard again. The engine missed for the second time.

'Your job?'

She nodded and repeated the starting sequence. This time the motorcycle stuttered noisily to life. The engine roared as she worked the throttle, then settled into a slow rhythmic throb.

'What kind of job?' Martin shouted over the noise.

'I'm a librarian,' she yelled, flipping down the helmet visor. She twisted the throttle again and they took off in a shower of stones and dust, Martin clutching frantically at his helmet with one hand and the sidecar with the other.

eight

Just before dusk they had hidden the motorcycle in some thick scrub off the road outside a small town. It was only a short walk to the caravan park they had seen advertised on a highway billboard. Faith crossed an empty car park to the manager's office to rent an overnight cabin, while Martin hid in the shadows. It was off season, so there was no-one around to see Martin sneak into the cabin five minutes after her.

'Have any problems?' he asked.

'Dead as a doornail this time of year,' she said, closing the door behind him, 'so the manager was grateful for any business. Told him my car broke down just outside town. Since I paid cash, he upgraded me to this luxurious *pied-à-terre*.'

Martin inspected the very basic fittings in the cabin. There was a combination living/dining room, a galley kitchen, and a separate bedroom with a double bed and an en suite bathroom. The cabin had obviously seen a lot of summers, and the wear and tear was showing.

'Crikey, what must the low-end accommodation be like?' he wondered.

'Think mildewed canvas, ex-army folding cots and chipped enamel mugs and you'll get the picture,' Faith said. 'Manager looked like the kind of bloke who might come sniffing around a single woman later, so I asked if there was a local pharmacy where I could get some lotion for crabs.'

She smiled brightly at Martin, who was stunned.

'Just a joke, Mr Carter, but it caused a definite loss of interest on his part. He is, however, letting me have one of their rental bikes. Probably apply a blowtorch and Dettol to the seat after I return it. So, you hungry at all?'

'I'm suddenly starving,' Martin said.

'Me too. We both left our lunches up on the mountain, if you remember. How about you keep a low profile and I'll cycle into town for some supplies?'

'Will you be all right on your own?' Martin asked.

'I reckon I might be. I'm a big girl, Martin.' Faith rummaged through her wallet. 'Bugger,' she said.

'Something wrong?' he asked.

'I spent the last of my cash on the cabin.'

'No problem,' he smiled, and handed her a wad of money from his back pocket.

'Why, Mr Carter,' she said, 'ten thousand dollars! Whatever can you be expecting?'

She was a funny bugger, this one, thought Martin. He glanced at the clock on the wall. 'I know all about country towns at seven-fifteen on a weeknight,' he said, 'so I'm not expecting a whole lot. A takeaway chicken shop, maybe.' He collapsed onto the shabby couch with a groan. 'I'm not usually much of a drinker but I could do with a serious belt right about now.'

Faith collected the bicycle from the park manager and pedalled into town. Martin was watching from the darkened cabin when she returned forty-five minutes later. The carrier basket was overflowing and several bulging plastic bags were hanging from the handlebars.

She unloaded barbecued chicken, coleslaw, bread and wine onto the bench in the kitchen. 'It's a two-chicken-shop town,' she said. 'Very high-tone. Not Too Fowl was closed, which I considered something of a blessing, but Chooks 'R' Us was still roasting.'

Faith put the foil bag containing the chicken into the oven, set it to low, and started pulling items from a plastic bag. 'Struck it lucky with a convenience store next door to the chicken man,' she said, reading the instructions on the back of a silver box with a picture of a glamorous blonde on the front. 'Go and wet your hair, Martin.' She held up a pair of scissors and a comb. 'The first thing we have to do is give you a different look.'

He retreated obediently to the bathroom, and when he returned she wrapped a towel round his shoulders and neatly trimmed his hair. Not a bad cut, Martin decided when she'd finished. Next she put on a pair of rubber gloves and shampooed an ammonia-smelling liquid through his still damp hair. She carefully applied some of the solution to his eyebrows with a cotton bud.

Setting the timer on the stove, Faith filled the sink with hot water and detergent and started scrubbing dishes and cutlery from the cupboards. Martin watched with the towel still around his shoulders.

'Food's probably okay,' she explained, 'but I'll bet these plates and forks could give you an interesting case of Delhi belly.'

The timer went off just as she finished the last of the dishes. 'Time for you to hit the shower, Martin. Way past time, in fact. You really stink.' She tossed him a garbage bag and shampoo. 'Put all your old clobber in this,' she said, 'and you'll need to wash your hair at least a couple of times.'

After locking the bathroom door, Martin stripped and stuffed all his clothes into the garbage bag. Just tying the yellow tape around the neck of the bag made him feel cleaner.

He looked in the mirror. Jesus, was that the same face he'd looked at twelve hours earlier? They say a day is a long time in politics – they should try armed robbery. His cheeks were red with windburn, which gave him a healthy glow, and he liked his new shorter haircut. It suited his face. His eyes looked really blue. Had they always been blue? He couldn't remember.

He turned and looked at his profile. Very solid, yes, but at least he didn't have a real beer gut and he had the height to carry it. C'mon, who was he kidding? Those extra kilos might have been spread evenly over his body but they were still there. Even Faith had noticed.

Faith. He couldn't figure her out. He looked at his reflection. C'mon, when had he ever been able to figure a woman out?

The towels in the bathroom were thin and threadbare but the water in the shower was surprisingly hot. Martin shampooed his hair first and then began to methodically scrub every square inch of his body. The first couple of times was to get rid of all traces of the bikie and his putrid clothing. The third time around even Martin couldn't be sure what he was trying to rub off.

When he came out of the bathroom, he found new socks, underwear, and a yellow and green tracksuit spread out on the bed. A pair of Dunlop Volleys were still in their box.

Back in the living room, Faith was setting out dinner on a coffee table in front of the TV. She looked up and smiled as he walked in wearing his new outfit. 'Here, try these.' She handed him a pair of heavy, black-rimmed glasses with lightly tinted lenses. 'You look like the man of my dreams,' she teased when he put them on.

Embarrassed, Martin adjusted the frames on his nose. 'You must have extremely limited expectations,' he said.

Faith laughed – that throaty laugh again. Martin decided he really loved the way she laughed. He found himself laughing with her.

'Those sandshoes fit?' she asked.

'They're fine,' he said, but his mind was miles away from the Dunlop Volleys.

'And the hipster briefs are okay? You didn't strike me as a boxers sort of guy.'

'No, they're good,' he said awkwardly.

'Size okay? Not strangling the scrotum, are we?'

Martin blushed.

'Oops, sorry. Didn't mean to embarrass you. Just wanted to make sure your boys were comfortable.'

'No, they're good . . . the hipsters, I mean. Not my . . . no, no, they're fine. Thanks,' he mumbled.

'Good. I also got you some sunglasses and a scarf for the road.' She reached for another bag. 'Squinting and picking grasshoppers out of your teeth tends to take the joy out of sidecar touring.'

'So I noticed,' he said, relieved that the conversation had taken another direction.

'We should eat.' She passed him a chilled bottle of chardonnay and a corkscrew. 'Wine going to be okay?

I wasn't sure how serious a belt you were looking for, but we probably shouldn't get totally blotto, given the circumstances.'

'Wine is fine,' he said. 'But given the circumstances, Faith, getting blind screaming legless on just about anything seems like a bloody great idea to me.'

They ate in silence, sitting on the floor in front of the TV so that no shadows showed on the drawn blinds. The infrequent news breaks made no mention of a major bank robbery that day, which Martin thought was odd. But apart from that, he was starting to feel a little less confused. Strangely, barbecued chicken and industrial coleslaw had restored a sense of normality to his day.

After the meal, they turned the sound down on the TV and Faith opened a second bottle of wine. Martin hadn't realised they'd already finished a bottle – the alcohol seemed to be having no effect on him.

'So, Mr Carter, what's your story?' she asked, stretching out her long legs.

Martin sketched a picture of his bleak five years of family life in Burrinjuruk, and the events leading up to the present. He was surprised at how easily it all came out in front of a complete stranger. Faith listened quietly, nodding from time to time and maintaining eye contact with him. He liked that. He tried to remember the last time someone, apart from Colin, had appeared to be genuinely interested in what he had to say.

'Now your turn,' he said when he'd finished his condensed life story. 'What exactly were you doing on a lonely mountain top with a crazed bikie?'

'Not a long story either,' she said. 'After my marriage fell apart, I chucked in my job, bought a second-hand motorcycle and decided to cruise. The bike broke down between towns and Prince Charming offered me a lift. It was stupid but I hopped right in. I guess I was paying more attention to the bike than the rider.'

Martin looked at her blankly.

'World War II vintage Indian. Military Chief and very cherry.'

Martin still looked blank.

'Before there was Harley-Davidson, there was the Indian Motorcycle Company,' she explained. 'Seriously cool bikes, and he was riding one. Military issue 344 Chief, with the 74 cubic-inch engine. Would have been lend-lease from the Yanks to us in '44. Pretty rare, especially in original condition, which this one was, apart from the crappy paint job. Streaky spraycan black all over the khaki. Plus that awful girlie picture. Bloody sacrilege.' She took a sip of wine. 'Anyway, it was hot, I was tired from walking my bike, not thinking straight, so I hitched a ride and I guess I fell asleep.'

'Next to that engine?' Martin was amazed.

'You're really not into bikes, are you?' she smiled. 'Anyway, when I woke up we were on the mountain and things started getting ugly. Then you showed up. My lucky day.'

There was a sudden thump on the roof of the cabin. Martin jumped to his feet, spilling his wine. 'Jesus,' he whispered, his face white, 'do you think it's the police?'

They listened for a minute, but all Martin could hear was his heart thumping in his chest.

Faith shook her head. 'Don't panic, Martin,' she said softly, 'there's no way anyone would know you were here. Especially not the cops. Not this soon anyway.'

Martin's heart rate began to return to normal. There was a scuffling noise from the roof. They listened, looking up at the ceiling.

'So what do you think, Mr Carter? Possum or pervy park manager?'

'Possum, I reckon. There'd be more snuffling and grunting if it was the manager.'

Faith chuckled and refilled their wineglasses.

That was the second time she'd laughed at something he'd said, Martin thought, like it really was funny. 'And what happened to your marriage,' he said, 'if you don't mind me asking?' He was surprised that he'd asked. Maybe the wine was kicking in after all.

'Normal stuff, I guess,' she said. 'He ran off with my best friend.'

'Oh, sorry. Why did he do that?' As soon as he said it, he realised it was a stupid question.

Faith sipped her wine. 'I think it was her tits.'

'She have really big ones?' he asked, staring into his glass.

'Not particularly. But she did have two.'

Martin looked at her, and saw something in her eyes that silenced him for a long time.

'Did you have chemo or radiation afterwards?' he asked finally.

'Bit of both. Lucky me, eh? Vomiting plus glowing in the dark.' She gave him an inquisitive look. 'You're unusually well informed for a country bank manager. And thanks for the "*really* big ones" comment,' she added. 'Me and my prosthetic are *really* quite flattered.'

Martin blushed scarlet. 'Sorry, I don't normally say things like that.'

'Don't apologise,' she smiled. 'I meant it. Nicest compliment I've had in a *really* long time.' She raised her glass and clinked it against his.

Martin finished his wine in one large gulp.

'Now tell me,' she asked, 'your working knowledge of post-operative oncology comes from?'

'I was married for fifteen years before the whole Burrinjuruk disaster.'

'Interesting. Teenage romance? With the requisite late-'60s unwanted pregnancy?'

He nodded. 'She lost it, but we were married by that stage. Never managed to get pregnant again. Not having a whole lot of sex might have contributed to that. Anyway,' he continued, 'one day I heard her crying in the shower. She thought if she ignored the lump it wouldn't be cancer and it would just go away. By the time she realised it wasn't going to disappear, it was all pretty hopeless.'

'Sounds like you hung around, though,' she said, raising her glass. 'Here's to kind-hearted bank-robbing bikie-slayers.'

Martin raised his own glass.

'Sorry, that makes you sound like a low-rent drive-in movie,' Faith said. 'Must be getting pissed.'

Martin spluttered and wine spilled down the front of his tracksuit. He laughed as he mopped it up with a handful of paper napkins. 'They do pretty good reconstructions these days, you know,' he said, recovering. 'I can give you the money.'

'Thanks for the offer. That's really kind of you.' There was a catch in her voice. She cleared her throat. 'I just figured I wouldn't have it done until I didn't need to. Does that make sense?'

'Yeah. Yeah, it does,' he said.

He decided to change the subject. 'So where were you headed before you ran into Mr Smooth on the Harley? Sorry, Indian.'

'Just north. My mum and dad bought a campervan and took off on the grey highway after he retired. I thought I'd follow their lead.'

'Where's the Grey Highway?' Martin asked.

'You know, Highway One. The coast road that runs all the way around the country.'

'I know Highway One, I just never heard it called the Grey Highway.'

'It's grey because it's chock-a-block with geriatric retirees in campers and caravans cruising their golden years away. Mum and Dad were just two more on the merry-go-round.'

'You trying to catch up with them?'

'No. Mum had a stroke near a north-coast town called Woodville on their second time around. They put her into a local nursing home. She died there last year.'

'I'm sorry,' Martin said. 'That must have been tough.'

'We were never really close,' she shrugged. 'I was in a pretty down situation at the time, so I passed on the funeral. Couldn't face it. Missing my old dad a bit now, though, so I thought I'd chase him up.' Faith stood up and crossed to the fridge.

'Where is he now?' Martin asked.

'He stayed on in a retirement hostel attached to the nursing home. Poor bugger. Mum made his life a misery, and now she's gone and he's wasting away with a bunch of boring old fogies.'

Faith opened the freezer and pulled out a couple of chocolate icecream hearts. 'Dessert?' Martin nodded and she tossed him one. 'Dad's the one who got me interested in motorcycles,' she said, crunching into the chocolate coating. 'He was a marine engineer on coastal freighters, and apparently a bit of a larrikin to boot. Used to hoon around on a 500cc Norton Dominator until he met Mum. No more two-wheels after that, though. Got me to love bikes to make up for it, I guess. Taught me all about them. I started saving on the sly for a Ducati when I was nine. Bought my first when I turned eighteen. That's an Italian bike,' she explained.

'Yeah, I figured that,' he said, biting off a chunk of icecream.

'Same make as the one that broke down and got me into all this trouble. Very Italian, very temperamental.'

'Why didn't you buy an Indian this time?' Martin asked.

'They're fantastic bikes but bloody expensive. Indian went out of business in the early '50s, so everything you see on the road these days has been restored. Nobody ever built a more beautiful-looking motorcycle, though. Maybe one day,' she sighed.

'So it was your old dad who made you a bikie?'

Faith nodded. 'But he wouldn't want to catch you calling me that. I'm a biker, and there's a definite difference.'

'He sounds like an okay bloke, your old man.'

'More than okay. One of a kind, old Wal. I missed him a lot growing up, when he was away at sea. Like I said, Mum and I were never really close.' She licked her icecream stick clean. 'Maybe you could pop in and meet him when we get to Woodville? If you've got a few minutes to spare.'

'We?'

'Well,' she said, 'you're heading north for that high-school reunion thing anyway. You'll be a lot less obvious travelling with me, and I sure as hell don't have anything better to do.'

'Sounds like a plan, I guess,' he agreed, surprised at how good this development made him feel.

'That's settled then.' Faith gathered up the debris of their dinner. 'Since I paid in advance, we can sneak out early. Got us some black spraypaint to give that fuel tank a bit of a makeover before we hit the road. Me straddling those pneumatic babes is probably not the look we should be going for.'

'Maybe we should get rid of HELLS ANGLES while we're at it?' Martin suggested. 'We don't want to get pulled over by the spelling police, you being a librarian.'

Faith laughed. She leaned forward and straightened the collar on his tracksuit. She was a very tactile person, he realised. And he also realised that he liked that a whole lot.

'So, what do you think of your new look?' she asked.

'Well, you obviously spared no expense,' he said. 'Genuine polyester, is it? God forbid I should wear a fabric that breathes.'

'In the spy game it's called trade craft, Martin. It's all about blending in. I suppose this means you'll be wanting your change back now?'

'Nah, you can keep it,' he smiled. 'I'm rolling in it.'

'That's exactly how you smelled in that bikie's jeans, like you'd been rolling in it. And it, whatever it was, had been dead for a week. We should bury that stuff off the road somewhere.'

'The sooner the better,' he agreed.

'Maybe we should ditch the rest of the armoury at the same time?' Faith suggested. 'Unless you've got one of those macho gun things happening?'

'I think I'm over guns for all time. They're too damn dangerous.'

Faith stood up and stretched. 'A shower and then hit the sheets, I think. It's been a very big day.'

'Sure has,' said Martin, fidgeting. He wondered what the sleeping arrangements would be in a situation like this.

Faith interrupted his thoughts. 'The couch turns into a bed. Not ideal, but for someone who's been jammed into a sidecar all afternoon it'll probably feel like heaven.'

'I'm sure I'll be fine,' Martin said, relieved that this was settled. He suddenly remembered something. 'Is it really your birthday?'

'Yep.'

'Mine was yesterday.'

She smiled. 'You can't beat not getting killed as a birthday present, eh? How old?'

'Fifty. And you?' He stopped himself. 'Sorry, that's a bit personal.'

She shrugged. 'No, it's not. I'm forty-five and grateful for every day of it.'

'Really? You don't look forty-five.'

'I've seen the million bucks, Martin, there's no need to sweet-talk me. And you're still on the couch.'

nine

Sergeant Colin Curtis was hosing out the satellite dish on the roof of the garage of the police residence. He did this regularly in the vain hope that a clean dish would somehow pick up less crappy programs. A black Commodore pulled into the police station driveway behind him. He noticed it had black tinted windows. Very black. The man who got out of the driver's door was wearing a suit. A very nice suit. Col might have been a country cop but he knew an Armani suit when it walked up to him at three in the morning. The suit and its owner had been nosing around the bank earlier, during the preliminary investigation. The armed-robbery cops from Albury had been deferential to its wearer, which was unusual. The armed-robbery cops from Albury weren't normally deferential to anybody. Everyone who had ever had dealings with them agreed that the armed-robbery cops from Albury were a pretty scary bunch.

'Had your car washed then?' Colin asked. 'The Albury wallopers do it for you?'

The man in the suit smiled at him. About the same age as himself, Colin estimated. And fit. Extremely fit. Colin decided he could take him, probably. But it wouldn't be easy. Someone would get hurt, and someone else would get very seriously hurt.

'Didn't wake you, I see,' said the visitor.

'I don't sleep.' Colin twisted the nozzle on the hose to off.

'Gotcha,' said the man. 'I know what that's like. How about we go for a little walk?' He nodded towards the residence. 'Wouldn't want to disturb the wife and sprogs.'

Col scanned the stranger's suit for evidence of a weapon. The man smiled and held his jacket open. 'Feel free to pat me down if it makes you happy.'

Colin swung his hip slightly to make sure the revolver on his belt could be seen.

'Must be your spare,' said the stranger. 'Word around town is the local bank manager took your service pistol off you.' He shook his head sadly and made tut-tutting noises. 'Not going to look too good in the old personnel file, is it?'

Colin shrugged. 'Bad day,' he said. 'It happens.'

The two men walked down towards the creek, which ran through a gully behind the station. The pale glow from an almost full moon washed an eerie blue light over the property; the ghost gums cast long shadows across the track.

'So what can you tell me about Martin Carter?'

Colin stopped at the question and looked closely at the man's face. He was silent for a long time. 'I gave all the pertinent details to the armed-robbery squad from Albury,' he said finally. 'And since I don't know you from a hole in the ground, I don't think I feel like saying anything else.'

'I'm from the government,' said the man in the suit.

'Federal, state, local or shire?' Colin asked. 'I'm pretty sure you're not the Burrinjuruk dog catcher because I think that's me.'

The man took a thin black leather wallet from his jacket and flipped it open to reveal an identity card inside a clear plastic sleeve.

'Sounds important, but I've never heard of it,' said Colin after checking the details on the card. 'Of course my twelve-year-old runs up IDs like that on her computer at school.' He squinted at the wallet again. 'Better than that, actually.'

The man in the suit closed his wallet. 'We're not a department that seeks out publicity, Sergeant Curtis, but we are tasked to report at the highest levels of government. Let's just say that if you ring the Federal Police Inter-Departmental Liaison Office in Canberra, they will confirm we exist.' His voice was suddenly cold. 'And I think they'll advise you that we're a department you don't really want to fuck with. So let's start again. What can you tell me about Martin Carter?'

'He's fat, fifty, confused and extremely cashed up.'

'Very droll. Anything personal you can tell me? Friends, relatives, acquaintances, accomplices?' The stranger paused for a moment. 'Any place you can think of that he might be heading for with all that money?'

Colin picked up a flat stone and skipped it across the shallow creek. It bounced twice and sank just short of the far bank. 'Why would a federal security agency be interested in a rural bank robbery?' he asked with his back to the stranger.

'Let's just say Mr Carter's name rang some bells.'

Colin turned back to him. 'Not buying it, pal. Martin's just some rural bank shit-kicker who went a bit wobbly. People like Martin don't ring bells. You're going to have to do a bit better than that.' Colin's face was blank, but his mind was racing. Why would someone like Martin be flagged in Canberra? He'd done a cursory check of police records the first time Martin came in to renew his licence for the bank pistol – nothing had shown up, and the state police computer was cross-linked to the federal police mainframe. Every bone in Colin's body was telling him that this bloke was ex-military, probably special ops. He'd be more likely to be out chasing terrorists than bank robbers.

Then suddenly it clicked. That was the connection. It wasn't Martin, it was the mad major. It had to be. Nothing else made sense. But why the hell would Stark's high-school friends and God knows who else be on a watch list? The list would go back over thirty years. Some serious kind of watch list, Colin mused.

The man broke into his thoughts. 'I can hear your brain working, Sergeant. Just confirm where Carter was headed and everything stays pleasant.'

'I really don't know,' Colin said, pulling himself together. 'And I don't like being threatened.'

The man picked up a stone and skipped it across the creek, watching as it bounced over the water's surface and continued into the scrub on the other bank. 'It may suit you to have the locals think you're just some laid-back dozy country copper, but we both know different. I don't care why you want to rot out here in the boonies, but I do know about the three police bravery commendations and your decorations from 'Nam.'

'Lot of people got medals over there,' Colin said. 'Doesn't mean much.'

'Yanks might have been chucking their gongs about like chook food, but our boys had to really earn 'em. And you certainly did. You weren't just some pogo hanging out at Vungers. One citation says you offed three nogs with your bare hands when your section ran out of ammo on a very hot contact in the Horseshoe.'

The access to his service records and the casual use of military jargon confirmed Colin's suspicions. Probably intentionally, he decided. This bloke was very, very good. Dangerously good.

Having reached the end of the track, they turned and started back towards the house.

'So where'd you serve?' Col asked finally.

The stranger smiled a cold smile. 'Here and there. You know. The Delta. Up north a few times. Got around a bit. Guess you could say I was a bit of a freelance operative.'

'I'll just bet you were.' Colin couldn't keep the contempt out of his voice.

'Someone had to do the really nasty stuff.'

'It was the bods who enjoyed doing the really nasty stuff who gave me the creeps.'

'Yeah, well, war is hell and all that bullshit. It's been nice talking over old times, but let's get back to tintacks. Where were we again?'

'I think I was saying I don't like being threatened,' Colin said.

'Right. And I believe I was indicating that I know better than to threaten a man like you.' His smile was now ice-cold. 'That's why I'm threatening your wife and kids.'

Colin lunged instinctively, but the man stepped back quickly and put up a hand.

'Let me just demonstrate something before we start getting all physical.' He raised his right index finger in front of Colin's face. A sharp red dot of light appeared on the tip of his finger, then disappeared as quickly as it had come.

'You prick!' Colin's eyes instantly scanned the house and the surrounding bushland.

'You won't find him,' the stranger said. 'He's very good.' He gave a nod and the red dot reappeared on his fingertip. He moved his finger around in a random sweep and the dot stayed precisely in place.

'The bullet hits where the red dot sits, and you know it takes one hell of a marksman to hold on a moving target like this.' Leaning forward, he placed his finger in the middle of Colin's chest. When he withdrew his finger, the dot stayed in place.

Colin looked down at the bright red dot over his heart. 'Bit obvious, though, isn't it?'

'Not when we switch to infra-red. Totally invisible, except to the shooter. Let's just say this is our demonstration model.' He handed Colin a plain white business card with just a name – A. Smith – and a mobile phone number on it. 'If he calls you, Sergeant, you contact me immediately. You do not call him. You do not try to warn him. If you do, believe me, we will know and there will be a price to pay. And you won't like it. Not one little bit.'

It was the calmness and cold certainty in the voice that Colin found most unnerving. He watched in silence as the man walked to his car and opened the door. Smith looked back at Colin. 'Don't disappoint me, now,' he said.

Colin held the man's gaze while he slowly ripped up the business card and let the pieces drop to the ground.

Smith pointed towards the house, where a single light glowed from the kitchen. Colin's youngest daughter had taped a crayon drawing of a clown to the fridge, clearly visible through the kitchen window. A glowing red dot appeared in the middle of the clown's forehead. It stayed for a moment, then rapidly moved up the side of the house to the roof and across to the garage. There was a thud, and a neat but surprisingly large hole suddenly materialised in the metal skin of the satellite dish.

Martin, you poor bastard, Colin thought. You are in some seriously deep shit.

ten

There were no roadblocks on the highway, but every few kilometres they passed police cars parked on the verge, with officers scanning the traffic through binoculars.

'What do we do if they flag us down?' Martin yelled over the roar of the engine.

Faith shook her head, unable to hear. She flipped up her visor and leaned down and Martin put his face close to hers.

'What happens if they flag us down?' he yelled again. He found himself distracted by how good she smelled.

'We haven't passed any roadblocks,' she yelled back. 'They just seem to be watching. It's very strange.'

Martin nodded and hunkered down as far as possible in the sidecar, keeping a wary eye out for the next sign of police. He found it impossible to get comfortable in the cramped space. The money that wouldn't fit behind the sidecar's seat was taking up most of the room in the nose, so he couldn't stretch out his legs. He complained about it at a roadhouse where they stopped for fuel and an early breakfast. He also complained about the quality of his breakfast, but his mood improved when he was able to swap the coal-scuttle helmet for something a little more conventional. A scooter rider heading for Sydney had been only too pleased to make the trade.

Just as they were getting ready to head back out on the road, a highway patrol car cruised into the service area. Martin, jammed in the sidecar once again, began to panic. He broke out in a sweat, even though the morning air still held a chill. Then he realised that the two officers were ignoring him, and were in fact much more interested in checking out Faith.

'Nice bike,' one said through the car window.

'You bet, officer,' Faith smiled.

'Looks like fun,' the second cop said.

'You really can't beat having something big, black and throbbing between your legs first thing in the morning,' she said, kicking down hard on the starter. The still warm engine roared to life and they pulled out onto the highway with Martin hunkered down even lower in the sidecar and regretting that he'd got rid of the German helmet. He'd almost been able to get his whole head into it, and right now he wanted to be invisible.

Around noon they pulled into the car park of a large shopping centre to get lunch. Faith thought a picnic would be a good idea, letting them eat and keep an eye on the bike and the money at the same time. Three police cars were parked by the entrance, so they found some shade and waited to see if the cops moved on. Sitting on the kerb under a large old bottlebrush, Martin asked, 'What made you become a librarian?'

'Now, there's a conversation starter you don't often hear,' Faith laughed.

'No, seriously, I'm interested. Ducatis to Dewey decimal – bit of a leap?'

'Not a lot of choices for girls back then – nurse, teacher, librarian ... I could read pretty well by the time I was three – Dad helped me sort words out. At five I realised I was thinking like an adult and at six I decided I was a lot smarter than most of the grown-ups around me. I started spending a lot of time in the library and I guess I never left. I loved the sense of order, I suppose.'

'Hiding out with the Famous Five?'

'That's a bit presumptuous,' she said with mock outrage. 'I was a Secret Seven girl! Actually, I'd read anything with words on it. Plus, when I read something it pretty much stays with me.'

'Like a photographic memory, you mean?' he asked.

'Something like that. Bit of a pain, really. My head's full of all sorts of often useless information.'

'Like what?'

'Okay,' she said, 'for instance, take your pills. ACE inhibitor for blood pressure, diuretic to make you piss and increase the action of the ACE inhibitor, and a statin to lower cholesterol.'

'Sounds like what the doctor said,' Martin agreed, craning his neck to check on the police cars, which were still parked at the entrance.

'I can do better than that,' Faith continued. 'The ACE stands for angiotensin-converting enzyme, and the inhibiting ingredient in the particular type you're taking is derived from the venom of a Brazilian brown tree snake.'

'Really?'

'Really. Which is why you don't want to be running around chopping down rainforests. Who knows what else is waiting to be discovered?'

'You must have been fun at parties.'

'I was once I learned to keep my mouth shut. And don't go anywhere with that statement,' she warned with a wry smile.

Martin grinned. He was starting to think she could read his mind. 'And why did you marry your ex?' he asked.

'Jesus, Martin,' she said, 'I thought banking required an ordered mind. Yours is all over the place like a mad woman's breakfast, with no disrespect meant towards women, the mentally ill, or the most important meal of the day.'

Martin pushed a stone around with the toe of his Volley. 'I spent thirty years trying to convince myself I was happy as a banker, and that I could think like one,' he said sadly.

'Didn't work, I see,' she said. 'Still, we need bankers in society so we know exactly when a fad is over.'

Martin affected a hurt expression. 'That's very cruel, Faith. And if you're referring to the diamond-stud earring period in retail banking, I was never a participant. I'm unpunctured.'

She let out a delighted laugh. 'Very good, Martin! You have the makings of an excellent travelling companion.'

Martin rather liked the concept of being a travelling companion. Especially hers.

'Now, back to your highly insensitive and grossly invasive question,' she went on. 'I married Giles because I was twenty-five and he had a shiny new engineering degree, an MGB and he asked me. Back then I thought that was love.'

'Really?' He turned to face her.

'I said I was intelligent, Martin, it just took me a long time to get smart.'

'Good old Giles with the MGB, eh?' Martin chuckled.

'I know, I know,' she said defensively, throwing up her hands, 'it's a name for a butler, not a lover. You're so hard, Giles. Slam it into me, Giles. Throw me onto the old four-poster and roger me rigid, Giles. It just doesn't work, does it?'

'Hey, keep it down, Faith,' Martin said, looking around uncomfortably.

'Why, Martin, did I embarrass you again?' she laughed.

He frowned. 'No, but there's a time and a place –'

'C'mon,' she said, 'this is a shopping-centre car park. It'll be full of shaggin' wagons as soon as the sun goes down. All squeaking down hard on their axles.'

He relaxed. 'You're right, I guess. But if Giles is a crook name, Martin isn't much better.' He glanced around furtively and lowered his voice. 'You're so hard, Martin. Slam it into me, Martin. Throw me onto the four-poster and roger me rigid, Martin – doesn't really work either.'

Faith touched his arm gently and looked into his eyes. 'If it really worries you, we can always get you a nickname.'

Martin stopped breathing, suddenly aware of his heart pounding savagely in his chest. It felt like it was going to explode.

Faith glanced at her watch. 'I don't know if these cops are ever going to leave,' she said, looking towards the entrance. 'I'm going to risk it. You just hang here and I'll get us some lunch.' She inspected Martin's face. 'And a bottle of sun screen. You're getting quite red.'

Martin suddenly remembered to breathe.

She stood up. 'With three carloads of cops here, there won't be a Chiko Roll, dim sim or donut left in the place. Just as well too, you could really do with losing some of that gut, Marty boy.'

Martin's heart stopped pounding.

*

After fifteen minutes, he began to be concerned. Then a group of uniformed police walked out of the mall entrance and gathered around one of the patrol cars. Ten minutes later, Faith came out carrying several large shopping bags. She walked in the direction of the police and then suddenly stopped, glancing around as if looking for someone. *What the hell is she doing?* Martin thought anxiously. After a minute or two, Faith made her way back to the motorcycle via a wide circle through the parked cars.

'Sorry about the wait,' she said as she put the bags on the ground, 'but I followed some of the cops around the mall to see if you were getting a mention.'

'Find out anything?'

She shook her head. 'Just that they'd all like to do it to the girl behind the counter in the jeweller's.'

'I nearly had a heart attack when you walked up to those policemen,' Martin said.

'Sorry, but they were listening to the radio, so I thought I'd see if you featured on any all-points bulletins.'

'And did I?' Martin asked nervously.

'Who knows? They were listening to the cricket. The West Indies just declared at six for 480.'

He laughed with relief. 'They're good.'

'And in theory you're really bad, Mr Carter,' Faith said, 'but no-one seems terribly interested. I can't figure out what's going on.'

They found a small park with picnic tables, shade, and a view over a dry creekbed. Lunch was crusty bread and a variety of cold meats, cheeses and salads. There was fresh fruit for dessert.

'This looks great, Faith,' he said, opening the bottle of mineral water she handed him.

'Hang about.' She rummaged in another bag and took out a complex-looking camera. After quickly checking the settings, she took a shot of him across the picnic table. 'They had a really great camera store in that mall,' she said. 'That's another reason it took me so long. I've got a thing about taking photographs.'

She took three more shots in rapid succession, changing her angle slightly each time. The camera's shutter clicked and the motordrive whirred with each frame. 'All great journeys should be documented, and what's life if it isn't a great journey?'

'It's too complicated for me,' he said.

'What, life?'

'No, that camera. But now you mention it, life is pretty damn complicated too.'

Faith handed him the camera. 'Take one of me.'

'Is it idiot-proof?' Martin asked, examining the settings.

'That all depends on the idiot,' she said. 'It's in auto mode, so it'll make all the decisions for you.'

'Fine by me.' Martin looked through the viewfinder. Everything was blurry.

'Just touch the shutter button lightly and it'll focus itself,' she said.

He did as she instructed but the camera fired.

'What happened? It went off before I was ready.'

'Life's like that sometimes,' Faith grinned. 'Try again.'

Martin gently touched the shutter button and Faith came into focus. 'Is it digital?' he asked.

Faith rolled her eyes. 'Of course not. I'm into preserving moments and emotions through the wondrous action of light on the silver halide crystal.'

'And that's not digital then?' Martin asked, looking over the top of the camera at her.

'Hell, no. Digital's just an unemotional recording of binary information.'

'Your old dad was a bit of a photo buff, right?'

She grinned. 'It shows, eh? We had a darkroom in an old shed where we used to hide out from Mum and make black and white prints and talk motorbikes. It was great.'

'Have you always had such strong opinions about every damn thing?' Martin wanted to know.

'Always had them. Only recently learned to voice them. I'm just making up for a lot of wasted years.'

The camera clicked and whirred.

'Got it,' Martin said.

'Great. Now, pass me a pickle.'

eleven

Even with his scarf and sunglasses Martin found it hard to pinpoint the joys of sidecar touring. The wind dried his eyes, forcing him to blink constantly, and he wondered if the steady hammering of the motorcycle engine in his right ear would make him deaf. The view was good, however, he had to admit. Cruising down the highway at ground level, without doors and windows, gave him quite a different perspective of the country they travelled through. Wide brown land was right, he mused. Even the green of the trees and the patches of pasture they encountered as they neared the coast was muted. It was as if everything was covered with a thin layer of dull ochre dust.

It was late afternoon when they finally reached Woodville. Faith suggested stopping for a drink before searching out the nursing home. They wheeled up to a pub on the main street where some three dozen motorcycles were lined up neatly outside. Several bikies lounging on the verandah watched as Faith dismounted, while Martin extricated himself awkwardly from the cramped sidecar. He was wary about leaving the money, but as Faith pointed out, the alternative was walking into a bikie pub with three garbage bags full of cash. She had a point. He tossed his leather jacket into the sidecar, hoping to partially cover the bags.

Faith looked down the line of bikes and whistled. 'Well, our little Chief should feel right at home among this lot. Quite a few Indians, and a couple of very nice ones too.'

Martin studied the parked motorcycles. She was right about Indians, he decided. The shiny, low-slung bikes with the Indian-head logo on their fuel tanks stood out as the most sleek and elegant.

The bikies on the verandah ignored them as they walked up the steps and into the saloon bar. It was noisy and smoky, predominantly male and almost exclusively bikie. A big-screen TV near the pool tables was showing a news bulletin. The sound was off, but Martin nudged Faith when a still of a red motorcycle appeared, followed by a photograph of her, looking very thin, with close-cropped hair and dark circles under her eyes.

'Thank goodness my ex is such a dill,' she said. 'Trust him to give them a photo of me at my very worst.'

The image cut back to a presenter, and the words 'Missing

Persons Hotline' and a phone number appeared across the bottom of the screen.

'Well, it's official,' she said. 'I'm missing. Just as well Dad doesn't watch the news any more.'

'His eyesight?'

'Gave up after the waterfront lock-out. His blood pressure went through the roof.'

They worked their way through the crowd to the bar. It was a riot of denim, leather, tattoos, beards, bald heads, and rotting or missing teeth. The majority of the men were wearing jackets or vests emblazoned with gang colours.

'Well, you certainly blend right in here, Martin,' said Faith, looking around.

A huge, bearded bikie came in at that moment and a small group discussion ensued. Someone pointed in their direction and the bikie walked purposefully over. Conversation stopped and all eyes followed him. A fat finger was pushed into Martin's chest.

'Are youse riding the Indian with the sidecar?' the bikie growled.

'No, actually I am,' said Faith pleasantly. 'What's it to you, dick breath?'

The bar was suddenly quiet, apart from the click of balls on the pool tables. The big bikie leaned down slowly and pulled a thin-bladed knife from his boot.

'You got a wicked mouth there, lady,' he said. 'You need a lesson in manners, I reckon.'

It felt somehow to Martin that everything was suddenly happening in slow motion.

'I want to talk to the president,' Faith said casually.

The atmosphere relaxed a little. Several bikies stepped away from the bar, leaving a gap between the pair and a fortyish man in faded colours. He had a full head of hair and also appeared to have a full set of teeth. Martin noticed that his jeans were held up by a beaded belt colourfully proclaiming: ELVIS LIVES.

'The name's Headjob,' the man said. 'I'm the president of this little band of merry men. How can I help?'

Faith held out a hand. 'Should I call you Head, or Mr Job?'

The president didn't take her hand. 'Let's not push it, lady,' he said coldly. 'You seem to know how the system works, but nobody likes a smart-arse.'

Faith shrugged. 'Your tubby mate seems to have a problem with my bike.'

The president shook his head. 'Actually, it's our bike,' he said. 'Bear recognised it, even with that crap spray job. It got stolen a couple of months back. Arsehole dog named Raymond took it after we turfed him out. Had a bad habit of taking things that didn't belong to him, which was what got him the elbow. How did you come by it, lady?'

'Raymond left it to me in his will,' she smiled.

'That's nice to hear,' the president said. 'How'd the prick die? Nothing too painless, I hope.'

'He fell over.'

'Fell over what?'

Faith looked him straight in the eye. 'A cliff.'

A chuckle rippled through the crowd.

'Fair enough,' said the president. 'As long as it's permanent.'

The atmosphere in the bar returned to normal. The president whistled to the barmaid. 'Three schooners, love. He's paying.' He indicated Martin and leaned over conspiratorially. 'Bear had a butcher's in the sidecar,' he said. 'He reckons you can afford to shout.'

Martin's beer was icy and delicious. Faith and the president downed theirs swallow for swallow. She tapped her empty glass on the bar and nodded to the barmaid. The president looked her up and down.

'So what brings you happy campers to Shangri La by the sea?' he asked.

'Family reunion,' Faith said. 'My old man's stuck in some rathole retirement village around here. Ocean View. You know it?'

'It's the only rathole for miles. Just out of town. What's the old coot's name?' the president asked.

'It's Walter. Walter Chance. For some reason he decided to hang around the joint after my mother died there last year. I just want to check up on him, make sure he's not too miserable.'

'Sounds fair enough,' said the president. 'We'd better find out then.' He yelled to a group at the pool table. 'Hey Wal, you old prick, you feeling miserable?'

One of the players turned from the table. He was wearing

the regulation faded jeans, boots, plaid shirt and sleeveless denim jacket. Thick glasses, a suntanned, wrinkled face, and a short grey ponytail completed the picture. A woman of about sixty put her arm around his waist.

'I'm doing okay, Pres,' the old man yelled back, 'but if you wanna buy me an' Doreen another coupl'a beers, I'll be doing even better.'

The president leaned back on the bar and smiled. 'There's some sheila here to see you,' he said. 'Bit younger than your usual. You can save your pension money, her bloke'll get you a beer. He's bloody loaded.'

The old man walked slowly to the bar and squinted. 'Well, g'day, Faith,' he said, 'what are you doing here?'

'Hello, Dad, just thought I'd check up on you.'

They hugged. The president looked at Martin and winked. 'This is a very touching moment,' he said. 'I think it calls for another beer or seven. Your shout again, I'm afraid. Club rules. Rich bastards pay.'

Martin signalled to the barmaid. 'And another round of whatever the old bloke and his lady by the pool table are drinking,' he said.

'So you got a name there, Mr Rockefeller?' asked the president.

'Martin,' he answered, and they shook hands.

'You around when Raymond fell over then, Martin?'

Martin swallowed. 'I have to admit to some slight peripheral involvement.'

'Definitely permanent, was it?' the president asked.

'And then some,' Martin replied.

The president sipped his beer thoughtfully and looked at Faith, who was still hugging her father. 'She's a bit lippy but that's a pretty nice arse,' he commented.

'Got to go along with you there,' Martin agreed.

'Looks like old Raymundo got way out of his depth with that one. She really a librarian like the old man reckons?'

'Apparently,' Martin said.

The president looked him up and down and shook his head sadly. 'Geez, mate, you're really going to have to lift your game.'

Martin finished his beer in a long swallow. 'Tell me about it,' he said.

*

The residents of the Ocean View Retirement Village and its associated full-care nursing home were obviously used to the thunderous arrival of some thirty-plus motorcycles. Nobody blinked an eye at the noisy cavalcade which now included the Indian and sidecar. Wal was riding pillion on the president's bike.

As he entered the foyer, Martin wondered if the lack of reaction was because the residents couldn't hear the bikes over the blaring sound system reverberating through the corridors. It was the Rolling Stones doing 'Street Fighting Man' at eardrum-jarring volume. Carrying the garbage bags,

Martin followed the president into an office marked 'Jesse James, Manager'.

The president pointed to a corner. 'Just chuck your pocket money over there,' he said, 'it'll be safe. Wanna beer?' He took two cans from a bar fridge without waiting for an answer.

'Won't the manager mind?' asked Martin.

'Shit no,' laughed the president, tossing him a can, 'I *am* the manager. Also the CEO. The club owns the joint through a shelf company. Cheers! You can call me Jesse,' he said, taking a swig of his beer. 'Usually only the boys call me Headjob. It's very touching and shows the high regard in which I'm held.'

'Jesse James?' Martin asked. 'Is that your real name?'

'It's Peter on my birth certificate, but when you run an outlaw motorcycle gang . . .' He shrugged.

Looking through the window, Martin saw a bearded, shaven-headed bikie in colours pushing an elderly lady across the lawn in a wheelchair. 'I'm not sure Faith was expecting anything like this,' he said. 'I certainly wasn't.'

Jesse finished his beer, belched, crushed the can and tossed it overhand into a bin behind the desk. 'I'll give you a tour while your sheila catches up with her dad. That old bugger's amazing. A real root-rat. Puts us youngsters to shame.'

As they walked, Jesse explained the set-up. When his mother had developed dementia five years before, he had been horrified at the level of nursing-home care on offer. He'd noticed a FOR SALE sign on Ocean View on a weekend run up the coast, and the club had purchased it.

'We were very liquid at the time, due to the success of some of our, er, other activities,' Jesse explained. 'The plan was to make a few improvements and let the place continue running itself, but it was as bad as all the others, so we fired the staff and took over.'

'Your mum still here?' Martin asked.

'Nope, she carked it a couple of years back. But we were all having such a good time we just kept the place going in her memory. Anyway, most of the members have oldies who are getting on a bit. Guess that goes for the members themselves.'

'Must have been a bit of a change for you?' Martin suggested.

Jesse guffawed. 'Mate,' he said, 'we're a motorcycle gang. Cleaning up piss and shit and vomit's nothing new. And at least we know in a few years' time we're all gonna end up in a place that understands us.'

A tall blonde nurse walked past carrying a tray of medication. She nodded to Jesse. Martin was goggle-eyed. She was beautiful, with a fantastic figure straining against her tight white uniform. From what he could see, which was quite a lot, she wasn't wearing much in the way of underwear.

Jesse saw him looking. 'What a stunner, eh? Got an

arse on her that would make a saint get a stiff one. Bit of a waste, really.'

'She married?' Martin asked.

'Worse,' Jesse said. 'She's a girls' girl.'

'Oh,' Martin said.

'We get all sorts working here,' Jesse explained. 'Gay, straight, pretzel-shaped. The ones that don't fit in most other places seem to drift our way. All we care about is they've got the right credentials and the right attitude. She held me old mum's hand while she died. I love her to death.' He turned and yelled after her, 'Hey Doris, Bear picked up that DVD for after dinner.'

'Not *Biker Molls from Hell* again, I hope?' she answered.

Jesse looked offended. 'Give the wrinklies a break, darlin', they like the classics.' He nudged Martin and lowered his voice. 'And she'll be watching with a hand up her frock, I'll bet.'

'I heard that, you prick!'

'Love you too, babe,' the president called.

As they walked down the corridor, Martin glanced through the doors of several rooms. Each one opened onto a sunny courtyard and had a TV, telephone and en suite. They were individually furnished and there were photographs and other personal mementoes on display.

Jesse stopped at one room where an elderly man was resting on the bed. He knocked gently on the open door. 'You feeling okay there, Mr Campbell?' he asked from the doorway.

The old man smiled. 'I'm fine, thank you, Mr James. Just a post-afternoon-tea nap. I think I rather overdid it on the lamingtons.'

'I can get Doris to pop in for a sec if you like,' Jesse suggested. 'Not that she'd do your ticker much good.'

'I'll be fine, Mr James. I'll see you at dinner.'

'Looks more like a holiday resort than a nursing home,' Martin observed as they continued on.

'Tell me about it,' Jesse said. 'We should have won Facility of the Year in the last annual nursing-home awards, but the government regulators like to pretend we don't exist.'

'The bikie thing?' Martin asked.

'Also our attitude to sex,' Jesse said. 'If the oldies want to shack up together or have the odd grope, it's none of our concern. Long as everyone's got all their marbles, they're both into it, and they keep the bloody doors closed so's not to frighten the horses.'

'Fair enough,' Martin laughed. 'Faith's old man seems pretty popular.'

'We've got ten sheilas for every bloke, like most of these places. Believe me, anyone with an X-chromosome and a pulse is popular. But, yeah, Wal's a great old bloke.'

They turned into a large sunny room with full-length windows along one wall. 'This is the main recreation room,' Jesse explained.

Martin was expecting basket-weaving or knitting. In the middle of the room was a partially dismantled motorcycle.

A leather-clad man with no teeth was demonstrating how to strip and clean the carburettor to an enthralled audience.

'When we took over, about half our guests were yanked out by their families,' Jesse went on. 'Six months later, they were begging us to let 'em come back. Crocheting or carbie-cleaning, we figure it's all stimulating activity.' He knelt down beside an elderly woman who was holding a can of WD40. 'Keep an eagle eye on him when he gaps those plugs, Clarissa,' he said. 'And don't forget to do up your helmet this time.'

Clarissa chuckled. 'Don't worry, Pres, I've learned my lesson.'

Jesse laughed as they continued on. 'The ones with reasonable tickers get to go on test drives after the tune-ups. That's the bit they really like. Costs us a bloody fortune in incontinence pads, but.'

In a clinically clean and brightly lit kitchen, staff were hard at work preparing dinner. Meals for the nursing-home patients were being loaded into mobile warming cabinets for delivery to their rooms. Martin tried to guess how many nationalities might be represented in this kitchen but gave up. The only common denominators were the spotless uniforms and the smiles.

'This is where we keep our boat people,' Jesse said as he walked through the door. He picked up a pot and began banging it on a bench, yelling, 'Immigration! Immigration! Raid! Raid!'

The staff ignored him, except for someone who threw a bread roll.

'This is Mr Tran.' Jesse indicated an elderly man in a chef's toque. 'Bogroll over there runs the kitchen, but Mr Tran keeps the menu interesting and makes sure Bogroll washes his hands at least once a week. That's why we let him wear the big hat.'

Bogroll, a scrawny figure in grubby jeans and a clean white jacket, was stirring a large pot. 'Fuck you, Headjob,' he said sweetly.

'Mr Tran taught philosophy in Saigon and drove buses in Sydney,' Jesse said. 'Figure that one out. We're looking after his wife, she's a bit ga-ga. Hell of a good cook for a uni professor, our Mr Tran. Learned off his mum as a kid in the old country. Started using the kitchen to make special dishes from home to cheer up the wife, and next thing everyone's demanding a plateful. Your Vietnamese here can cook French, Asian – of which Vietnamese is the most healthy – and Australian, if you explain it to them slowly. Right, Mr Tran?'

Mr Tran smiled politely. 'Fuck you, Headjob.'

'Plus they know their place.' Jesse laughed as he put his arm around the older man's shoulder. 'Mr Tran's daughter June is our on-call medico. She's got a clinic in town. Great doc, we're bloody lucky to have her. Good-looking too. Bear goes to see her when he dislocates his shoulder. Used to just pop it back in all by himself before he met our June.

Now he's suddenly a great big wuss who needs his hand held. It's really quite pathetic. I'm starting to think he keeps falling off his bike on purpose.'

Jesse picked up a ladle and had a taste from the large pot Bogroll was stirring. 'Mmm, *pot-au-feu*. Not too bad, Bogroll. Your stock is getting to be as good as Mr Tran's.' He glanced into the pot again. 'Not as crystal clear, though. Must try harder.'

He looked at his watch. 'You and the sheila should have dinner with us. We're fully licensed, got a cellar full of Grange, and nobody cares if you dribble. And if you need your food cut up, you'll be in the majority. But mostly that's just my boys.'

twelve

The community of Bowser was 300 kilometres as the crow flies from just about anywhere. The crows didn't fly to Bowser, though – they had more sense. At the side door of Clancey's Country Carvery, a man in grease-spattered chef's whites leaned against the wall and dragged deeply on his cigarette. Thank God the lunchtime shift was over – that fecken kitchen was like an oven. His eyes swept the flat, treeless landscape. Why the hell would people choose to live out here? he wondered. Why was he here? Well, that was pretty obvious – he'd drunk his way out of jobs in some of the better restaurants in Dublin, so he had no-one to blame but himself.

The town was tiny, only about a dozen houses, and the restaurant was its main activity, along with the pub and the wheat silo. A lot of the customers were regulars, but he couldn't figure out where they all came from. Not that he really cared.

He saw the car as a speck in the distance and watched as it drew closer. Drive past, you bastard, drive past. The vehicle slowed and then turned into the driveway. The cook ground out his cigarette on the doorpost. Arsehole, he said to himself.

There was a clearly marked disabled parking space outside the main entrance and the black Commodore drove straight in. Smith stepped out and carefully removed his suit jacket from the rear seat. He noticed an elderly woman staring disapprovingly at him and he turned slightly to make sure his holstered pistol was visible. She quickly looked away. He slipped the jacket on and adjusted his shirt cuffs.

The restaurant was almost empty and Smith chose a table where he had his back to the wall and could watch the entrance and keep an eye on his car at the same time. The waitress, a pretty girl of about sixteen, smiled at him. He ignored her and the offered menu and ordered a steak sandwich, medium, with the works, and a glass of water. Then he got up from the table and walked to the men's toilet. Inside he checked all the empty stalls before methodically washing and drying his hands. Using a tissue from his pocket, he avoided touching the door handle with his bare skin on the way out.

He had just sat down when the waitress brought his

water, and some cutlery rolled up in a paper napkin. He took out the knife and fork and inspected them, then polished both implements with the napkin. Satisfied, he flipped his mobile phone open and punched in a number. He was answered immediately.

'It's Smith,' he said, 'put me through.'

A gruff voice came on the line. 'What's going on, Albris?'

'It's not him, sir,' Smith said.

'Well, that's good news,' the voice said. 'You certain?'

There was a loud scream from near the entrance. Smith looked up. Two young boys, aged about three and five, were fighting over possession of a coin-operated amusement ride in the shape of a vintage steam locomotive. An exasperated mother was trying to get the older boy to climb down. She gave up and put another coin in the slot. The machine began shaking and tooting and the smaller child started to cry.

Smith turned his attention back to the phone. 'Sorry, sir,' he said, 'the natives are restless. Local forensic bods want to do DNA, but I know it's definitely not him, so we're still in play.'

The waitress placed a large white plate in front of him. The steak sandwich was huge, and surrounded on three sides by chips. He looked up at her. 'What are these?' he asked.

'Chips,' the girl said.

'Did I ask for chips?'

The girl shrugged. 'It comes with chips.'

Smith shook his head and carefully pushed the chips off his plate onto the table with his fork. He carried on with his phone call. 'A big chunk of his bicep got chopped off on impact and thrown clear before the fire took hold. The only bit of him that wasn't burnt to a crisp.' He looked at the girl again. She turned pale and walked away.

'Tomato sauce!' he called after her. Then, 'No, I'm in a restaurant. Late lunch. Autopsies always give me an appetite.'

The waitress grabbed a red plastic squeeze bottle from a nearby table, plonked it in front of Smith and hurried off as he continued his conversation. 'The arm belonged to someone who was heavily suntanned and hadn't washed for about a week. Plus there was a tattoo. Amateur job, prison design, almost certainly done in the slammer. Doesn't really fit our man's profile.'

He listened to the gruff voice on the other end of the phone and nodded. 'Sounds good,' he agreed. 'But we don't know what to look for. I didn't think he'd have the smarts to pull off a switch like that. He might have changed his appearance, for all we know.'

Smith took the top slice of bread off his sandwich and squirted sauce over the steak as he listened.

'Well, I still think the weak link is that local copper,' he said. 'I've got the landlines and all mobiles covered. If there's any attempt to make contact, we can pinpoint him.'

He took a small, careful bite out of the corner of the sandwich and nodded in response to the voice on the phone.

'I'm almost positive that's where he's headed,' Smith said. 'Nothing else makes sense in his situation, and the cop knew more than he was saying. So we just keep an eye on all roads heading up towards Cooktown.'

He ate as he listened, chewing slowly and deliberately. 'I understand that,' he said. 'Kid gloves. He'll never even know we're on to him. Total discretion. You can rely on me, sir, one hundred per cent.'

He closed the phone and finished his sandwich, then walked to the till to pay. The waitress didn't bother smiling this time. Smith counted his change and didn't leave a tip.

Near the door, the two young boys were still fighting over the mechanical ride. Smith smiled at the mother, who was having coffee and cake with a friend at a nearby table. She smiled back. She could see it was an expensive suit. You didn't get too many well-groomed and stylishly dressed men in this town, even if he was a little old for her. He went across to the ride, smiled at the boys, leaned over and whispered in the ear of the older one. The boy obediently climbed down and walked quietly over to his mother with a serious look on his face. Beaming excitedly, the younger child scrambled into the cab of the locomotive. Smith put a coin into the machine and the ride started. The boy was ecstatic.

The woman gave the man a friendly look. 'You must have kids,' she said.

He shook his head.

'Well, you've certainly got a way with my boy. Jarrod here usually won't listen to anybody.'

'It's all in the way you explain the situation to them,' Smith said, and walked out the door.

The woman turned to her son. 'And what did the nice man say to you?' she asked.

Jarrod was very pale and when he spoke it was almost in a whisper. 'He said if I didn't give my little brother a turn, he'd rip my fucking heart out.'

thirteen

The Eldorado Motel was located behind a large service station, just a short walk down the highway from Ocean View. The motel, abandoned for years, had been bought by the bikies along with the service station. They ran the latter as a business and also used it to work on their motorcycles. The motel's '60s façade and rooms had been restored, and a neon sign flashed: ELDORADO MOTEL. NO VACANCIES. BUGGER OFF!

Martin and Faith were given adjoining rooms, which were reserved, according to Jesse, for 'dignitaries, honoured guests, or anyone looking for a quiet spot for a quick shag'. Martin was wary after the president offered to phone ahead and have them burn the old bedding and throw a few flea bombs in, but the rooms were spotless and well furnished.

Dinner was at six, and after a shower and shave, Martin knocked on the connecting door. Faith was wearing a long white terry-towelling bathrobe, and her damp hair hung loosely around her shoulders. Martin whistled. She pulled the front of the robe tight up to her neck and smiled.

'It came with the room,' she said. 'It's Christian Dior. For a motorcycle gang, these guys have great taste.'

She asked for ten more minutes. Martin was waiting outside when Jesse ambled up.

'Sorry about eating so early, but we can't break the oldies of the habit.' He lit a cigarette. 'Nice to see the Indian's still in good shape. She was almost cherry when Raymond nicked her. Full military specs and an OD paint job.'

'What's that?' Martin asked.

'Olive Drab, Yank military colour. Not quite khaki and not jungle-green.'

'So Harleys aren't compulsory then?'

'The heavy guys reckon if it's not a Harley, it's a postman's bike.'

'And you guys aren't heavy?' Martin asked

Jesse took a long drag on his cigarette. 'We have our standards, but we aren't your full-on psycho outlaw motorcycle gang. We probably slot in somewhere between the Hell's Angels and the Double Bay Mid-Life Crisis Motorcycle Club.'

'So how did you get into this?' Martin asked. 'Ever done anything else?'

Jesse leaned against the sidecar of the Indian. 'Ran away with the circus when I was fifteen. Well, carnival anyway. Drifted for a while. Brickie, builder's labourer, bit of scaffolding work when I needed to earn a crust. Brother who's a corporate banker and boring as batshit, and a flaky sister who works in advertising in the big smoke. Peter Jesse James, this is your life.'

'Sorry,' Martin said. 'I didn't mean to pry.'

'That's not prying, mate,' Jesse said, 'that's conversation. In our world, prying's when two blokes hold your arms and a third hits you in the guts with a pick handle till you tell him what he wants to hear.'

Faith stepped out of her room and Martin's heart jumped at the sight of her.

'Sorry we haven't changed for dinner, but we're travelling a bit light,' she said.

Jesse ground his cigarette out under his boot. 'A million in cash and a change of socks and underdaks. Works for me.'

'Not all that in touch with your feminine side then?' Faith said.

'Wouldn't say that, love. The socks and undies always match,' he grinned. 'But tell you what, a couple of our sheilas own the surf shop in town. You could get Martin to buy you a nice frock tomorrow. They're more than happy to accept cash.'

'I'm up for it,' Martin said. 'We'll pop in after breakfast and you can knock yourself out.'

'Just how did I get to be such a lucky girl?' Faith asked, linking arms with the two men. 'Let's eat, boys, I'm famished.'

*

Like everything else at Ocean View, the communal dining room for the retirement-village residents was not quite as Martin expected. The menu was à la carte, served by the bikies on a roster system, or the residents could line up at a large barbecue where Bogroll was cooking steaks and seafood to order under the watchful eye of Mr Tran. Faith was already seated, deep in conversation with Wal, so Martin joined Jesse among the zimmer-frames in the barbecue line. There were about equal numbers of residents and bikies in the room, and Martin noticed how gentle and patient the bikies were with the older people. He watched as a huge tattooed Maori pulled out a flick-knife and carefully carved up a char-grilled pork chop for a blue-haired lady in a pink cardigan.

'A lot of these old buggers can demolish a mixed grill like there's no tomorrow,' Jesse said, 'which in some cases is actually true. But statistically, our meat-eaters stay out of the nursing home longer.'

'Better for you than creamed spinach, I guess,' Martin said as he ordered a porterhouse, rare, with salad.

Jesse ordered a medium T-bone with chips and more chips. And a side order of chips.

Martin thought for a moment, then added chips to his

order. He glanced around the packed dining room. 'This is amazing,' he said.

'Saturday nights are formal,' Jesse said. 'The boys put their teeth in. Sometimes it's a fresh seafood buffet, and we usually have a few of them rising up out of their wheelchairs. It's like a miracle, my son, the miracle of the prawns.'

He took a handful of chips from the plate of a passing bikie, who snarled at him in mock anger. 'You don't want to stand between some of them and the oyster bar. Especially not bloody Wal.'

'I don't see how this place makes any money,' Martin said as they collected their huge meals and headed back to the table.

'Well, we do have a lot of volunteer labour,' Jesse said, 'plus several alternative income streams, though we're now restricting our activities to aged care, retail, and the income from our stock portfolio and real-estate investments.' He gave Martin a sly look. 'You could say that in the early days we were subsidised in part by a grateful and very wide-awake long-distance trucking industry.'

At this point Martin decided he had more than enough information. He attacked his steak, which was incredibly tender.

Wal leaned over to him. 'Faith tells me you're a bank robber on the run.'

Martin glanced quickly at Faith. She seemed embarrassed.

'Sorry,' she said, 'it just came out, and I swore him to

secrecy.' She glared at her father. 'Fat lot of good that did.'

Wal ignored her. 'And she reckons you're heading up north to see the mad major,' he continued.

Jesse nearly choked on his chips. 'Jesus, Martin, you're a dark horse. That all true?'

'I guess,' he said sheepishly. 'There was no plan, though, it all just sort of happened.'

Jesse was impressed. 'You sly dog. And here's me thinking you made a million in cold cash by honest labour and the sweat of your brow.' He poured the last of a bottle of red into Martin's glass and stood up. 'I'll get some more plonk,' he said. 'You okay for white there, Faith?'

Faith gave him the thumbs-up and Jesse ambled off to the bar. Wal got up and followed and the two men had an animated discussion while the barman was opening another bottle.

'If you're still thinking of heading up north, Martin,' Jesse said as they sat down, 'Wal just had a bit of a bright idea, which is pretty surprising since I thought he'd shagged himself totally senseless. Why don't you leave the bike here and take his old campervan? You'll be a lot more comfortable and a hell of a lot less obvious.'

Wal nodded enthusiastically. 'She's a good little van, Martin. A genuine Coolibah camper/cruiser. The deluxe model. Got a chemical toilet and a shower with hot-and-cold pressurised water. Radio, microwave, gas stove, plus you got a 12/240-volt power supply. Bunk beds, unfortunately, but you can probably bodgie up a double if you get lucky with some hot hitchhiker.' He winked.

Faith looked at Martin. 'Sorry,' she said, 'he used to be such a charmer.'

'I still am, darlin',' Wal said. 'Ask around.'

Martin was uncertain about the van.

'You should think about it, mate,' Jesse urged. 'We made a few modifications to the camper after Wal stopped using it, and it's a pretty sweet ride. And there's a compartment for your cash that'll be safer than in that sidecar. Very safe, in fact. Almost totally impossible to detect.' He took a sip of wine and gave a sly smile. 'And believe me, our vehicles tend to get searched by experts on a fairly regular basis.'

'I think we should take them up on it, Martin,' Faith said.

He looked at her. 'We?' he said. 'I thought you were only coming north to catch up with your dad?'

'Well, Dad's got himself sorted out here. According to the TV news, I'm missing, and as long as Dad knows I'm okay, that's just fine with me. In fact I think I might already be cramping his style. Apparently some poor lady missed out on her afternooner while we talked over old times.'

Wal was winking at a woman at the next table. Faith leaned over and took Martin's hand. He felt the now familiar electric tingle run along his spine.

'The van sounds great, Martin,' she said, 'let's do it. It'll be great cover if anyone's caught on to the motorcycle by now.'

Martin looked around the table and raised his glass in a toast. 'Sounds like a done deal to me,' he said. 'Cheers.'

'You two watch your step up north,' Wal said. 'I looked Stark up on the Net. That psycho-wanker's bunker is supposed to have booby traps and landmines from arsehole to breakfast. We can't have Faith here losing any more bits, can we?'

Faith glared at her father again. 'Dad!'

'Don't mind him, Faith,' Jesse laughed, 'he doesn't know what he's saying half the time. All the pussy he's getting has addled his brain.'

'Bugger you, Pres,' Wal huffed. 'I was seventy-three before I found out about oral sex and I'm just making up for lost time.'

'Whoa!' Faith said, shaking her head and shivering. 'Way too much information.'

'Did I see a delicious-looking pavlova by that espresso machine, Faith?' Martin asked with a fixed grin. 'What say we go check it out?'

fourteen

Martin ran the campervan into a ditch at about ten o'clock in the morning. Before they left Ocean View, the bikies' mechanic had warned them about the van's 'bad habits'. The problem apparently lay in the replacement of the original small diesel engine with a turbo-charged V-6.

'Woulda loved to whack a V-8 in, but there wasn't room,' Spark Plug the mechanic explained with a sigh of regret. 'Bugger'll go fast and we gave her wider tyres and lowered and stabilised the suspension, but she's still just a granny flat on wheels, so you gotta watch yourself.'

He patted the side of the van and smiled. 'If you gotta outrun anyone, try doing it on a straight bit of road,' he warned them, 'cos she's a real bastard on turns. Old girl's got the cornering characteristics of a slice of lemon meringue pie.'

The 'old girl' was an all-white cab-over-camper conversion. She was airconditioned and as nicely fitted out as Wal had claimed. A cunningly concealed space behind another cunningly concealed space in the ceiling cabinets of the van held the loot from the bank. As Jesse explained, the logic was you should always give searchers something to find to make them feel they'd done their job. Then they'd stop looking and your second hiding place would be safe.

Posing with Wal next to the van for a photograph before their departure, Martin and Faith looked like typical holiday-makers heading north for the sunshine. Faith had changed from her motorcycle leathers into hipster cargo pants, a white singlet and a light hooded sweatshirt. Martin was wearing an extremely colourful yellow and red flower-patterned shirt, very long shorts and white sneakers. His hair was red. Their second day at Ocean View had given Faith a chance to work this transformation, with the assistance of the local hair salon which the bikies also owned and ran.

During the afternoon, Martin had learned more about motorcycles from Jesse than he really wanted to know, while Faith spent time catching up with her dad.

There had been quite a send-off from the bikies and the residents of Ocean View. The van's engine started with a throaty exhaust roar, which settled into a deep and resonating rumble on idle. Spark Plug smiled proudly.

'Might look pretty fuckin' ordinary,' he said, 'but there's that huge donk hidden away for when you really need it.'

'Just like the original owner,' said Wal, who was standing with his arms around the shoulders of two women.

'Jesus, Dad,' Faith said, 'give it a rest.'

'Good idea, love,' Wal said, 'I think I'll have a bit of a lie-down as soon as you've gone. Feeling a tad weary.'

Both women grinned. Wal kissed them on the cheek in turn. Faith took a photograph.

Jesse shook Martin's hand and then grabbed Faith, kissing her full on the lips.

On the highway, it took Martin a while to get used to the idea that the van could overtake almost everything on the road. Spark Plug had fitted cruise control, so they were travelling at a steady 85 kph, causing delays on some stretches and getting the finger on a regular basis from truckies and hoons in hotted-up sedans and utes.

'The best way not to draw attention to yourself in a campervan is to keep getting in everyone's way,' Faith had advised him.

Around nine a.m. Martin suggested they leave the highway for some of the less crowded rural roads.

'Sounds like a plan,' said Faith. She poured coffee from a thermos and handed him a cup.

The back road was in good condition, but the frequent dips and curves required a lot more concentration from the driver. There was very little other traffic.

Faith spoke after half an hour of silence. 'I like a man who doesn't feel he's got to talk.'

'Sorry,' said Martin, glancing over at her.

'No, I really mean it,' she said. 'I love just sitting and watching the road go by. It's why I like bikes. My ex always figured if you weren't talking, you were fighting.'

'Can I ask you something?' Martin said.

She turned to face him. 'Sure.'

'Why are you still here?'

She turned back and watched the countryside roll past for a couple of moments before replying. 'When you hear the cancer word, you either flip out or suddenly see everything pretty clearly. I'm here because I want to be here. Live in the moment and bugger the consequences.'

'Like mouthing off in a bikie bar?' he asked.

'Well, I have to admit I did go a bit over the top there,' she said.

'Not all that much. Getting involved in robbery and mayhem seems a bit more extreme.'

'Hey,' she laughed, 'I'm a librarian. The history books are full of our outlandish escapades, erotic adventures and deeds of derring-do.'

'None of the history books I've read.'

'Of course not,' she said. 'We keep them in a special sealed section.'

Martin turned to her and smiled. She looked back into his eyes. She didn't smile.

'Spark Plug warned you about the over-steer, remember?'

'Sorry, what?' Martin asked. Then, 'Oh shit!'

'Better hold on tight,' Faith said.

Martin swung the wheel hard, trying to correct as they began sliding into the curve. He pumped the brakes. The van fishtailed another hundred metres down the bitumen before coming to a juddering stop on the side of the road, tilted at a steep angle towards a ditch. Martin turned off the engine. His hands were shaking.

'Nice save,' said Faith.

Martin breathed a sigh of relief. 'No damage done.'

The van suddenly shuddered, groaned slightly, then toppled slowly over onto its side. There was a noisy clatter from the back, followed by complete silence.

'Bugger,' Faith said. 'Mum's priceless collection of Royal Doulton. My inheritance.' She was lying on her side with Martin hanging above her, suspended in his seatbelt.

'Shit,' Martin said. 'I'm sorry, Faith. I'll replace it all, I promise.'

'Joke, Martin,' she laughed, 'it's all plastic. Everything my mum had was unbreakable. Even me, pretty much.'

Martin undid his seatbelt and instantly fell on top of Faith. Their faces were pressed together, his lips on her cheek. It was the softest thing he had ever felt. He didn't ever want to be anywhere else.

'Smooth move, Martin,' she said.

It seemed to Martin that she didn't much mind the situation either. After a moment he said, 'I think we'd better get out, Faith. There could be an explosion.'

'You're right, Martin,' she said, making no effort to move. 'And the van might blow up too,' she added quietly.

Exiting the overturned van was difficult as they had to climb up to the driver's door. Faith helped by putting her hands on Martin's butt and pushing hard. On a scale of one to ten, he decided, this particular crash rated about a twelve.

*

There was no obvious damage, but the van would need to be winched back onto its wheels. Being off the main highway meant there wasn't much passing traffic, so they got out the picnic rug and sat on the verge. Faith photographed the clouds while Martin checked out Mr Tran's picnic basket.

'Yum, meatloaf sandwiches,' he announced.

'You mean the *pâté de Campagna* on a baguette?'

'Yeah, that's what I said, meatloaf sangers,' Martin grinned, hoeing into the baguette.

After eating, they lay back and looked at the sky.

'Why did you do it – the bank thing, I mean?' Faith asked after a long time.

'To tell you the truth,' Martin said, 'I really don't know. I got up that morning and was sick of my life. Just wanted it to be over. Drank my morning coffee in the garage while wondering if I should put the rifle under my chin or between my eyes. Then I thought about playing Russian roulette with the bank's pistol during the morning smoko.'

'Revolver or automatic?' Faith asked. 'The bank's pistol, I mean.'

'Automatic, I guess. Why?'

'Because you can't play Russian roulette with a semi-automatic pistol, Martin. Incredibly bad odds. Every contestant loses, every time.'

'Oh,' he said, rolling onto his side. 'You know what's funny? I just realised I had two coffees that morning and almost killed myself after each one.'

'Instant coffee will do that to you,' Faith said.

He sat up. 'How do you know it was instant?'

'You're a bank manager,' she said, 'you wear brown suede shoes and you just order coffee when you go into a cafe, without looking.'

'Looking at what?' Martin asked. 'You usually order tea, anyway.'

'I love coffee and I'd actually rather have coffee, but you have to pay attention,' Faith insisted.

'Pay attention to what?'

Faith sat up as well. 'Do they have a professional-quality espresso machine? You need to check out the make, the type of grinder they use, the roast of the beans. Does a waiter or the person on the cash register make the coffees, or do they have a dedicated barista? How well do they pack the ground coffee into the portafilter? Do they tamp, and if so, how hard?'

Martin gaped at her. 'Portafilter?'

'That's the handle part you put the ground coffee in,' she explained. 'It locks into the group, which is in the actual coffee machine and which ideally should be made of brass for better temperature control. Tamping is packing the ground coffee down into the portafilter, and just how hard you should do it is a matter of some debate.'

'C'mon, Faith,' Martin complained, 'we're just talking coffee, aren't we?'

'Good heavens, no!' Faith said in a shocked voice. 'We're talking espresso. And if the boys and girls at the Istituto Nazionale Espresso Italiano could hear you, they'd be pretty cheesed off.'

'There's actually an Italian institute for coffee?'

Faith nodded. 'They set the standards to aim for,' she said. 'The perfect espresso should use seven grams of freshly ground coffee, hit by water at 90 degrees Celsius under nine atmospheres of pressure to give you twenty-five millilitres of coffee at about 67 degrees Celsius in the cup. And this should take precisely twenty-five seconds of extraction time.'

'Whoa,' Martin said, 'you're kidding, right?'

Faith gave him a look that said she'd never kid about coffee.

'Coffee's a lot more complex than I realised,' Martin said.

'Sure is. And we haven't even mentioned *crema*, which is a whole other debate. The Turks think coffee should be black as hell, strong as death and sweet as love. The Spanish like a *carajillo* in the morning, which is coffee with a dash of brandy – the size of the dash is open to interpretation – and the Italians think you have to understand the four Ms before you can fully appreciate coffee.'

'The four Ms?'

'*Miscela*, or the blending of the beans; *macinatura*, which is the grinding of the blend; *macchina*, which refers to the espresso machine; and *mano*, for the hand of a skilled barista.'

'Instant coffee does sound a little easier, Faith,' he said.

'Martin, please, you're a millionaire now, you have to have standards. Life's way too short to be drinking instant coffee.'

'Good point,' he said. 'Do you think they serve real coffee in prison?'

Faith considered this. 'Interesting. The one place where time is not a consideration and I bet they use instant. Now, that is a conundrum, I must admit.'

There was a long silence.

'I'm not sure how I'll cope with prison,' Martin said.

'I wasn't sure how I'd cope with cancer,' Faith said, 'but you just have to keep going. No matter how you look at it, life's a death sentence. No way round that little fact. Just ask Jim Morrison.' She slapped him on the shoulder. 'Anyway, you should cheer up, mate. They have to catch us first.'

Martin shook his head slowly. 'I did the robbery and shot our bikie friend. You could say I held you hostage. You could just walk away, you know.'

'I'm not sure that scenario will play, Martin. Imagine the headline: BANK MANAGER HOLDS LIBRARIAN HOSTAGE. Could be a hard sell to the girls at Librarian HQ. Besides, I'm enjoying this. I'm starting to like you.'

'In spite of the brown suede shoes?'

She leaned over and ruffled his hair. 'Maybe even because of them,' she smiled.

The familiar tingle ran up Martin's spine. It appeared to him that she withdrew her hand very quickly, as if she'd felt the same thing. Neither of them spoke for a long time.

Finally he said, 'Faith, I have decided to piss away my million dollars.'

'Good for you, Martin!'

'If they catch me – us – I want the headlines to read: POLICE UNABLE TO TRACE ANY OF MISSING MILLION.'

Faith gave him the thumbs-up. 'Now you're cooking with gas, Martin.'

'Pulling us out of this ditch should be worth about ten grand, don't you think?' he asked.

'Easy. And no more instant coffee?'

'Not a drop shall pass these lips,' he vowed. 'And if I want to wear brown suede shoes, I'll wear brown suede shoes.'

'Way to go, Mr Carter. Of course, not a lot of women want to have wild sex with men who wear brown suede shoes, but it's your decision and a valid choice.'

Martin stopped. He was suddenly confused. 'Am I missing

something here, Faith?' he asked. 'We were talking about coffee and now we're talking about sex, right?'

'Mmm. Wild sex. But we're actually talking about not having it. You'll have to try to keep up with the conversational shifts if this relationship is going to work.'

Martin was relieved to hear the sound of an engine in the distance. 'I think I hear a tractor,' he said.

'Ten grand to pull a van out of a ditch,' Faith said. 'Here comes a man whose day is going to change rather suddenly and dramatically.'

'And I for one, Faith, know exactly how he'll be feeling!'

fifteen

Faith made morning tea with Bev Porter in the farmhouse kitchen while the three men inspected the campervan. Fred Porter had been checking the mail when he noticed the van in the ditch down the road from his front gate. It had only taken him and his offsider Shariffie five minutes to haul it back onto its wheels with the tractor, and then he'd suggested driving up to the farmhouse and checking the suspension.

Now Shariffie was under the van with a lamp on a long lead that ran from the equipment shed. Fred and Martin were squatting in the shade of the van.

'Shariffie was a mechanic in Afghanistan,' Fred explained. 'He's good. I'd given up on that tractor, but he got it going.'

Martin looked around. 'Not the kind of place you expect to find an Afghan.'

'We've got quite a few round here. Mostly they're on temporary protection visas. Good workers. They brought the local meatworks back to life. Running two shifts now. They've even got a halal certification. Export lamb for the Middle East. We get paid bugger all per head, but it's better than watching your stock starve to death.'

'How long since it's rained?' Martin asked, looking around at the parched paddocks.

'Going on two and a half years,' Fred said. 'Good downpour right about now would spoil a perfectly acceptable drought.'

He stood up as Shariffie slid out from under the van. 'Just telling Martin about our drought,' he said.

Shariffie nodded as he wiped his hands on an oil-stained cloth. 'It is most definitely as dry as a dead dingo's donger around here,' he declared.

Fred winked at Martin. 'We try to help them fit in with a few lessons in English as she are spoke.'

'The van is good,' Shariffie announced. 'Very excellent job on the underneath. Bloody beauty, digger. You should be having no worries, mate.'

Fred chuckled. 'In another six months we reckon we'll have him eating Vegemite.'

'No way José,' Shariffie said with a shudder.

'Tea's up,' yelled Faith from the screen door in the flywire-enclosed verandah.

They sat at a table in the huge kitchen. While Faith poured the tea, Bev offered Martin a plate of small oval cakes.

'Thanks, Bev, these look great,' he said

'Don't thank me,' Bev said, 'they're Fred's famous friands.'

Martin bit into his cake and looked at Fred with surprise. 'This is bloody beautiful, mate!'

'Thanks. I got the recipe off the Internet. They come up a treat in the old slow-combustion stove.'

Shari jumped up at the word 'stove'. 'I must get some more wood. Back in the shaking of two lambs' tails.'

Bev smiled. 'My gran had Italian POWs help her run Granddad's place while he was in the Middle East fighting Rommel,' she said. 'Now we've got an Afghan helping us keep this place going. Funny old world, eh?'

'They're not getting any grief from any of the locals?' Faith asked.

'Nope,' Fred said. 'Our blokes were pretty well settled in when all that Children Overboard bullshit started. We kind of knew what it was all about by then. You always get some whining, but we had a meeting at the pub on RSL night where they talked about what they were getting away from back there.'

'That must have been interesting,' said Martin.

'You're telling me,' said Fred. 'Bloody "queue jumping". As if it's that simple. Couple of the old diggers wanted to drive down to Canberra and form a queue to biff a few politicians. Reckoned this wasn't why they went off to war in '39. It got quite heated.'

Bev reached across the table and took Fred's hand. 'Let's

just say some people got more heated than others.'

'Shari's a good bloke,' Fred said defensively. 'So are all his mates. I don't know if we could have kept this place going without him.'

Shari backed into the kitchen with his arms full of firewood. He dumped the logs into a basket next to the stove.

'You did us a good turn, Fred,' Martin said, 'pulling us out of that ditch, and I can see times are tough around here. How about I repay the favour with some cash to tide you over?'

'Sure, mate,' Fred laughed, 'thirty-five grand would get those bastards at the bank off my back for a bit.'

'I know all about those bastards at the bank, believe me,' Martin said. 'I can give you the thirty-five.'

Fred and Bev looked at each other, stunned. Fred turned to Martin.

'I was joking, Martin, I didn't help you out for any reward.'

'Well, I'm not joking,' Martin replied. 'I'll give you the money.'

Bev shifted in her chair. 'This was Fred's dad's place, and his dad's before that,' she said. 'Same goes for most of the farms in the district. All third- or fourth-generation. We're all in the same boat, which, given the lack of water, is a pretty silly phrase. The money would be nice, Martin, but we wouldn't be able to look our neighbours in the eye. Thanks, but we'll get by.'

Faith joined in. 'Hey, if Martin here is so intent on

splashing his cash about, is there anything we can do for the whole area?'

Fred considered this. 'Maybe the library needs some books or something.' He glanced at Bev. 'What do you reckon, love?'

'I'm your girl, if that's the way you want to go,' Faith said.

'Well,' Bev said, 'I reckon what this community could really do with is the piss-up to end all piss-ups. Sorry, Shari.'

Fred nodded towards the Afghan. 'He doesn't drink,' he explained. 'The Koran is pretty down on it. Apparently they're a lot like Methodists that way.'

'Please,' said Shariffie, 'don't mind us. Afghan people love a good party. Shall we have Cheese Twisties?'

'You're taking the piss, right?' Martin said.

Shariffie smiled innocently. 'Of course! I study my new home very hard. I don't wish to look like boofhead. My friends and I shall cook for the party. We shall do lamb in the way of my country.'

'Good-oh,' said Fred.

'You're on, mate,' said Martin.

sixteen

Lesley Bogan was pulling the tarpaulin back over his truck when the campervan rolled into the car park of the Golden Sheaf. Lesley was known as Bogie to his friends, and being the local beer distributor, he had a lot of friends. He was surprised to see a campervan. From the noise of the engine, he had expected some big Yank tank. A red-headed man in a loud shirt leaned out of the van.

'G'day, mate,' Martin said, 'got any grog to spare? I'm throwing a party.'

'Maybe,' Bogie said. 'How many you expecting?'

'Dunno. How many people in the area?'

Bogie scratched his head. 'Sign on the highway says the shire's got 347 residents. It's a newish sign, so it's probably right. I knocked the old one down when I was pissed last Christmas.'

'Let's say 350 then,' Martin said. 'You up for a beer?'

Bogie proudly patted his protruding stomach. 'Wadda you reckon?' he asked.

'Great. Let's call it 351. Cash okay?'

'"cun'oath,' Bogie said, flipping the tarp back off the load. 'I'll get the keys to the forklift and have Kelly open up the coolroom.'

Kelly, licensee of the Golden Sheaf, had been leaning on the door during this exchange. He walked out into the sunlight and tossed a set of keys to Bogie. Faith and Martin got out of the van and walked over to Kelly.

'Fred and Bev reckoned you'd be the man to see about a party,' Martin said.

'Too right,' he said with a broad smile. 'Fred rang already. Since you've bought all that grog, me and the missus can organise the rest for twelve grand. Food, soft drinks and a band. The local Chinese fangatorium and the ladies from the bowls club and CWA will pitch in.'

Kelly had the broadest Australian accent Martin had ever heard. He also appeared to be Chinese. 'You're not from round here, are you?' Martin asked.

Kelly Kwan shook his head. 'Nah, family's originally from Dubbo. How could you tell?'

'Just a wild guess,' Martin said. 'Anyway, twelve grand's not quite the figure I had in mind.'

Bugger, Kelly thought to himself, too high. 'I'll do it for ten then,' he said.

Martin shook his head. 'What'll I get for twenty?'

Kelly didn't blink. 'The pub, my car, the wife and kids, my dog, and the best night this town's had in a very long time.'

'Just the party will be fine, thanks,' said Martin holding out his hand. 'I'm Martin, this is Faith, and I've never thrown a do like this before. Where do we start?'

Faith tossed him the mobile phone. 'Why don't you park the van and see if you can track down an electrician and some party lights?' She turned to the publican. 'And once that beer's on ice, maybe you can chase up some charcoal and spits,' she suggested. 'The local Afghan community are bringing some lamb.'

Kelly rubbed his hands together. 'Bewdy, I've had Shari's lamb before. De-fuckin'-licious.'

Faith glanced around. 'Where do I find your wife? We've got a lot to do.'

Kelly pointed towards the pub. 'She's probably in the back bar. Name's Dawn.'

Martin and Kelly watched Faith as she ran up the stairs and into the pub.

'Doesn't muck about, does she?' Kelly said. 'I like her.'

Martin nodded. 'Yeah,' he said, 'I like her too.'

✱

Late that afternoon, with the party preparations well under way, Faith and Martin walked across the paddock to the dam behind the pub.

'Must be a great place for yabbies when it's full.' Martin tossed a clod of dirt into the murky brown water.

Faith seemed to have something on her mind. 'Fred collected a week's worth of papers from his letterbox after he pulled us out of the ditch,' she said. 'State and local. I checked through them while you boys were out farting around with the van.'

'And?' Martin asked.

She shrugged. 'It seems very odd, but somehow a million-dollar armed robbery, a missing bank manager, and a body in a burned-out police car don't rate a mention.'

Martin kicked at the dry dirt.

'The cops out along the highway are definitely looking for someone,' Faith continued, 'we can see that. But they're keeping a really low profile. What's going on?'

'Beats me.' Martin threw another lump of crumbling clay into the dam. Then he suddenly remembered the mobile phone. 'How about I call Col and see what's going on?' He reached for the phone in his pocket.

'Good idea.'

Martin turned the phone on and checked for a signal.

'SMS him, though,' Faith suggested. 'And keep it short. Just ask him what's happening with the cops. The digital network is theoretically safe from prying eyes and we're probably part CDMA out here, but you never know.'

Martin looked up at her quizzically.

She shrugged. 'I like to keep up with technology.'

seventeen

The text message from Martin was short and to the point: 'What's going on?' Colin stared at the screen and wished he knew exactly what was going on himself.

His thoughts were interrupted when the phone rang and the screen flashed 'private number'. Colin answered it with a sharp, 'Curtis.'

'Don't even think about replying,' was all that Smith said, then the phone went dead. The coldness and certainty in the man's voice was chilling.

Colin sat in his new patrol car, trying to come up with some kind of plan to make contact with Martin. These bastards had obviously plugged into every mobile-phone transmission in the area. It was smart of Martin to keep the message short, but even so, Smith would have an idea of his approximate position very soon. What Colin needed was a way of getting a warning back to Martin, but it couldn't come from him and it would have to be sent from outside the local call zone.

Just then his radar chimed and he glanced at the display. One-seventy. The culprit was a silver BMW barrelling down from the crest of the hill. Col hit the lights and siren and rolled his car out onto the highway from its hiding place under a willow. Thanks to Martin, he now had a nice new turbo-charged pursuit car with power to spare and very, very comfortable seats.

The BMW's nose dipped sharply as the driver saw the flashing lights and hit the anchors. No fishtailing, though, Col noted approvingly. German automotive design and engineering at its very best. He wondered exactly what made Beamers so popular with fuckwits like this bloke. The luxury sedan rolled to a stop and Col climbed out of the police car with his infringement-notice book. He noted the tinted glass and mobile-phone aerial. As he approached, the electric window whirred smoothly down on the driver's side. Cold air, loud music, and the sweet smell of marijuana washed out. The driver was a man of about thirty, ashen-faced, clutching the steering wheel and staring straight ahead. Col knew that look. What a dill!

'Licence, please,' he asked politely. He studied the laminated card the driver passed through the window. This was going to be fun. 'Wanna save me a radio call and tell me how many points you've got up?' he asked. 'Be the nice thing to do.'

The driver looked at the floor. 'Eleven,' he said quietly.

Col whistled and opened his ticket book. 'Congratulations,' he said, 'this is your lucky day. You only need one more demerit point to lose your licence, and you'll get three for speeding, plus a ginormous fine for doing 170 in a 110 zone.' He took a pen from his shirt pocket. 'That's before we get to the dope and the playing of that mindless techno music at high decibels on a public road. All very serious crimes on my patch.'

The driver groaned and put his head in his hands.

'Definitely looks like we got you driving HUA,' Colin said.

The driver stared at him, bewildered. 'HUA?' he asked.

'Head up arse,' Colin translated. He nodded at the mobile phone in a cradle on the dash. 'That thing working, Fangio?' he asked.

'Hey, come on, be fair,' the driver protested. 'I wasn't talking on it and I always use the hands-free anyway.'

'Whoop-de-fuckin'-do,' said Col. 'I'm sure the magistrate will be tickled pink.' He clicked the top of his pen and leaned towards the window. 'Now, listen to me very carefully,' he said quietly. 'I can write you a ticket or I can arrest you, but whatever I decide to do, you are in some seriously deep shit right now.'

Another low groan came from the car.

'However,' Colin continued, 'I could also pretend to write a ticket and ask you to do me a favour. You agree, and I send you on your way and we forget anything ever happened here.'

'Do I have a choice?' the driver asked warily.

Col shrugged. 'Doesn't seem much like it to me,' he said, 'but hey, you might be even dumber than your current situation would indicate.'

The driver considered this and then conceded. 'What do you want me to do?'

Colin smiled and started writing. 'Well, it may look like I'm filling out a speeding ticket, but in fact I'm writing a mobile number and a text message. When you get exactly five hundred k's from here, I want you to pull over and SMS the message to the number. Easy as that. Then you destroy the ticket.'

'How?' asked the driver.

Colin shook his head. How could someone this thick possibly afford a BMW? he wondered. 'Listen, sport,' he snapped, 'I really don't give a rat's. Eat it or burn it or roll it into a joint and smoke it, for all I care. Just as long as you destroy it. Then you drive on into the sunset and forget I ever existed.'

'Cool,' said the driver, smiling.

'Not so cool,' said Colin coldly, leaning in the car window and handing over the ticket and driver's licence. He took off his sunglasses, looked the driver directly in the eye and spoke very slowly. 'I now have your name and address.

If this message is not sent exactly as written, I will know about it, and I'll find you. And when I do I'll shove this shiny Bavarian-built auto up your arse, blunt end first. Just imagine what that'll do to your snazzy metallic paint job.'

The driver meekly took the ticket, folded it and put it in his shirt pocket. He zeroed the trip counter on the instrument panel. 'Five hundred k's, right?' he asked.

'You got it, champ,' Colin said, straightening up. 'That's about five hours if you obey the speed limit, and believe me, you will be obeying the speed limit. Right?'

The BMW pulled sedately back onto the highway as Colin folded up the ticket book. He saw a brief glint of light from a patch of scrub way off to his left. The watchers were good, but back in the jungle Colin had discovered a sixth sense for being observed. He climbed into the car and reversed off the roadway into his shady hiding place.

These seats were a bit too comfortable, he decided, rubbing his shoulder against the headrest. He glanced towards the patch of scrub and flicked his radar unit on. There was still an hour till sunset, and unfortunately he was going to have to ruin this perfectly nice day for a few more drivers. Just for the sake of appearances.

eighteen

By seven that night the hotel's car park – or the dusty paddock that served as the car park – was pretty well full.

'Bushies don't mind an early start to a party,' Kelly explained.

A bush band was setting up in the main bar, and the local amateur DJ was rigging some loudspeakers out over the back balcony. Trestle tables dotted the withered grass that passed for a lawn. Cut-down 44-gallon drums overflowed with beer and ice, and a group of men were erecting hessian screens around some portable toilets.

A dozen lamb carcasses, stuffed with rice, carrots, raisins and spices, were already turning on spits over banked-up charcoal fires, the heady aroma wafting back into the hotel. Urns, plates, cutlery and trays of food were appearing out of the backs of utes and four-wheel drives.

'You gotta love the bush,' Kelly laughed. 'They can't help themselves. They always have to bring a plate.'

'Dawn's set up a space for the teenagers to dance,' said Faith, who'd just joined them. 'And a spot for the little kids to crash. Good thing it's Sunday tomorrow.'

'That reminds me,' said Kelly, picking up a bucket, 'time to start collecting.'

'Hey, I'm paying, remember,' said Martin. 'We don't need donations.'

'Car keys,' Kelly explained. 'I've barely got enough regulars as it is. Don't like having to pull any of them out of wrecked cars. I'm on the local volunteer rescue squad.' He walked off in the direction of a large group of party-goers.

'Might I say, Mr Carter, you look spiffing,' Faith said.

Martin was wearing black jeans and riding boots and a colourful shirt. 'You look very nice yourself,' he said.

She had changed into riding boots and moleskins and a crisp white fitted shirt.

Martin picked up a jumbo bag of Twisties from a trestle table. 'That lamb is starting to smell pretty good,' he said, 'and I think it's time to teach Shari a lesson.'

'Good for you, Martin. We can't allow refugees to come to this country and take the mickey out of hardworking white-collar criminals.'

'Faith, please, I'm an armed robber. There was nothing white-collar about my crime!'

'And I guess I'm your moll, then?' Faith said.

'Are you? Really?'

'It's starting to look that way,' she replied.

Martin liked that answer a whole lot.

*

At ten-thirty Fred and Kelly declared the party a raging success. Forty-seven seconds later, Fred passed out. Kelly then decided to see if there was enough water in the dam for an attempt on the world record for the hundred-metres freestyle. Luckily for Kelly, Shariffie had thought to post one of his friends on the bank as a lifeguard.

Faith and Martin were leaning on the rail of the front balcony of the hotel.

'Quite a night, eh?' Martin said.

Faith took his hand and nodded. 'Quite a night indeed. For a first-time party-giver, you've done an excellent job, Martin Carter.'

He was chuffed at the compliment – and amazed at the rush of emotions he felt with her hand in his. 'Thanks, but I think you and Dawn deserve most of the credit.'

'She's a dynamo, that Dawn,' Faith said. 'And who'd believe it? She looks more Asian than Kelly and she's got an even broader Aussie accent.'

'Did you get the story?' Martin asked. 'Goldfields?'

'Yep. Both great-grandfathers came out for the Ballarat rush. Every generation intended to go back to China but none of them made it. Kelly's just a Dubbo boy, born and bred. Dinki-di to the bone.'

'And that would be a lamb bone,' Martin said. 'Did you see him at that spit? Wild man.'

'I didn't,' Faith said, 'I was watching you.'

Martin nestled a little closer. 'That's rather romantic.'

'You spilled tomato sauce down your shirt,' Faith said, pointing to a spot on his chest.

Deflated, he looked down at his shirt, but couldn't see a stain. Faith flicked him under the nose with her finger.

'Made you look,' she said playfully.

'I can't believe I fell for that!' he laughed.

'Hey, I'm just busting your chops, Martin.' She rested her head on his shoulder.

Martin really didn't care what she busted as long as she didn't let go of his hand.

'You hear something?' she asked suddenly, breaking away and leaning over the balcony, her eyes scanning the night sky.

'If you mean country and western music, then I've heard way too much already,' he answered.

'No, I thought I heard a helicopter. Listen.'

Martin listened. He couldn't hear anything over the noise of badly duelling banjos. 'They probably use choppers out here for mustering stock,' he said.

'Not in the middle of the night,' she said. 'And not in the middle of a drought.'

There was a beep from Martin's pocket. He pulled out the phone and read the message, Faith looking over his shoulder.

"Bang. Bang. Bang. Lose the dog,' she read out. 'What the hell does that mean?'

'It's Col,' Martin said, 'firing three warning shots for me. It means the ammo dump's gone up, which is his way of saying the shit's hit the fan.'

'And the dog?'

'The dog and bone,' Martin said, 'the phone.'

'Of course!'

'This means they're on to us,' Martin said. 'Shit!'

'But why isn't there anything on the news?' Faith asked. 'This is very, very strange.'

Martin ran his hand through his hair. 'I know. It doesn't add up.'

Just then a campervan pulled in off the highway.

'Hello,' said Faith, 'what have we here? Coolibah camper/cruiser. Same colour and model as ours.'

Martin nodded absently, his mind on Colin's warning.

A couple in their sixties climbed out of the van and came towards them, the man taking the woman's hand as they walked.

'Ah, that's nice to see,' Faith said.

'We're looking for a caravan park,' the woman said when they reached the balcony. 'Anything close by you know of?'

The woman's hair was an interesting shade of blue.

Martin blinked hard several times to make sure he wasn't hallucinating again.

'G'day,' Faith said, 'I'm Faith and this is Martin. I like your hair, by the way.'

Martin breathed a sigh of relief. He wasn't hallucinating.

'Ta, love. I'm Hazel and this is my hubby, Cliff. Having a party?'

'You got it in one, Hazel,' Martin said. 'Can't help you with a caravan park, but we've got free grog, free music, free dancing, and the best damn barbecued lamb you ever had in your life.'

Cliff sniffed appreciatively. 'You can smell that bloody lamb about ten k's down the road,' he said. 'We are a bit peckish. A cold beer would be pretty good too. What can I get you, Haze? The usual?'

While the men searched out the drinks, Faith and Hazel headed for the food. Faith saw her staring at the men tending the spits. 'They're Afghans,' she said.

Hazel nodded, then strode up to the men and began talking in some language Faith didn't recognise. Shariffie stared at her and then his face broke into a huge smile. Suddenly the blue-haired woman was surrounded by a group of grinning, chattering men.

'Hazel did some volunteer work with refugees after we retired,' Cliff said, handing Faith a beer. 'She's real good with languages, got an ear for it, they reckon. Put too much heart into it, though. Quack reckoned the stress would kill her before too long, so we hit the road.' He held up a bottle of Scotch. 'Hey, hon,' he yelled, 'got you a drink when you're ready.'

Hazel smiled and waved back.

'So which way you heading, Cliff?' Faith asked.

'Inland. Maybe do some opal fossicking. Just cruising, really.'

Faith noticed that Martin was looking at the text message on the phone again. 'You and Hazel have a mobile phone in the van for emergencies?' she asked.

Cliff shook his head. 'Gotta watch the pennies, love, you know how it is.'

'Martin's got a spare he doesn't need any more,' Faith said. 'You're welcome to it if you want.'

Martin erased Col's message and handed the phone to Cliff.

'Gee, thanks,' Cliff said, 'that's real nice of you. But aren't the calls a bit expensive from out here?'

'This one's got free calls,' Faith reassured him. 'You can use it as much as you like.'

'Jeez, Hazel'll be in clover. She can call the grandkids without us having to stop.'

'We've got a charger for the car too,' Faith added. 'Plugs right into the cigarette lighter.'

'You little beauty. Thanks, love,' Cliff said. 'You sure?'

'Absolutely,' Faith smiled. She looked around. 'Seen that electrician who put up the lights?' she asked Martin.

'I think he's passed out in the back of his ute.'

'Wonderful,' she said. 'He's got a nice little electric screwdriver I need to borrow.'

As she walked off, Martin looked up at the night sky. She'd been right about that helicopter earlier. He could hear it now.

Back behind the hotel, the party was slowing under the weight of all the food and alcohol consumed over the past few hours. With the band on a break and the DJ nowhere to be found, one of the Afghan men produced a small drum and another began plucking on a stringed instrument.

'The drum's called a *tabla* and that other thing's a *rebab*,' Hazel explained when Martin and Cliff joined her and Bev on the back verandah.

Shari and a group of his friends formed a circle and, hands raised shoulder-high, began to dance. One of the dying barbecues suddenly flared into life, the flickering firelight illuminating Shari's swirling tunic and beautifully embroidered vest. Cliff put his arm around Hazel's waist and the party-goers watched the dancing in silence, under a star-dotted sky.

This is a bloody funny country, Martin said to himself with a wry smile.

nineteen

Cliff and Hazel were making excellent time. Both early risers, they had left the hotel car park before dawn, after a quick cup of tea. They usually tried to get in three or four hours on the road before the day got too hot. Cliff was driving and, as usual, wishing the old Coolibah had cruise control. Soon be time for lunch though, he was thinking. Cold roast lamb and some of Hazel's homemade mustard pickle in a white-bread sandwich. Yummo.

The camper was cruising at a steady ninety k's through a desolate landscape when Cliff leaned forward and squinted. A thin black line crossed the highway a couple of hundred metres ahead. Too damn big and straight to be a snake basking in the sun. Hazel, in conversation with one of her grandkids on the mobile, noticed it too. 'Gotta go now, sweetie. Love to mummy.'

'Shit,' Cliff yelled, slamming on the brakes just a touch too late. They were still sliding forward on locked-up wheels when the front end hit the spikes and the tyres disintegrated. The van covered another thirty metres in a haze of smoke, dust and sparks, dragging the spikes under the front wheels, before it finally stopped.

'Bugger me dead,' said Cliff, switching off the ignition. Then, 'You right there, Haze?'

Hazel nodded and unfastened her seatbelt. They climbed out to inspect the shredded tyres and Hazel was the first to notice the men in suits. There were four of them, and three were carrying military-style assault rifles. She coughed and indicated them with a tilt of her head. Cliff whirled round.

'You stupid pricks have totally rooted my two best tyres!' he yelled. 'Who's going to pay for them? What if you've bent the rims, you bastards?' He strode towards the men. There was a metallic click as someone pulled a bolt back, cocking his weapon. Cliff kept walking. 'You and your poofy plastic rifles don't scare me. I fought in Korea. The Short Magazine Lee Enfield – now, that was a real rifle!'

'Cliff got the Military Medal,' offered Hazel cheerfully.

The man without a rifle stepped forward, pulling his suit jacket open to reveal a pistol. 'Where's Carter?' he asked.

'Who the hell is Carter?' demanded Cliff. 'And who's paying for my new tyres?'

They turned at the sound of a whistle. One of the men

was standing at the door of the van, holding up a mobile phone. 'It's the right phone,' he yelled. 'The van's clean.'

'Course it's clean,' snarled Cliff. 'Hazel scrubs it out every week. You could eat your tea off Hazel's floor.'

'Thanks, darl,' said Hazel brightly.

'You're driving Carter's van and using his phone,' Smith said calmly.

'It's my van,' snapped Cliff. 'Got it with part of my super payout.'

Hazel looked at the men. 'We found that phone in a rest stop about a hundred k's back,' she said. 'And we've had the van since Cliff retired. We've got pictures in an album inside.'

'Van's got Carter's plates,' Smith said.

Cliff and Hazel looked at the licence plate on their van. 'Never seen that before in my life,' Cliff said. 'Some bugger musta done a switch. Who gives a rat's anyway? It's my van. And what are you going to do about these tyres?'

'Screw your tyres, Grandad,' Smith said dismissively.

Hazel walked up to them. 'Now, I think we'd better calm down before someone gets hurt,' she said soothingly.

Smith ignored Hazel, talking over her head to Cliff. 'You should really listen to your old lady, Pops.'

Hazel positioned herself directly in front of Smith. 'I was actually talking to you, shit-for-brains,' she said.

Smith suddenly stiffened, inhaled sharply and looked down. Hazel's right hand was between his legs. His mouth gaped open, his face reddened, and he began breathing in short gasps. Hazel leaned in close to his face.

'Now, we want a tow truck, money for new wheels and tyres, and a night in a nice motel to get over our trauma,' she said. 'Or I can squeeze harder. You choose.'

Smith winced, coughed and gasped all at the same time.

At that moment a large tour bus appeared over the crest of the hill and the road spikes and automatic weapons magically disappeared. From somewhere off behind a sand dune came the sound of a helicopter starting up. The bus pulled up with a loud hiss of air brakes and the door slid open.

Smith reluctantly pulled his wallet from a back pocket and pushed a wad of notes into Hazel's free hand. She smiled and released her grip. His sigh of relief was short-lived as her knee connected with his already traumatised testicles. He went down hard.

'It's not nice to frighten vulnerable old pensioners and war veterans,' Hazel said as she counted the money.

Cliff, the tour bus driver and a group of elderly men were standing around looking at the van's front end. Hazel surreptitiously showed Cliff the cash. He was impressed.

'When we add that to the ten grand we found in the fridge this morning, we're doing all right, old girl,' he whispered.

*

'You swapped licence plates with Cliff and Hazel?' Martin asked in amazement.

Faith pulled a small electric screwdriver from the glove compartment and pressed the start button. It whirred. 'Not a straight swap, of course,' she said, 'that would be pointless. Our plates on their van, their plates on Red's ute, and his plates on our van.'

Martin glanced at her. 'Red?'

'The unconscious electrician from Taree. I didn't think he'd mind after what we paid him for the party lights. Every little bit of confusion helps.'

'I'm beginning to see that,' he said. 'I think.'

They were heading through greener bush and down towards the coast, a route Faith had suggested since Hazel and Cliff were taking an inland road. They had left the pub just a little after Cliff and Hazel, not having done much drinking at the party. Around nine, they pulled into a truck stop to refuel and have breakfast, although after last night's feast they didn't feel much like eating.

'That lamb of Shari's was really fantastic,' Faith said. 'I'm still stuffed. And those Afghan boys can certainly put it away.'

'Fred told me that since it was certified halal, it's kosher for them,' Martin said, taking a seat at a laminex-topped table.

Faith gave him a bemused look.

'I don't think that came out right, did it?' he asked.

'A magnificently mangled metaphor, Martin,' she laughed. 'Now, how about trying to flag down a waitress while I'm in the loo.' She glanced towards the counter. 'Mine's a cappuccino and raisin toast, thanks.'

Martin waved to get the waitress's attention, and when Faith returned, the table held two plates of raisin toast, a cup of tea and a cappuccino.

'Tea, Martin?' Faith asked. 'And not even attempting the artery-clogging breakfast special?'

'I saw it passing – a steak, eggs, tomato, chops and chips combo – but it just didn't seem to have that magic glow about it.'

'Jeez,' she muttered, 'every second middle-aged bloke in this country is living out a fantasy of the Great Roadhouse Breakfasts of their youth. You just have to say the word breakfast and they all start whining like a ute with a rooted diff.'

'Steady on, Faith,' Martin said in mock outrage.

'The great Aussie roadhouse breakfast is a myth, Martin,' she went on. 'When you were a kid you went on a holiday trip to the hills or to visit your Uncle Jim's farm and stopped in some country cafe and had the most fantastic breakfast of your life. But it was just greasy bacon and eggs. It was a treat because it was so different from the Vita-Brits with warm milk and the toast and Vegemite your mum made, you thought you were in heaven. But it was just breakfast on the road. Get over it.'

She took a sip of her coffee and suddenly spluttered and gagged.

Martin laughed, his face full of mischief. 'I watched them

make it while you were in the loo,' he said. 'They use one of those frill-free supermarket instant coffees. Flavour-free too, from your reaction.'

Faith looked at the big red espresso machine taking up a large part of the counter. 'But that's a La Pavoni! And I heard the pump running.'

'They just froth the milk with it,' Martin chuckled. 'I think the giveaway was probably when the waitress said, Here's your wife's cup of chino.'

Faith grimaced, wiping her lips on a paper napkin.

'Not quite the cup of coffee of your youth then, Faith?' Martin smirked.

She smiled sweetly. 'Fuck you, Martin Carter.'

'I think that might be very nice, Faith,' he smiled back, holding her gaze.

She looked into his eyes for a long time. 'Indeed it might, Martin,' she said evenly.

Martin leaned back in his chair. 'Whining like a ute with a rooted diff?' he said, raising an eyebrow.

'I'm nothing if not colourful,' she said.

*

Back on the road later that day, Martin noticed Faith examining a driver's licence. 'Whose is that?' he asked.

'It belongs to Red, the electrician,' she said, tossing the licence back into the glove compartment. 'I nicked it when I got that screwdriver.'

Martin looked across at her. 'Okay, I'll bite. Why did you want his driver's licence?'

'Well, we've got his plates on the van and I noticed he looked a bit like you, so I figured we could use it as ID.'

'He looked like me?'

'Not as handsome, of course,' she said, 'but taller and better built.'

Martin patted his stomach. 'I think I'm losing weight, Faith. And if I put my mind to it, I'm pretty sure I could get taller.'

'Well, you certainly took that like a man, Martin', she smiled.

'You won me over with handsome. But tell me, exactly why do I need ID?' he asked.

There was no answer. Martin glanced over to see Faith staring intently into the passenger-side rear-view mirror. He glanced into his mirror. The police car was about half a kilometre behind them on the narrow country road and closing fast.

'How's our speed?' Faith asked.

'Ninety,' Martin answered, looking at the dash. 'Well under the limit.'

'Shit!'

Martin looked back in his mirror. The lights on the roof of the police car were now flashing red and blue. Then the siren started.

'Want to try to outrun them?' Martin asked.

'We just passed a sign saying we're coming up to twenty k's of winding road. We'd never make it.'

'Well,' Martin said, 'I guess it was great while it lasted. Let's go with the story that I kidnapped you, eh?'

Faith shook her head. 'No way. We're in this together. Anyway, we eighty-sixed all the guns, remember? You want to try telling them you've been holding me hostage with one of Mum's souvenir cheese knives?'

Martin kept his eye firmly on the rear-view mirror. 'You've got a point. But it has been fun,' he said, 'apart from that bit on the mountain. I've never met anyone quite like you, you know.'

'Same here,' Faith said, looking into the side mirror, which was now filled with blue flashing lights.

'Really, you mean that?' Martin asked.

Faith put her hand on his thigh. 'You're a pretty interesting bloke, Mr Carter,' she said. 'And you have a very nice smile.'

The police car was right behind them now, siren wailing, and the driver began flashing his headlights.

'This looks like it then,' Martin said. 'Guess I'd better pull over.'

As the campervan moved over to the verge, the police car was suddenly beside them, then just ahead of them, and then pulling away in the distance.

'Jesus,' Martin said, 'I thought we were gone.' He exhaled slowly.

'You and me both,' Faith said, sinking back into her seat.

Martin slowed the van down and rolled into a rest stop. He switched the engine off. The lights of the police vehicle disappeared rapidly over a hill. They sat in silence, breathing deeply.

'So you really don't think I could have pulled off that souvenir cheese-knife thing?' Martin said at last.

Faith burst out laughing. After a moment, Martin joined in. It was a full five minutes before they managed to calm down.

As he eased the van back onto the road, Martin suggested they find a caravan park and sleep off the excitement.

Faith took out Red's driver's licence and held it up. 'I think we should check into some schmick motel as Mr and Mrs Taree Electrician, have a great dinner and a couple of drinks, and then go to bed. Together.'

'Oh,' Martin said. And then, after a pause, 'You sure about this?'

'I was sure before those cops turned up, but now I'm absolutely certain.'

Martin took the licence from her and slipped it into his shirt pocket. 'Mr and Mrs Taree Electrician it is then,' he smiled. They drove on into the twilight in silence.

Twenty minutes later, a motel sign appeared.

'The Jolly Roger,' Faith said. 'Nope. Too obvious.'

'You don't think it will look a bit odd driving a campervan into a motel?' Martin asked.

'Happens all the time,' Faith said. 'Even dedicated

caravanners need a bit of luxury now and again. Besides, Martin, what do you care about how it looks? You're a hardened criminal.' She paused. 'At least that's what I'm counting on.'

Martin nearly choked and Faith had to grab the wheel and steer until he recovered from his coughing fit.

*

Some time later, he read another sign as it flashed past. 'EUREKA MOTEL. 20 K'S AHEAD. IN-ROOM MOVIES, SPA BATHS, WATERBEDS. Mmm, maybe not. I get seasick.'

Faith swung around in her seat to face him. 'Martin, this is going to be a bit odd for me. I know I might come on a bit strong occasionally, like some kind of wild woman –'

'Occasionally?'

'Okay, most times,' Faith acknowledged, 'but right now I'm actually pretty nervous. Giles and I were never really hot and heavy after the first couple of years, and this boob business put the total kybosh on what was left of our sex life.'

'That's okay, Faith,' Martin said. 'I understand. We can just cuddle if you like.'

'You know, I think you do understand, Martin. And I don't want to just cuddle. But I don't want to be totally naked and I'd like the lights out. That okay with you?'

Martin shot her a sly glance. 'So I guess "Eureka" at the Eureka Motel would be me yelling, "I've found it"?'

'Hey, come on,' she said, 'we're not teenagers trying to figure out how all the bits go together.'

'Speak for yourself, Faith. It's been a long time for me too, and I was never really sure whether I was any good at it anyway.'

'Terrific,' Faith said, shaking her head, 'what a couple we make. But it's just incompetence you're worried about, not one of those size-of-your-dick things?'

'Christ, Faith,' Martin groaned. 'Be gentle. You know, I'm not good at talking about stuff like this in broad daylight.'

'Oh, lighten up, Martin,' she laughed. 'I'm sure we can fumble through.'

'Great. I've just gone from worrying about premature ejaculation the next time we hit a bump to regretting not taking your old man up on his offer of Viagra.'

'I knew the randy bugger had a secret!'

The van crested a rise and a motel appeared on the left. A large illuminated sign flashed: COUNTRY CHARM MOTEL – VACANCY.

'Mmm. Country Charm. Heated pool, fully licensed restaurant and a trampoline. That's for me,' Faith said. 'Pull in here, please, driver.'

Martin swung the wheel hard to the left. 'I hope there's a major minibar,' he muttered.

twenty

After checking in, they dined in the motel's restaurant. Airfreighted Sydney rock oysters were featured on the menu. Faith suggested a dozen each, followed by grilled West Australian crayfish in a white wine and sambuca reduction with chopped fennel.

'We owe it to all the other bank robbers on the run to live well,' she pronounced.

The oysters were cold, salty and delicious. When the crayfish arrived Faith inspected her plate. 'Goodness, this part of the world has certainly changed! The first time I came up this way, you knew you were in a high-tone establishment if there was a pineapple ring on your hamburger.'

They ate silently, savouring the meal.

'That sauce was fantastic,' Martin said, wiping his mouth with a crisp linen napkin.

'Anchovy,' Faith said. 'Just a hint, but it really took it into another realm.' She picked up the dessert menus and handed him one. 'Now, what are you having for dessert, Martin?' she smiled. 'Besides me?'

Martin's dessert, a delicate blue-cheese bavarois with mango coulis, was delicious, but he had a hard time giving it his full attention.

The waitress suggested coffee. Faith considered this for a moment. 'If he has coffee now he'll be up all night.'

Martin shifted uneasily in his chair, waiting for the other shoe to drop.

'A double espresso, darling?' she asked innocently.

'Just the bill, thank you,' he said firmly.

*

They strolled arm in arm along the frangipani-fringed path to their room. 'How come this feels so right?' Martin asked. 'But also kind of scary, somehow.'

'Beware of your belonging,' Faith said, plucking a frangipani from a tree and inhaling its heady perfume.

Martin looked at her quizzically.

'It was a sign in a Chinese restaurant in Sydney,' she explained. 'Great yum cha. Prawn gow gee to die for. Must have been a literal translation from the Cantonese, warning customers to keep an eye on their valuables. And it was taped up over a bloody great dried shark fin on display by the door, which I thought was a touch ironic.' She waved the frangipani gently under his nose, sharing the fragrance.

'Beware of your belonging,' he mused.

'I just found something about the grammatical incongruity of it quite charming. And somehow it seemed to sum up love. Mixing up longing and belonging and being wary and watchful.'

At the door to their room Martin put his arms around her. 'You're a very intriguing woman, Faith.' They kissed. They seemed to melt together somehow and Martin felt a sense of happiness and completeness he'd never known before. They kissed for a long time, then Martin finally broke away and opened the door. 'Why don't I have a quick shower while you get ready?'

'Great. That'll give me time to fold back the bedclothes and squirt some oil on my handcuffs.'

Martin couldn't stop smiling as he let the warm water run over his body. He felt oddly calm and wildly excited at the same time.

When he came out of the bathroom, the room was in darkness, apart from some candles on the dresser. A gentle breeze blowing through the open balcony door made the curtains sway. There was an almost-full moon and he could see Faith on the bed. She was wearing a creamy silk top with thin shoulder straps. And nothing else.

He took off his watch and put it on the bedside table. The time was 11.12 p.m.

At 11.27 p.m. Martin thought he was going to die. And die very happy. But he didn't.

At 12.41 a.m. Faith said, 'Mmm, tastes like mango. How very odd.'

At 1.20 a.m. Faith told him to hold that thought while she rolled over.

At 2.46 a.m. Martin asked if she knew of any medical device for the unclenching of toes.

At 3.51 a.m. Faith wondered if he was still up and discovered he most certainly was.

At 4.47 a.m. Martin considered risking a quick phone call to Colin to boast. But he fell asleep.

*

They checked out late and headed for breakfast. Faith ordered pineapple juice, eggs over easy, extra-crispy bacon, sausages, grilled tomato, hash browns, mushrooms and toast. And a cappuccino. Martin ordered orange juice and muesli with fresh fruit.

'You've got quite an appetite,' Martin commented.

'Thank you. And I like a big breakfast too.'

Martin grinned. 'My life is in total uproar and you're in the middle whipping things up and it's freaking me out, but somehow I don't think I want to change a thing. What happened to me and who the hell am I?'

Faith reached across the table for his hand. 'That's very sweet, Martin. And freaking out is so '60s, you little stud-muffin.'

'See, that's what I mean,' Martin said. 'You say something nice and romantic and bust my chops all at the same time.'

'My, we are sensitive this morning,' she smiled.

'No, we are not.' Martin lowered his voice. 'I'm almost completely numb. I'm surprised I can still walk. At one point last night I thought my legs were going to turn to jelly.'

Faith looked disappointed. 'Only at one point?' she asked. 'I'm letting the side down. There were at least three points last night when I thought I might require urgent medical assistance.'

'I guess I did okay then,' Martin said.

'*We* did better than okay. In fact we did great. We might have even broken a record or two.'

'Ah Faith, I think the waitress can hear you.'

Faith glanced around. 'Let her find her own stud-muffin,' she said. 'Grab the tomato sauce off that table, will you, spunky buns?'

Martin handed her the sauce and took a spoonful of his muesli. He looked at Faith's plate.

She gave him a black look. 'Yes, I am going to finish all of this. Order your own. You're the aficionado of the highway breakfast and this is very, very good. Why are you eating muesli, anyway?'

Martin took a sip of his orange juice. 'The level of, ah,

physical exertion in my new lifestyle,' he said. 'I do have high blood pressure. I'm not supposed to start any strenuous exercise regimen without consulting a doctor.'

'Yeah, right,' Faith laughed. 'Sounds like Medicare fraud to me. You just want to boast to someone.' She speared a sausage with her fork and offered it to him. 'Want a bite? Fair's fair. You let me nibble –'

'Jesus, Faith,' Martin whispered, taking the sausage, 'keep your voice down.'

'You're a fine one to talk about keeping things down,' she said, biting into a piece of crispy bacon.

Martin took a sip of Faith's cappuccino. 'I have to admit I was pretty impressed with last night,' he said. 'I'm not even sure I did anything like that in my twenties.'

'I'm surprised. I'd have thought that a gangly young teller in flares and a bri-nylon bodyshirt would have been a real chick magnet,' she said with a straight face.

'We weren't allowed to wear – oh.' Martin caught himself mid-sentence and smiled. 'I really can't tell when you're serious and when you're joking, Faith.'

'Might take you years to figure that out,' she said, polishing off the last of the bacon.

'Do I have years?' he asked seriously.

'Who knows what anyone's got, Martin. I'm forty-five, I've had cancer, and I don't really see any point in dicking around.'

'And I'm on the run for robbery and murder,' he said.

She shook her head. 'It was self-defence, Martin. He was going to kill both of us.'

'Okay,' he agreed, 'but I'm still not exactly a prime candidate for a long-term relationship.'

She took his hand again. 'When I was a little girl I wrote one of those Prince Charming lists about my ideal man.'

'Let me guess – handsome, rich, riding a white stallion?'

'Close. Okay-looking, saves my life, million in cash, and drives a white campervan.'

'Only okay-looking?' Martin asked.

'Oh, all right. Better than okay-looking,' she said. 'And rogers me rigid all night long. Happy now?'

'Perfectly,' Martin smiled. 'But you're busting my chops, right?'

'You bet,' Faith said. 'You're taking it well, though, which is a very good sign.'

*

'Bingo!' she said.

Martin looked up from the map he was studying. Faith was driving.

'Did we win the jackpot?' he asked. 'Or have we avoided another radar speed trap by travelling at close to the speed of light, thus becoming invisible?'

'I am not a recidivist speedster,' she protested, 'despite your accusations. I just thought we should know exactly what this van was capable of for future reference.'

'It was the sonic boom from breaking the sound barrier that got the Concorde banned from travelling over land, you know,' Martin said

'Cheap shot,' Faith replied, 'and anyway, that little aberration was hours ago. I would have thought the blood would have come back to your funny bone by now.'

'We don't want to draw attention to ourselves.'

'Look at the speedo, Martin. One-fifteen in a 110 zone. We're almost going backwards.'

'Faith, it's a campervan, remember?'

She considered this. 'You make an excellent point, fearless leader,' she said, saluting and easing off the accelerator. 'And there's this nice little town coming up, as you can see,' she continued, 'which was what my "Bingo" was about, actually. We passed a sign advertising the presence of the Minerva Cafe, so perhaps we should decelerate from warp speed to late-lunch mode.'

Martin checked out the shops along the town's main street. The place reminded him a little of Burrinjuruk, but it was a quite a bit larger and appeared to be a lot more prosperous. 'You know this Minerva joint?' he asked.

'No, but the name's Greek, and the sign said "Established 1928". Everything points to a classic, late-deco country cafe. I'm seeing booths, real Aussie hamburgers with egg and bacon and beetroot, and thick malted milks in icy metal containers dripping with condensation.'

'You reckon they'll still do breakfast?'

'Such optimism,' she sighed, pulling into a parking space at the kerb.

Inside the cafe Faith was in raptures. The Minerva was an almost perfect time capsule of the 1930s. A worn but well-polished wooden floor, panelled walls, and deep, comfortable booths. A long counter ran the length of the room and behind it there were mirrors, stainless-steel and chrome refrigerator cabinets, brass soda-fountain heads and shiny milkshake mixers. The walls were covered with framed black and white photographs, some dating back to the '30s and '40s, showing the local district, large family groups and visiting celebrities.

It was well past two and they had the place to themselves. A young woman came out of the kitchen and smiled at them. Olive-skinned, dark-haired and attractive, she was dressed in a 1930s waitress uniform, including a white apron and cap. Her name tag said 'Diana'. She bore a strong resemblance to some of the faces in the photographs.

'*Yasu*,' Faith said.

'*Yasu*,' Diana replied.

'That's pretty much the extent of my Greek,' Faith said. 'Except for souvlaki and tsatziki. And retsina, of course.'

'Mine too,' Diana said, 'which is a real bugger when I go back to Greece to visit the rellies.'

They sat in a booth and Diana brought them menus, reproductions of the original Minerva menu and proudly boasting in bold type: 'Only our Prices have Changed'.

'I know it's late, but any chance I can still order breakfast?' Martin asked apologetically.

'No worries. As long as there's an egg and a frying pan in the kitchen, you can have breakfast. You want the full disaster, with the lamb's fry and the steak and the chop?'

'Take it easy,' Faith said, patting Martin's hand, 'you'll have him in tears in a minute.'

Martin ordered his eggs sunny side up, his bacon crispy, and put himself in the chef's hands for the rest. Diana scribbled busily on her order pad. She looked at Faith.

'I'll go with lunch. What do you reckon, the mixed grill or your Big Bloke's Burger with the works?'

'Well, the mixed grill's awesome, but unless you intend driving a big rig right through the night, or digging a few ditches, I'd go with the burger.'

'The burger it is. So tell me,' Faith asked, 'what's a nice Greek girl like you doing in the bush anyway?'

'My great-grandad built this place in the late 1920s, and my grandad and dad ran it after him,' Diana explained. 'The old man closed up one evening a couple of years back, sat down in a chair and died. Mum passed away a few years earlier. I was in Sydney trying to be an actress and waitressing in a cafe where my boyfriend was the chef. We drove up here one weekend to close the joint and sell it, and somehow we never left. Place sort of grows on you.'

'You resisted the urge to renovate?' Faith said.

'Barely. We had an architect friend come up from Sydney and he took one look and fell in love.'

'I can see why,' Faith said.

'He reckoned touching one bit of the place would be sacrilege. So we just tarted the old girl up a smidge and kept the doors open.'

Diana headed for the kitchen. Martin was examining a chrome jukebox selector on the wall at the end of their table.

'Wow, I haven't seen one of these for years,' he said. 'Got a twenty-cent coin?'

Faith flipped through the metal-framed pages behind the glass cover. 'Looks like they converted them to decimal in the early '70s,' she said, 'and that was the last time they changed the record selection. Whoa, Elvis doing "Blue Suede Shoes". Are we in a country town or what?' She looked at Martin. 'So what's it to be, sweet thang? My treat. "Galveston" by Mr Glen Campbell? How about Bobby Goldsboro's "Honey"? Some early Joe Cocker from the Mad Dogs and Englishmen tour? Leon Russell tickling those ivories on "She Came In Through The Bathroom Window"? Don't tell me, Neil Diamond's "Song Sung Blue"?'

'Hey, look, they do hot fudge sundaes here!' Martin said, in a desperate attempt to change the subject.

'Don't be ashamed to admit it,' Faith laughed. 'There was a time when every second household in the country had the *Hot August Night* LP on their turntable.'

Martin adopted a mock-serious tone. 'It's like drugs, Faith. Just because everybody's doing it doesn't make it right.'

Faith beamed at him. 'Right on!' she said.

'Boy,' Martin laughed. 'LP, turntable and "right on". That really dates us.'

She dropped a coin in the slot and pressed two buttons on the selector. There was a long pause and then music blasted out of the speakers at the far end of the cafe. Diana poked her head out of the kitchen and Faith pointed an accusing finger at Martin. Diana shook her head sadly.

'ELO?' Martin said.

'The Electric Light Orchestra performing "Livin' Thing" for your listening pleasure,' Faith said. 'Just a shot in the dark.'

Martin looked at her and slowly smiled, his head starting to bop with the music.

'Sing along if you want, Mr Carter.'

So he did.

twenty-one

The next day they clocked up 200 k's by mid-morning and the highway rest stop looked inviting. There were toilets, barbecue facilities, panoramic views of the distant coastline, and, best of all, no other vehicles in sight. Martin parked the van near the safety fence and Faith took out her camera.

'Sun's still a little too high but I might find a nice angle,' she said.

They walked over to the lookout and she put the camera to her eye. A moment later she took it down. 'Nah, doesn't do anything for me.'

They both turned at the noise from behind. A low-flying helicopter was heading rapidly towards them, rotor blades flashing as they caught the afternoon sunlight. Faith had the camera to her eye again and she was shooting as the chopper flew over them and headed down towards the coast.

'Police?' Martin asked.

'Wasn't marked,' Faith said, 'and they usually have one of those big spotlights mounted underneath.'

'He sure was in a hurry to get somewhere,' Martin said.

Faith packed up her camera. 'Well, we're not, so do you fancy a cup of tea?'

Ten minutes later, Faith stepped out of the camper with a teapot and cups on a tray. Martin set up two folding aluminium chairs he'd discovered in a locker in the van.

'Bring back memories, Faith?' he asked. 'Those holidays from hell of your childhood?'

'God, yes,' she agreed. 'We used to go to Jackson's Inlet and camp on the foreshore. Same spot, same neighbours, same cheesy carnival, same New Year's Eve fireworks, same pimply boys trying to grope me, same bloody dreary holiday every year.'

'Brothers and sisters?' Martin asked.

'Nope, I was the classic only child. What about you?'

'Couple of brothers,' he said. 'Malcolm's a plumber and Morris is a signwriter.'

'Good heavens,' Faith said. 'Malcolm, Morris and Martin. How cute. Melanie was no doubt earmarked for any little girl that might show up. Close family?'

Martin sipped his tea. 'Not really. We just sort of tolerated each other until we drifted apart. No animosity, just nothingness.'

'I know that feeling,' she said.

'But we all had nice, safe, secure jobs,' Martin continued, 'just like Mum wanted, and we all got married to nice pregnant girls and everything worked out for the best.'

'Did it?'

'Well, Malcolm kept getting divorced when his wives figured out all those after-hours calls weren't about blocked drains. Old Mal gave the plumber's snake a bit of a bad name, I'm afraid. And Morris paints signs all day and drinks cask wine all night because he'd rather be in Paris on the Left Bank with an easel and a beret, but the five kids and the mortgage make that a little impractical.' Martin threw up his hands. 'I guess I'm the success story of the Carter family, and that truly shocking statement about sums it up.'

Faith sat up straight. 'Well, this is a grim little turn in the conversation. Subject change, I think. Tell me about the mad major.'

Martin relaxed back into his chair. 'Not a lot to tell, really. We met in second year at high school. I guess we were both a bit sensitive for Box Forest Boys High. And I don't mean the love-which-dares-not-speak-its-name kind of sensitive.'

'You're starting to read my mind, Mr Carter.'

Martin looked at her. He really loved the sound of that voice. Why hadn't anyone ever told him you could feel like this about another person? he wondered.

'Anyway, I was a bit weedy back then and used to get picked on. We had some real dickheads at our school. Jack and I didn't fit in for different reasons, so we sort of gravitated to each other. That stopped the bullying pretty quick. He had a great left hook. We kind of watched each other's backs after that.'

'Why didn't he fit in?' Faith asked.

'Reffo,' Martin said. 'Jack Stark was the shortened version of his name. He was actually born Iliya Jakob Starkovsky. We Australianised it for him one day.'

'Did it help?'

Martin shook his head. 'Not a lot. You know what kids are like. His grandparents were Russian; they'd lived in Harbin in Manchuria. Jack's dad was born in Harbin. He moved to Shanghai when he was eighteen, spent the war there under Japanese occupation, got turfed out when Mao's communists took over China in '49, went to Hong Kong and finally wound up in Australia.'

Faith was intrigued. 'Russia to China to Hong Kong to Melbourne. Now, that's a hell of a journey.'

'His old man told us some incredible stories, usually after a few vodkas. Sometimes, when his parents were out, Jack used to open up this steel trunk in the attic and pull out the most amazing stuff. Knives, medals, flags, dirty postcards, a hand grenade, and even this funny-looking Mauser pistol with a round wooden grip.'

'Hmmm,' Faith said, 'sounds like you two should have

been able to take care of the school bullies with an arsenal like that. Those old broomhandle Mauser automatics were supposed to be very persuasive.'

'I have to say, we considered it,' Martin said. 'But we just stuck it out until we got our Leaving Certificates, then I joined the bank as a junior. Jack seemed a bit lost until the Vietnam conscription ballot got him. His dad was rabidly anti-communist, which is understandable, so Jack getting called up wasn't the worst thing in the world from the family's point of view. I heard he was doing really well in training, and then we lost contact. Just different worlds, I guess.'

'So we're heading north to meet someone you haven't seen or spoken to in over twenty-five years?' Faith asked.

Martin nodded. 'Seems a bit pathetic,' he said, 'but I really don't have anywhere else to go. Things haven't quite worked out the way I thought. And the last fifty years don't seem to have added up to a hell of a lot.'

'There's still time, Martin,' Faith said. 'Don't rush it. Samuel Johnson said, "Excellence in any department can be attained only by the labour of a lifetime; it is not to be purchased at a lesser price."'

'Not even at Kmart?' Martin raised a cheeky eyebrow.

'Not even on their mark-down days,' Faith laughed.

'You're a funny bugger, Faith. I haven't talked to anyone like this for as long as I can remember. Maybe never. It feels great. I think everything that's happened in the last few days just caught up with me. What's really weird is that it felt like the right thing to do, and meeting you has made it seem complete. Very confusing.'

Faith rested her hand on his. 'After my diagnosis, I was in shock, I suppose,' she said. 'I took a ride on that bloody awful monorail in Sydney, which is something I wouldn't usually do in a fit. There were two elderly couples – retired, I guess – in my carriage. The men looked out the window and droned on and on about the virtues of leaf-blowers. The women just stared ahead, and the look on both their faces really horrified me. They were in shock, like me, I decided. We were all facing death. Mine possibly had a specific timeframe attached, but theirs was indeterminate. In our own ways, we were all thinking, What the fuck happened to my life? They'd probably spent fifty years married to these men, living their lives through them, and didn't even really know them. Now they had to live out the twilight of their lives with them.'

'Well, that's certainly cheered me up, Faith,' Martin said. 'Good work. Any chance there's a bottle of hemlock in the pantry?'

She laughed. 'I just mean, win or lose, we've both made a choice and a change. I don't know where this road is leading, but I like the ride. I'm glad I made the choice I did.'

'Me too,' Martin said.

*

A large sign at the border read: YOU ARE NOW ENTERING QUEENSLAND. Underneath, someone had spraypainted: PLEASE TURN CLOCKS BACK 20 YEARS.

'They really should work on their material,' Faith said. 'They've been painting the same graffiti for twenty years.'

Just past the sign, they overtook an old man walking along the road. He was wearing threadbare track pants, a flannelette shirt over a faded T-shirt, ugh boots, and a red and black football beanie over his wispy white hair. His arm was extended and his thumb was up.

'Why don't we give the old bloke a lift?' Faith suggested. 'I wouldn't want my old man wandering along the road way out here.'

Martin slowed and backed up and Faith wound down her window. 'You okay?' she asked. 'Need a lift?'

'That'd be great, darl,' the old man said. He clambered onto the bench seat and Faith slid closer to Martin.

'Name's Len,' said the old man, shaking their hands. 'Thanks for stopping. The car carked it on a side road. You heading to the coast?'

'You bet,' said Martin pulling back onto the roadway.

'Want us to have a look at the car?' asked Faith. 'Might be something simple.'

The old man scratched his bristly five-o'clock shadow. 'Nah, thanks anyway,' he said. 'I think the bloody turbo's cactus. Teach me to buy a dago car.'

Faith flashed Martin a look of mild amusement.

'You two on a second honeymoon then?' Len asked after a while.

'Something along those lines,' Faith said and she squeezed Martin's knee.

'I'm hoping to catch up with an old friend from high school a ways up the coast,' Martin said. 'Sort of a surprise visit. Haven't seen him for thirty years.'

The old man grunted. 'Not a big fan of the surprise visit myself. Sometimes they don't pan out the way you hoped.'

They rounded a corner half an hour later and came to the edge of an escarpment looking down over the Pacific Ocean. Sparkling blue water, miles of golden sand, and towering high-rise buildings stretching towards the horizon.

'You know,' the old man said, 'when I first came up here after the war, there was bloody nothing and no-one. Just empty beaches, palm trees, and maybe a small fibro fisherman's shack every five or ten miles.'

Martin looked at the hotels and apartment buildings stacked ten and fifteen deep back from the beach. 'God, what a tragedy,' he said.

'Too fuckin' right, it was,' the old man said. 'Clearing contractors hooked up huge chains between pairs of bulldozers and ripped bloody great swathes through the scrub. A couple of blokes could clear fifty acres on a good day. Just look at it now. Isn't she a beautiful sight?'

'Yeah, just look at it now,' Faith said, her voice heavy with irony.

'You two are coming to my place for tea,' Len suddenly announced. 'We can carbonise some chops on the barbie. I think there's probably a couple of bottles of half-decent plonk somewhere in the kitchen. Red okay?'

Faith looked at Martin for confirmation. He nodded.

'Sounds good, I guess,' she said. 'We're up for it.'

They cruised down the escarpment and on into a thriving suburbia. Wide, divided roadways took them past expensive low-rise housing, some of it on a network of manmade canals. Closer to the beach it was all high-rise apartment canyons, the massive structures already casting dark shadows across each other and the sand in the early afternoon light. Martin wasn't sure exactly what Len's place would look like, but he wasn't expecting a high-walled compound occupying several blocks of waterfront.

'Hang a hard left just down here,' the old man ordered, pulling a small remote-control from his pocket.

High steel gates swung open. Speechless, Martin negotiated the circular driveway up to the main entrance of a two-storey Italianate mansion. A tall man in an elegant suit opened the van door on Len's side.

'Car trouble, Mr Barton?' he asked.

Len grunted as he climbed out. 'Fucking Testarossa,' he said. 'Redhead is right; bloody acts like one. That Ferrari dealer's gunna have a red arse when I get through with kicking it.' He headed up the steps to the front door, yelling back over his shoulder, 'That's Albris. Leave the keys and he'll park the van and give it a bit of a wash if you like. Tea's at six. You'll stay the night. Stick 'em in the Agung wing, Albris.'

Martin and Faith stared at Len's back disappearing through the carved double wooden doors.

'So that's Arthur Leonard Barton,' Martin said. 'Well, I'll be buggered!'

'I thought he looked vaguely familiar,' Faith said.

Albris was sizing up Martin. 'About a thirty-six regular, sir?' he asked.

Martin looked blank. 'Excuse me?' he said.

Albris steered them towards the house. 'Dinner, if a touch early, is always formal,' he explained. 'Mr Barton can be somewhat eccentric in his entertaining, so we have a variety of dinner wear on hand for his guests.' He studied Martin again. 'Something double-breasted, I think.'

A slight, golden-skinned woman in a sarong and kebaya appeared in the doorway. She bowed elegantly.

'This is Tamila, ma'am,' Albris said to Faith. 'She will assist you with anything you need. Perhaps a classic Dior sheath?' he suggested to Tamila, who nodded in agreement.

As Albris led them down a cool, dark, marble hallway, Martin and Faith exchanged looks behind his back. Martin raised an eyebrow as if to say, What's going on here? Faith shrugged.

At the end of the hallway Albris paused and opened a set of double doors, revealing an exquisite suite of rooms.

'The architect's brief here was something airy with a Balinese influence,' he announced, sliding open two wall panels and allowing the golden afternoon light of the Pacific to flood the room. 'There are interconnecting doors to an identically appointed suite, should you wish individual privacy.'

On the terrace outside their suite were two swimming pools shaded by frangipanis. The pool to the right, Albris explained, was heated. If swimming costumes were required, they were in the walk-in wardrobes. Though, as he pointed out, the pools were screened from view and completely private.

'We were originally somewhat overshadowed by the main tower of the old Breakers Hotel,' Albris said. 'Mr Barton had it removed for his guests' comfort and convenience.'

'That must have been a hell of a messy demolition job just for the odd skinny-dipper,' Faith said. 'Wouldn't it have been easier to roof in the pool?'

Albris shook his head. 'Explosive demolition,' he said. 'We blew it up on a Monday morning and the site was cleared by Thursday.'

'I think I saw it on the news,' Martin said. 'The whole building just sort of fell in on itself. Must have been a heck of a big bang.'

'Not really,' Albris said. 'The trick with explosives is not how big a charge you use, but exactly where you place it.'

'My thoughts exactly,' Faith said, smiling at Martin.

Tamila silently appeared bearing a *dulang*, a carved

Balinese wooden stand used for temple offerings to the gods. It was stacked high with tropical fruit.

'The mangosteens are particularly good at the moment,' Albris suggested. 'Just press two on any phone for the kitchen. It's staffed twenty-four hours. Please feel free to order anything.'

'Anything?' Faith asked.

'Anything,' Albris responded.

'How about a crème brûlée and a pot of coffee?'

Albris smiled. 'Of course. Our chef uses a hint of ginger in his crème brûlée, which is quite intriguing. Today's coffee is a double-A Yauco Selecto.'

'Puerto Rican, and a damned fine coffee, I believe,' Faith said. 'I'm very impressed, Albris.'

Albris nodded. 'We do try, madam,' he said. 'Rather than a brewed pot, which won't really do justice to the beans, might I suggest an espresso, or perhaps a macchiato.'

'A long macchiato is possible?'

'Anything is possible, madam,' Albris said evenly.

'You don't agree with the long macchiato concept, Albris?'

'I am something of a traditionalist,' he replied. 'I find the long macchiato to be something of a Melbourne affectation. But madam may of course order anything she wishes.'

Faith shook her head. 'Nothing right now, thank you,' she said. 'I was just checking. I'm going to save myself for dinner, which I have a feeling will be superb.'

'An excellent decision,' Albris said. 'If you would like to relax, Tamila and I will return at four to arrange your dinner clothes. Tamila will make any necessary adjustments.'

Faith called after Albris as he walked to the door. 'That's rather a beautiful suit,' she said. 'Armani?'

'Exactly right, madam.'

'You've got a bit of a limp there, Albris,' said Martin.

'A sporting injury, sir. Nothing serious.'

'Football?' inquired Martin.

Albris's face wrinkled in a thin smile. 'Something very like that, sir,' he replied.

twenty-two

Faith and Martin had fallen asleep in separate rooms. There was an unspoken agreement that this would be the way to play it. Martin woke to the sound of Faith doing laps in the pool, but he didn't look out. He had a lot on his mind. It puzzled him that he hadn't been caught yet, and was it only a week ago that he'd thought about ending it all? Now here he was about to dine with Australia's richest man. The dinner-table conversation should be interesting: 'So tell me a little about yourself, Martin.'

'Well, the first fifty years of my life were pretty ordinary, but the last few days . . .' His reply would be one to remember if he actually told the truth.

There was a discreet knock on the door and Albris entered, wheeling a clothes rack. Ten minutes later, he left with a pair of dress trousers pinned for Tamila to take up. Martin had a dinner jacket, new shoes chosen from a selection of sizes, a shirt, cummerbund and bow tie. While Albris was kneeling to fit the shoes, his jacket had gaped open and Martin saw the pistol in a holster strapped under his arm.

'Len pretty strict about the dinner at six thing then, Albris?' he asked.

Albris looked up quizzically. Martin pointed at the pistol. Albris adjusted the front of his jacket. 'A man like Mr Barton attracts the attention of a wide variety of people,' he said, 'not all of whom wish him well. I need to be prepared for any eventuality.'

'You use that thing a lot then?' Martin asked.

'No, sir. Generally just the once is enough. If you aim very carefully.' He smiled, but there was no humour in his eyes.

Albris took his leave and Martin showered and shaved in a bathroom almost as big as his house in Burrinjuruk. When he came out his complete dinner suit was laid out on the bed. A beautifully wrapped hibiscus sat on the side table. At five-fifty Martin had everything under control, except for the bow tie. There was a gentle knock on the connecting door and he went to open it.

His mouth moved but no sound came out. Faith was wearing a long, black, tightly fitted evening dress with a cropped, three-quarter-sleeved jacket. Her hair was pulled back into a sleek French roll. Martin tried to find the words.

'Why, thank you, Martin,' Faith smiled. 'I'll take your gasping for air like a stunned mullet as a compliment.' She put down an elegant beaded clutch purse and deftly tied his bow tie.

'You look absolutely fantastic!' Martin finally managed to stammer out. He remembered the hibiscus and pinned it to her jacket. They looked at themselves in the full-length mirror.

'You know, we scrub up okay for an ex-librarian with one tit and a bank-robbing fugitive,' Faith said.

'We sure do, don't we?' Martin put his arm around her waist and looked in amazement at the couple he saw in the mirror. Was that really him?

Faith glanced at her watch. 'Almost six,' she said, breaking away to fetch her purse.

'We'd better hustle then,' Martin said, turning to admire his profile. Nothing like a beautifully cut tux to make a man feel debonair. 'Apparently there are extreme penalties for latecomers.'

'How extreme?' she laughed.

'Albris is packing heat,' he said, turning to check his other profile.

'Packing heat, Martin? A touch *film noir*-ish, don't you think?'

'He definitely had a piece, a shooter, a gat, a rod, a roscoe, a heater,' he went on mischievously.

'Are you sure you're new to all this, Martin?'

'Too many late nights watching Humphrey Bogart reruns, schweetie,' Martin drawled in his best Bogie impersonation.

'You'd know how to whistle then,' she purred in a soft American accent. 'Just put your lips together . . . and blow.'

Martin grinned. She'd be a hell of a poker player, he decided. She'd just seen his Bogart and raised him a Bacall.

*

'My first job was trainee manager on a Pommy rubber plantation in Malaya just before the war. I was only seventeen, but even then I thought every damn thing they did was wrong, except for dressing for dinner. I liked that idea.'

Len sipped on a very old single malt. He was freshly shaved, well groomed, and wearing a beautifully tailored dinner suit. They were relaxing on overstuffed lounges on an upstairs terrace facing the ocean. When Martin had indicated he would have whatever the older man was drinking, Len nodded approvingly.

'Good choice,' he said. 'It's a thirty-year-old Glenfarclas. Close to four hundred bucks a bottle and worth every cent.'

Martin tried to guess the value of the smoky golden liquid in his glass and made a special effort not to spill any.

Faith sipped on the best Manhattan she'd had in a long time. 'It's very kind of you to lend us the clothes. They certainly add to the occasion.'

Len grunted. 'Not a loan. Keep 'em if they fit. Even as we speak, the wife's in Paris scorching the plastic. She gets a range of sizes knocked up. Doesn't like grotty changing rooms much, I guess.'

'I'm pretty sure where she shops the changing rooms would have parquetry flooring, Persian rugs, chandeliers and Louis Quatorze chairs,' Faith suggested.

Len shrugged. 'I humour her. It's only money, and I've got a ton of it.' He raised his glass to Faith. 'Worth it to see a frock like that worn the way it should be.'

Martin raised his glass as well. 'I'll go along with that,' he said.

Albris announced dinner and led them to a table set up at the other end of the terrace. There was a waiter to serve each of them. The first course, a gateau of smoked salmon with cucumber coulis served with an unwooded chardonnay, was superb.

'Nobody's a bloody vegetarian, I hope,' Len said when the main course of filet mignon was announced. 'Too many bloody vegetarians in this country. Just had to close my abattoir at Burrinjuruk this month because it wasn't making money,' he added.

Faith snuck a look at Martin. His face was impassive.

'How do you two want your steak?' Len asked. 'Rare, very

rare, or blue?' He finished the last of his wine and the waiter replaced his glass with a new one. 'I took this Hungarian cook up to the Kimberley in the '50s,' he went on. 'All the bushies on my stations liked their meat burnt to a cinder. Used to be that way myself. This bloke would tell 'em they had a choice of a bloody steak or a bloody nose. Meant it too. Tough bastards those reffos.'

'Rare,' said Faith.

'Me too,' said Martin.

The bottles of red in the kitchen that Len had mentioned turned out to be '82 Grange. The wine was decanted and served by Albris, who also placed a jar of Keen's English mustard in front of Len.

The old man smiled at Faith. 'You can take the boy out of the bush . . .' he said.

The steak, served with a mushroom and port sauce, and potatoes cooked with spinach, macadamia nuts and cream, was unlike anything Martin had ever tasted. Faith commented on the tenderness.

'Comes from my feed lots in the Northern Territory,' Len explained. 'The best of it goes to the Japs. The very best of it comes to me. Exquisitely marbled and beautifully hung.'

'Exactly the way I like it,' Faith said, squeezing Martin's thigh. He finished his glass of wine in one gulp.

Faith turned to Albris, who hovered nearby. 'And the mushroom sauce?' she asked.

'Sautéed shallots with star anise and juniper berries reduced in red wine and port before adding a *demi-glace*,' he informed her.

'Fresh and dried mushrooms?' she asked.

Albris nodded. 'Porcini, shitake and morels.'

'And trompette de la mort?' she asked.

'Among others,' he agreed. 'Well spotted. Madam has an excellent palate.'

She smiled. 'Thank you, Albris,' she said brightly, 'I certainly know a mushroom from a toadstool.'

There was a much-needed pause after the main course. Martin asked Len about the range of his business interests.

'Started off in construction, then diversified. These days it's mainly beef, TV, newspapers and magazines,' he said.

'Well, Len,' Faith smiled sweetly, 'I guess you're in the bullshit business whichever way you look at it.'

Len guffawed. 'I like your style, girlie!'

Martin shot Faith a glance. She was still smiling but he saw the flicker of annoyance in her eyes.

Dessert was a quince *tarte tatin* with King Island cream, served with a botrytis semillon. Albris placed a tiny crème brûlée in front of Faith along with her coffee. It was excellent. She knew the touch of ginger was lifted from Tetsuya's in Sydney, but it was a fine effort nonetheless.

They retired to chaises longues after the meal. Martin took a cigar from the humidor Albris presented. Len pulled out a packet of Tally-Ho papers and rolled a cigarette.

'That was a superb meal,' said Faith. 'Could you convey our compliments to the chef, Albris.'

'Certainly, madam. Mr Barton lured him away from the Sultan of Brunei. Quite a coup.'

Len belched. 'Yep, your slopes make your best all-round chefs,' he said. 'Now, anyone for a palate-cleansing ale?'

Faith sat up in her seat. 'Len,' she said quietly, 'I really don't like that.'

'You don't like the fact that a bloke can cook better than a sheila?' he asked.

Faith held his gaze. 'You know exactly what I don't like,' she said.

Len tightened his lips and whistled. Albris appeared. 'Bring us a couple of beers, chop chop,' he ordered. 'There you go, love,' he said to Faith. 'I'm an equal-opportunity abuser.'

Faith sipped her coffee. 'Not good enough,' she said. 'That was just for show.'

'Listen,' Len said. 'I'm old. I grew up in a different country, girlie. We were white, British and proud. That was until I actually worked with the Poms and found out what they were really like. Then the war came. I'd learned to fly Tiger Moths when I was a sprog in the bush, so I joined the RAAF and got sent to Europe to fly bombers. My younger brother went up to Singapore with the army. He arrived just in time to get surrendered to the Japs by the fuckin' Poms. We think he was murdered on the Sandakan death march, but we'll never be sure. Killed the old lady, never knowing how he died, or even if he had a decent burial. I sell the Japs my beef, but it doesn't mean I have to like 'em. I built dams and hotels for Viets and Thais and Indos in the old days, but that's because it was what I did. It's just business. I like the fuckin' Thais, they're okay. In Thailand. Same with Afghans, Cambodians, whatever. I'm sure they're just bloody great in their own countries. It's when they show up on our doorstep that we get problems.'

'Do you know how many immigrants and refugees this country accepts every year?' Faith asked him.

Len looked her in the eye. 'Sure do, girlie. Too bloody many. I reckon I grew up in a better country than my grandkids will ever know. I don't need to watch my TV stations or read my papers to know that crime in this country is out of control and whose bloody fault it is.'

Martin had been sitting back quietly, his eyes flicking between Len and Faith. Now he saw Faith's face take on a cold calmness he hadn't seen before.

'Talk like that going unchallenged is part of the problem,' she said. 'I grew up in Parramatta on the same street as the jail. It was a bloody big sandstone prison that was built a long time before we had any kind of non-white immigration program. To hear people talk, you'd think there was no crime in this country before 1970. Jesus, this whole joint started out as a penal colony, and the land of milk and honey you seem so wistful for grew out of that.'

She took a deep breath. 'And one more thing. If you call me girlie again, Mr Barton,' she said quietly, 'I will kick you in the balls. Very hard.'

Martin coughed. 'Three nine five, Faith,' he said.

Faith acknowledged Martin with a nod, then turned back to Len. 'I'm sorry, Mr Barton, Martin has just reminded me of my manners. We are, after all, your guests.'

'I'm an old man,' Len said, leaning back in his chair and taking a slow drag on his cigarette. 'And I'm stinking rich, so I sometimes forget my own manners. But if I don't like something, then I speak my mind. As do you, which is fair enough. There's a lot of things happening in this country that I don't like, so I say so.'

'That's all very well, but it was those Hungarian reffos and wops and Balts and Greeks and Lebbos and all manner of displaced persons from Europe who built this country after the war, and made you a very rich man in the process. Now that you're set, you think it's time to pull the ladder up and slam the doors shut and I'm all right, Jack.'

Len raised his glass. 'Why don't we just agree to disagree then?' he said.

Faith raised her own. 'The problem with that, Mr Barton, is that I'm a retired librarian with a single vote and you're a billionaire with newspapers and a national television network.'

'You've got me there,' he laughed. 'I have to admit, when you're a billionaire you do have the prime minister's ear.'

'And when you're a billionaire with newspapers and a television network,' Faith said, 'you probably also have the prime minister's balls.'

Len smiled and exhaled, watching Faith through the cloud of smoke.

Martin stood up. 'It was a lovely dinner,' he said, 'but I think we might want to make an early start in the morning.' He put down his drink and shook hands with Len.

'Yes,' Faith said, doing likewise, 'it was a unique evening.'

*

Albris was standing by the terrace doorway as they left. He walked over to the balcony railing where Len was leaning, looking out to sea.

'Never liked the sea at night, Albris, not after the war. Coming back over the channel after an op was always the worst part for me. Hated it. That was a bloody stupid war, in Europe. White men killing white men. What for? Stupid.'

'Yes, sir,' Albris said.

'Two tours with Bomber Command, Albris, fifty ops all up, and try as they might those fucking Krauts never managed to get me.' Len looked around into the empty hallway. 'I like her. Pity. Is it done?'

'Everything as we discussed, sir.'

'And the tracking device?'

'Activated,' Albris said. 'We can stand down the watchers

and just use the satellite information. It will place them accurately to within ten metres.'

'Not too much longer then.' Len flicked his cigarette over the balcony.

'It won't be the same,' Albris said glumly. 'Not at arm's length like this.'

'Safer this way. He's too damn dangerous to fuck with close up. You should bloody well know that by now. This time it has to be hands off and clean.'

Albris was about to say something but changed his mind.

'Someone bring the Ferrari back?' Len asked.

'It was driven to the dealer's. They'll keep it out of sight till the coast is clear.'

Len stretched. 'Better let the little prick in Canberra know what's happening, I suppose. They all wanna be kept in the loop, Albris. Silly buggers don't realise the loop is a ring through their noses. Get him on the phone.'

Albris looked at his watch. 'It's well after midnight in Canberra, sir.'

Arthur Leonard Barton shrugged. 'He needs my newspapers and TV stations and he knows it. Wake him up.'

*

The beds had been remade with fresh linen in both rooms. A bottle of chilled Piper-Heidsieck champagne rested in an ice bucket in Faith's room, near the connecting door. Faith took off her jacket and wandered into the bathroom, returning with a glass of water. She sat on the bed next to Martin.

'Well, that certainly was an evening to remember,' she said.

Martin put his head in his hands. 'I didn't drink all that much but my head is spinning.'

She kissed him gently. 'Three ninety-five, eh?' she said. 'Manners and etiquette. Nothing turns a librarian on more than a man who knows his way around the Dewey decimal system.'

'I used to work in the library in high school to get out of sport,' he explained.

'Hidden depths, eh?' she said, laughing. 'And I think you're right about getting an early start, Martin. We should probably go to bed.'

He looked at her.

'Separately,' she said. 'There's a very bad vibe here. I keep getting the feeling we're being watched.'

'I know what you mean, this place is pretty weird,' Martin said. 'But at least you scored a free dress out of it.'

'I don't want it,' Faith said, and she shivered. 'What a thoroughly ugsome man.'

Martin kissed her gently on the forehead. 'Cheer up,' he said, 'I've still got close to a million dollars, you know. Next Kmart we come to you can knock yourself out.'

'I might hold you to that,' she laughed, and gave him a long, lingering kiss. 'Goodnight, Martin.'

He walked reluctantly to the connecting door.

'Martin,' she called, 'I've decided to keep the underwear. It's La Perla.'

He turned. She was wearing a black bustier, stockings and suspenders. He felt his heart jump. 'Struth,' he whispered.

She smiled, a wicked gleam in her eyes. 'Hold that thought. See you in the morning.'

He grinned and blew her a kiss.

'If you're taking a shower,' she said, 'the cold tap's on the right.'

twenty-three

Driving in two-hour shifts, and with regular stops for food, fuel and fornication, they had made excellent time in the four days since leaving the Gold Coast. Faith now claimed to be able to judge the quality of a motel by the number of adjectives used in its roadside signs.

They were rapidly closing in on their destination and the countryside was tropical, with weather to match. Clumps of palm trees and sugar cane and banana plantations whizzed by the windows, and every roadside stop offered the chance to purchase exotic fruits and vegetables. Inside the van, airconditioning kept the heat and humidity at bay.

'You didn't finish telling me why you never had kids,' said Martin.

'We were interrupted yet again by your quest for the

Holy Grill, as I recall,' Faith laughed. Her bare feet rested on the dashboard as she expertly sliced into the purple skin of a mangosteen.

'Scoff if you must, but I know the great highway breakfast is out there.'

'One to top the Minerva?' She peeled away the skin of the fruit to reveal its creamy segments.

'I admit it was very, very good, but I'm afraid I can still only give it nine out of ten.'

'And so we continue to seek out that subtle and ineffable difference that will carry us to breakfast nirvana?' she asked, slipping a segment of mangosteen into his mouth.

'Mmm,' Martin pondered, as he savoured the fruit. 'I think perfection may rest with just the right relish.'

'With a big greasy banger wallowing in it, no doubt,' she shuddered.

'Mmmmm, big greasy banger with relish,' Martin said with a wicked smile, imagining exactly that.

'Okay, Homer!' Faith grinned. 'Now, where were we? Me and kids, or lack thereof. Never really wanted them, I guess is the short answer. Suited my ex too. He had very definite plans for our retirement, right from the age of twenty-five. It was actually a bit creepy when I think about it now.'

'Doesn't really sound like the kind of person you'd marry, Faith.'

'Well, to be fair, he did have a lot of good qualities. It's just that his later behaviour made me forget most of them. One day I looked at him and suddenly realised I was married to an old man of thirty. And he was wearing a cardigan.' She popped the last segment of mangosteen into her mouth and wiped her hands on a tissue. 'Not really sure why I stayed after that. Inertia? Fear? Pity? None of them particularly good reasons.'

'I've worn the odd cardigan in my time, Faith,' Martin said, shifting uncomfortably in his seat.

'I don't mean literally, Martin, I mean on the inside. Under his skin, he was wearing a sensible cardigan and comfortable slippers.'

'Now, that is a seriously creepy concept, Faith.' Martin shivered.

'I know,' she agreed. 'Nothing surprised me more than when he left me for Gillian.'

'The girl with the two tits?'

She nodded. 'I was actually impressed on some level. I didn't know he had it in him. Seriously crook timing, though.' She opened a bottle of water and took a sip. 'And what about you and kids, Martin?' she asked, offering him the bottle.

He took a drink and handed the bottle back without taking his eyes off the road. 'Dunno,' he said, 'just never happened. I don't think I mind not having kids, but then again I suppose I wouldn't really know. I wasn't much chop with the step-kids, that's for certain.'

She patted his knee. 'Don't be so hard on yourself. You

were behind the eightball right from the start on that one. With the right woman, I think you'd have been a fantastic dad.'

They drove in silence for a few minutes.

'Okay, anything else you want to talk about then?' Martin piped up. 'Sex, maybe?'

Faith laughed her wonderful throaty laugh. 'Keep your mind on the road, Mr Carter.'

'And my eyes peeled for the next motel?' he asked with a cheeky grin.

She turned to look at him, enjoying the playfulness in his expression. 'This whole boob thing doesn't worry you at all, Martin, does it?'

'I'm very sorry that it happened, for your sake,' he said, 'and that you had to go through it, and what it did to your relationship, but no.'

'Very good answer, Martin.' Faith leaned over and kissed him on the cheek. 'You should have seen them when I was twenty – very perky. I couldn't walk past a building site without being vocally encouraged to display them in their natural state for the entertainment and edification of members of the hardworking fraternity of high-rise construction engineers.'

'I never understood the rationale of yelling "Show us ya tits" to complete strangers myself.'

'It was an invitation I always found quite easy to resist. Obviously more so these days.'

Martin found her hand and gave it a squeeze. 'Hey, you're here and you're alive and I'm having the best time I've had in my life. Let's make the most of what we've got for as long as we've got. Breasts are nice, but you've also got a very horny brain.'

'Stop the van!'

Martin's head snapped round, his foot covering the brake pedal.

'I have to call the *New England Journal of Medicine* to report the world's first successful bankmanagerectomy. You're cured. The first sign was that urge to give money away, then you started making jokes, and now *real* romance, free and unafraid.'

'Are my chops being busted here?' Martin asked, relaxing back into his seat.

'Ever so delicately and from a place of love,' she answered, smiling.

'You want to drive, don't you?' Martin said knowingly.

'You see right through me, stud-muffin.'

Martin shook his head. 'We're trying to keep a low profile, and you have the definitive lead foot, Faith.'

She waved a brochure. 'My trusty motel directory says there's a Country Charm just over a hundred kilometres ahead,' she said. 'If you drive it's sixty minutes. If I drive it's forty-five. A lead foot does sometimes have its advantages.'

'And what if the cops pull us over for speeding?'

Faith considered this. 'The odd thing is we haven't seen a police car for days. Not that I'm complaining, mind, after that last scare. But anyway, if they did pull us over they'd understand the situation.'

'You reckon?' Martin asked.

Faith smiled and batted her eyelids. 'They'll just take one look at gorgeous me and then at the front of your trousers.'

Martin looked down. 'Oh! Right,' he said. He pulled the van over to the side of the road and opened his door.

'Just scramble over, it's quicker,' Faith said, unbuckling her seatbelt.

'I'll walk around. It's safer.'

'You could just pole-vault across,' Faith smiled innocently.

*

A faded sign read: MAX'S GENERAL STORE. The building was a ramshackle weatherboard shack with a single battered petrol pump out front. It had a lush, tropical backyard garden and a gravel path leading to an equally ramshackle wooden jetty jutting out into the bay. A twenty-foot cabin cruiser was moored to the pilings at the far end. As the van pulled up, a barefoot, weatherbeaten man in a blue singlet and stubbies wandered out onto the verandah. Martin and Faith stretched after getting out.

'Morning,' said Martin.

The man leaned on a verandah post and nodded.

'We drove all night,' Faith said.

'Waste of good sleeping time then,' said the man. 'Nothin' round here worth driving all night for.'

'What are the chances of some breakfast?' Faith asked.

The man on the verandah considered the question. 'Well,' he said, 'if your name's Max and you've run this place for thirty years and been married to my wife for twenty-five of 'em, then probably pretty bloody good. Otherwise I think you'd find you'd be shit out of luck.'

'We need petrol, can you help us with that?' Martin asked.

'It's self-service,' Max said, indicating the bowser. 'You start pumping petrol and people expect you to wipe their windscreens and check their oil. And then they want to use the dunny.'

Martin started to fill the tank. 'We're looking for the major,' he said. 'Is this the right road?'

'Road ends here, mate,' Max answered. 'We got a major bay out there and a major mangrove swamp where you can pick up some major muddies. Apart from that, I think you'll find this place is a major disappointment.' He scratched his chin. 'I might just have to move one day soon.'

Martin replaced the nozzle in the bowser. 'They said back at the roadhouse twenty-five clicks past the Dolan Bridge. We've done ten so far.'

Max shrugged. 'They'll tell you at the roadhouse their burgers are a hundred per cent real beef, but you don't want to believe everything you hear.'

'Isn't that a road?' Faith asked, pointing to a red dirt trail continuing past the store.

'Nope, that's a bush track. The shire council grades it once a year, if they remember. A good rain turns it to mud three feet deep, and we get a lot of rain around here. People sometimes go up that track and never come back.'

'What do you reckon we'd find if we drove another fifteen k's up that way, then?' asked Martin.

'Dunno,' shrugged Max, 'never done it myself. Head-hunters maybe? Amelia Earhart? The wreck of the *Hesperus*?'

'You mean, in thirty years you've never gone up there?' asked Faith.

Max shrugged again. 'Guess I'm not the inquisitive type,' he said. 'Don't go poking around in places that don't concern me. You keep healthier that way.'

Martin paid for the fuel. Max counted the money carefully and gave him some change from his pocket. They climbed back into the van.

'If we find anything interesting we'll send you a postcard,' Martin called back to Max as he started the engine. 'Broaden your horizons.'

Max pulled a pipe and tobacco pouch from his shorts. '"I am not ashamed to confess that I am ignorant of what I do not know,"' he said, and then he smiled. 'You watch where you walk up there, Sonny Jim.'

Martin waved and pulled onto the red dirt track. He glanced in his side mirror at Max, still on the verandah.

'Well, old Max is certainly one of a kind.'

'Sure is,' Faith agreed. 'A bushie quoting Cicero, no less.'

'What?' Martin asked. '"You watch where you walk up there, Sonny Jim"? Was that Cicero? I was sure it was Samuel Johnson.'

Faith hit him with the rolled-up motel directory.

Back at the store, Max watched the track until the red dust had settled. He scratched at the stubble on his chin and pulled a mobile phone from his pocket.

*

The dirt track ended at a wire gate. Numerous signs and placards were attached to the posts and the gate. Martin turned off the engine as Faith started reading the signs out loud.

> KEEP OUT! NO VISITORS! ATTACK DOGS ON PATROL!
>
> ARMED GUARDS WITH ORDERS TO SHOOT ON DUTY 4 NIGHTS A WEEK. YOU GUESS WHICH NIGHTS!
>
> IS THERE LIFE AFTER DEATH? TRESPASS HERE AND FIND OUT!

Martin climbed out of the van.

> ANYONE FOUND HERE AT NIGHT WILL
> BE FOUND HERE IN THE MORNING!
> THERE IS NOTHING PAST THIS GATE WORTH YOUR LIFE!

Faith joined him. 'This school chum of yours isn't displaying that old-fashioned country hospitality we've come to know and love.'

'Maybe it was Vietnam,' Martin suggested. 'Post-traumatic stress syndrome.'

'Grumpy-old-bugger-living-alone-in-the-scrub-too-long syndrome, more likely,' Faith said.

The dense green vegetation continued up the hill. There was a narrow track just visible past the gate. Martin walked around to the passenger side of the van and opened the door for Faith.

'Keep the doors locked and wait for me,' he said. 'If there's any sign of trouble, honk the horn.'

Faith climbed into the van. 'You sure about this?'

'No,' he answered, 'but we've run out of road.'

'Know anything about landmines and booby traps?'

'Nope, and I hope to keep it that way.'

She blew him a kiss. 'Remember what Cicero said – Watch where you walk up there, Sonny Jim!'

There was a large white styrofoam box by the gatepost. Martin carefully lifted the lid, glanced inside and quickly replaced the cover. Faith wound down her window.

'Live mud crabs,' he yelled. 'Big buggers. So someone's come up this track recently, despite what Max says.'

He climbed over the gate and then stopped. The path or the jungle? He decided it would make sense to mine a path, so keeping to the jungle should be a safer bet. He walked slowly, putting his feet down carefully and looking for trip-wires. That seemed to be the technique that worked for Chuck Norris, he recalled. The Burrinjuruk video shop carried a lot of Chuck Norris movies.

Progress was slow, and eventually he glanced at his watch. He now knew three things: it was twenty minutes since he'd left the van, he was very thirsty, and he was completely lost. He turned to retrace his steps and heard a metallic click somewhere to his left. He froze.

A voice came out of the bush. 'Do not move a muscle, and keep that foot off the ground.'

Martin slowly put his hands up.

''kay, now just walk out of there slowly,' the voice said. 'Step exactly in the footprints you made going in.'

Martin did as he was told. After about ten paces, the voice said, 'Hold it right there.'

Martin could make out a shadowy figure in the thick undergrowth. The man stepped into the light. He was wearing combat boots, jungle camouflage battledress, and a soft bush hat.

'Well, bugger me dead,' the man said, 'it's Martin Carter.'

Martin slowly put down his arms. 'Hello, Jack.'

The two men sized each other up.

'You've packed on a few pounds since I last saw you, Martin. Nice shirt, though.'

Martin jumped at the sound of another metallic click.

'You look a bit thirsty, mate,' Jack said, handing him an opened can of Foster's.

'It's a bit early for me, Jack, but I'll make an exception because it's you,' he said, taking a long drink.

Jack held up his beer in a toast. 'This is the tropics, mate,' he said. 'It's not drinking, it's rehydrating. Medical necessity.'

'You know, you're a hard man to find,' Martin said.

Jack winked. 'Which is why I'm still breathing.' He threw an arm around Martin's shoulder. 'You really don't want to be blundering around in the bush by yourself, sport,' he said, glancing towards the thicket Martin had just exited. 'That was a wee bit too close for comfort. Stopped you just in time.'

Martin's throat constricted. 'Landmine?' he asked.

Jack shook his head. 'Herb garden,' he said. 'You almost trampled all over my fuckin' coriander, you dick.'

twenty-four

Faith watched the two men walk down towards the gate. When Martin waved she unlocked her door and climbed out. The man in the camouflage outfit was about Martin's height, tanned and very fit-looking. He used the tip of his machete to lift the lid on the styrofoam box.

'Bewdy, old Maxie never lets me down,' he said. 'You can stay for dinner, Martin. We've got heaps.'

Faith walked up to the two men and put out her hand. Martin did the introductions.

Faith smiled warmly as she shook hands with Jack. 'The mad major,' she said.

Jack returned her smile. 'The sex-crazed librarian.'

For once Faith blushed scarlet.

'Lying bastard said you were good-looking, Faith,' Jack

said. He turned to Martin. 'She's bloody gorgeous. How did a porky prick like you manage to pull her with a measly million bucks?'

'Luckily for him, Martin has other attributes besides a big mouth,' Faith said. Martin grinned.

'More than I need to know, Faith,' Jack laughed.

'Now, you guys didn't see a dog on your travels?' Jack asked. 'Beagle name of Biggles?'

'The killer attack dog of legend?' Faith asked.

'Not exactly,' Jack said. 'But he will give your leg a near fatal humping on my command. Or if he fancies you. Or just about any old time, really.' He glanced around. 'Not like him to go wandering off for this long, though. Old Biggles is a bit of a homebody usually.' He took a small walkie-talkie from his pocket and put it to his ear. 'No sign of the pup,' he said into the radio handset, 'but I've got a couple of friendlies for breakfast.'

There was an answering click from the handset and Jack put the radio back in his pocket. He picked up the styrofoam box. 'Let's chuck this in the van and head up to the house,' he said. 'As you've probably worked out, Faith, I had a little chat with Martin on our walk down the hill. He's brought me up to speed on the broad detail of this sordid little saga.' He shook his head sadly. 'I must say, neither Martin nor I reflect much glory on the hallowed name of Box Forest Boys High. I'll drive.'

Martin held the gate open until the van was inside, then

jumped in. Faith sat between the two men on the bumpy ride up the hill. Every so often Jack would stop, open his door and pull in some roots or greenery, which he piled in Faith's lap.

'Lemongrass, galangal, kangkung. I'm very impressed, Jack,' Faith said, rummaging through the stalks.

'I grow my chillies nearer the house since we use them the most.'

'"We" would be the gorgeous blonde twins who sate your every desire?' asked Faith.

Jack laughed. 'Don't believe everything you hear about me. "We" is me and Van Tuan. He was a mate in the 'Nam. Used to be General Ky's personal helicopter pilot when he was the main man in the government of the week. VT flew one of the last choppers out of Saigon in '75.'

The hillside grew steeper towards the crest, and the van surged forward as Jack gunned the engine. 'Boy, this boat's certainly got some grunt,' he said.

At the top of the rise Jack gave a long blast on the horn. The house was a low-rise bungalow with a corrugated-iron roof and wide verandahs. Two water tanks sat behind the house, and steps at one end of the verandah led down to a large swimming pool.

'That looks inviting,' Faith said.

'Gets a bit warmish,' Jack commented, 'but the nearest accessible beach is a bit of a hike. And between the stonefish, sharks, saltwater crocs and stingers, I can never remember which month it's safe to go swimming. I think it's anything with a Q in it.'

The van swerved around behind the house. A heavy steel roller door was opening in an otherwise blank concrete wall. Jack drove in and killed the engine. Behind them the roller door began to close. Large banks of overhead fluorescent tubes lit the garage. Grey 44-gallon drums lined three walls, with red drums on the fourth.

'Diesel for the generators,' Jack explained, climbing out. 'The red ones are petrol for the cars and motorbikes.'

Martin counted seven bikes, two four-wheel drives, and an old ambulance painted dark green.

Jack patted the mudguard on the ambulance. 'Yank. World War II vintage. Still runs like a dream.'

'What the hell is this place?' Martin asked.

Jack smiled. 'Your tax dollars at work, sport. The government built this in the 1960s to house some top-secret, long-range radar facility. Supposed to be able to spot a mosquito taking off from Sukarno's arse in Jakarta, but it was the usual flop. The only part of the contract that was fulfilled was the contractors making millions. The house up top was built for cover, but it's a real house.'

Martin gave a low whistle.

'This is nothing,' Jack laughed. 'There's another five floors below us. I've got a great armoury. We can shoot off some submachine guns after breakfast, if you fancy. Ever fired a bazooka, Faith?'

'Careful, Jack,' Martin said, 'I've learned to be very wary about asking her questions like that.'

'Are we talking the 60-millimetre M1A1, or the M9, Jack?' Faith asked mischievously.

'Right,' Jack said, nodding to Martin, 'I see what you mean.' He took the box of mudcrabs from the van. 'Let's get cleaned up and see what we can rustle up for breakfast,' he suggested.

Martin and Faith followed Jack across the garage.

'So, exactly how mad are you, Major Jack?' Faith asked.

Jack was sprinting up a set of steel stairs. He stopped and looked back. 'I like you, Faith,' he said. 'Very direct. We'll talk about that after we eat. Come up and meet VT.'

The stairs led up to a cool, well-lit kitchen which opened onto a dining area with picture windows looking out over the jungle and down to the ocean. A marble bench held eggs, bacon, sausages, ripe red tomatoes, and what looked and smelled like freshly baked bread.

'Welcome to Casa del Nutso,' Jack said. 'I'm about to cook us a fabulous breakfast, the equal of any highway-truckstop cafe in the country. And wait till you taste my homemade tomato-chilli relish.'

Martin gave Faith an I-told-you-so look. 'Faith thinks the famous highway-truckstop breakfast is just some deranged male fantasy,' he said to Jack.

Jack threw up his hands. 'Women, mate, what can you do with them?'

Faith noticed a gleaming silver espresso machine. 'A Pasquini Livia,' she said, 'very nice. We don't get truckstop coffee then?'

'I'll agree with you on that point,' Jack said. He flicked a coffee grinder on and off. 'Arabica beans, from Bali. Got a small roaster downstairs. Gas-fired and computer-controlled for consistency. Took me a hell of a long time to get the grind just right, though. Humidity up here makes it tricky.'

Faith studied the espresso machine. 'What temperature do you use?' she asked.

'Smidge over 90 Celsius seems to work best,' Jack said, looking bemusedly at her.

'And the pressure?'

'Around nine atmospheres,' he said.

'Sounds good,' Faith smiled.

'Well,' Martin said, 'I think you've passed that test, Jack.'

A tall, slender Vietnamese man entered the kitchen. He was wearing a light cotton shirt and sarong and carrying several large fluffy towels and some folded sarongs.

'Welcome to our home. You might like to freshen up while we prepare breakfast,' he suggested.

Jack put his hand on the man's shoulder. 'Faith, Martin, I'd like you to meet Van Tuan, VT for short.' He leaned over, ruffled Van Tuan's hair, and kissed him on the cheek. 'VT's the one who sates my every desire,' Jack said, slipping an arm around his waist.

'Well, I guess that answers your question about what you can do with women, Jack,' Faith laughed.

'You might wanna close Martin's mouth there, Faith,' he said. 'We get a lot of big flying bugs this far north.'

*

The one sour note at breakfast was Martin's sarong coming adrift as he reached across for more papaya.

'Lose the lard if you want to wear a sarong, my boy,' Jack suggested. 'Charles Laughton and the South Seas were never a good visual mix.'

'I'll have you know Martin here is well on his way to a slimmer, trimmer physique,' Faith said in mock outrage.

'Must be all the push-ups,' Jack suggested innocently.

They adjourned to the verandah for more coffee. VT, who had eaten lightly, announced he would go looking for Biggles. Jack reminded him to take a pistol.

'Snakes,' he explained. 'In the grass.'

'And sometimes other places,' VT said as he headed down the stairs.

'That was a fantastic breakfast, Jack,' Faith said, lolling back in a big cane chair. 'Although the presence of fresh fruit and the absence of buckets of grease may take it out of the truckstop category.'

'The homemade tomato-chilli relish was something else,' Martin said. 'You could bottle it and make a fortune.'

'Mmm,' Jack said, considering the suggestion. 'Crazy

Auntie Jack's Fruity Homemade Condiments. We could open up in Sydney. Be big on Oxford Street at least.'

'This whole gay thing is a bit of a shock,' Martin said.

'Really?' Jack said. 'And didn't I say to VT just the other day that I wouldn't be surprised to see my old cobber and school goody-goody Martin Carter turn up on the run from the cops for armed robbery with a hot blonde on his arm? Surprise is a two-way street down this particular block.'

Faith laughed. 'Give him a break, Jack. A week ago he would have been catatonic about you being gay.'

'Yeah,' Martin said, 'give me a break, Starkie. How are the parents then?' he asked.

'Passed on about ten years back,' Jack said. 'The old lady had a stroke and lasted about a week. Dad went about a week after that. Doc said he just died in his sleep, but I reckon he made arrangements not to wake up.'

'Sorry to hear that,' Martin said quietly.

'And yours?' Jack asked.

'Still the same,' Martin said. 'Always the same.' He leaned forward. 'Now, what the hell is going on in your life, Jack? That local cop I told you about was a Vietnam vet. He told me some very odd stories about you. I think you're probably as crazy as you ever were, but I'm not sure you're mad. What's the story on this World Wide Web psycho business, mate? What gives?'

Jack put down his coffee cup. 'Just one of a number of

weird stories to come out of the 'Nam, I guess. Just before it all started going tits up in Saigon, I was sent to Washington. My exploits in Indian country caught some people's attention.' He looked at Faith. 'I finally found something I was good at, but it turned out to be a pretty odd thing,' he explained. 'Vietnam Counter-Insurgency and Counter-Terrorism Specialist looks weird on the CV.

'Anyway,' Jack continued, 'way back when, someone working in Projections and Forecasts for the CIA read a paper from some bod out here about how domestic and international terrorism would develop over the next few decades into being the major problem after communism. Thousands of small cells and single-issue groups that would be almost impossible to infiltrate or control.'

'The last couple of years have shown that to be a pretty good guess,' Faith said.

'And how. Back then, though, it was only a theory, but some pretty powerful people got behind it. They decided to create a fictional super-nut who could become a focus for all these groups. And for my sins they chose me.'

'You mean you're a total fraud?' Faith laughed.

'Careful, girl,' Jack said, 'someone still has to wash all those breakfast dishes.'

'But how would you even begin to go about setting up something like that?' Martin asked.

'Easy,' Jack answered. 'With enough time and enough money, you can do pretty much anything.'

'Cure cancer, feed the hungry, house the homeless...' Faith suggested.

'Okay,' Jack conceded, 'with enough time and enough money *and* the political will, you can do pretty much anything. And these guys had the political will. Psychologists and psychiatrists produced suitable profiles for my fall from grace, with disillusionment turning to paranoia and the inevitable turning against the system that made me.'

'But if it was a Yank project, why base it here?' Martin asked.

'Distance,' Jack explained. 'Both physical and political. Australia is far enough out of the way to discourage most drop-in visitors, and that allowed plenty of time to set up suitable displays for the people we wanted to impress. And if it all went pear-shaped, the Yanks had a pretty good case of plausible denial and we'd take the heat.'

'And how did it actually work?' Faith asked.

'It was low-key in the beginning. The Echelon communications spy network was initially good enough for intercepting radio and other signals traffic. The Internet was what really made me. I railed online against one-world government, super-capitalism, the Club of Rome, fluoridation, and, hey presto, my website became an essential bookmark for Nut Jobs 'R' Us. I was getting cake recipes, bomb recipes, calls for advice, assassination suggestions, and, best of all, boastful emails before and after operations seeking my blessing or congratulations.'

'You *were* getting?' Faith asked.

'The disillusioned-warrior profile they set up turned round and bit them in the arse. I started asking awkward questions because I was getting really uncomfortable about a few things. They cut me out of the loop and it all started going through Canberra.'

'Uncomfortable about what?' Faith asked.

'Well, there was this one operation, a plane hijacking, which we knew all about and would have stopped in our normal roundabout way.'

'Meaning what?' said Martin.

'Well, we couldn't just arrest the hijackers because someone would eventually work out where the leak came from. So it had to be a wee bit subtle. We might arrange for the ringleaders to be killed in a road accident, or something similarly innocuous where there was a high level of plausible denial. Shit happens, and sometimes very conveniently.'

Martin looked startled. 'You could make stuff like that happen?'

'Sure,' Jack said, 'easy as pie. In Europe we used this old Kraut named Rollo Kleindorf who could flip your car off the autobahn and into a tree before you knew what was happening. He looked like a doddery old grandddad in a clapped-out Audi, but he was an Afrika Corps veteran and bloody lethal at the wheel.'

'Jesus,' Martin whistled.

'Didn't work this particular time?' asked Faith.

Jack shook his head. 'Didn't happen at all.' He glanced

at his watch and scanned the hillside. 'The hijacking went off just as scripted. Special Forces troops stormed the plane on the runway in Zurich during negotiations – killed the hijackers where they stood in the aisles.'

'All the passengers got out?' Faith asked.

'Five dead. Not too bad in the scheme of things, I guess. Unless you happened to be one of the five. Or related to them.' Jack was silent for a long time, and when he spoke again his voice was soft. 'It was only afterwards that I realised that the deaths of a couple of those passengers happened to be very much to the advantage of some of the people running our little play group.'

Faith shivered. 'You mean politically?'

'I mean commercially,' Jack said, 'which makes it even worse somehow.'

'That is seriously disturbing, Jack,' Martin said.

'I called for an investigation. They maintained that blocking the operation would have compromised security, which was bullshit of course. I got stroppy, made a few comments, and bingo, I was out of the loop and headed for early retirement.'

'But all this stuff still happens?' Martin asked.

Jack checked his watch again, got up, and moved to the edge of the verandah. 'Very much so – and in my name, but I have no part in it. Which is weird. They receive, analyse and answer, and people still think it's me.'

'But they let you stay on here?' said Martin.

'Not exactly. Circles I move in take a dim view of two things – unauthorised memoirs and early retirement. Retirement is only on their terms, and if you piss them off the terms can sometimes be a little less than favourable.'

'Sounds like you definitely pissed them off, Jack,' Faith said.

'It's a fatal flaw in my character, Faith,' Jack replied with a wry smile. 'Literally. The only reason they haven't retired me yet is because they can't figure out how to get a hit team in here to give me my gold watch.'

'They want to kill you?' Martin was incredulous.

'You bet. If I were to open my mouth and spill the beans on this project, there'd be a lot of red faces and some rapidly terminated high-profile careers on both sides of the Pacific. And I don't just mean in government either. This thing goes deep into the private sector too.'

'Pretty powerful incentive to shut you down permanently,' Faith said.

'It's not like they haven't tried. We've had the odd nocturnal visit over the past couple of years, but they figured out it wasn't a cost-effective method after a while. They trained me in counter-insurgency and I'm pretty bloody good at what I do. None of them have ever got within sight of the house.'

'Dead?' Martin asked.

'Dissuaded, mostly,' Jack said with a tight smile. 'We'd have a bit of a chat and they'd usually come round to my point of view that a man's home is his castle.'

'That must have been some chat,' Faith said.

'VT and I can be very persuasive when we put our minds to it.'

'They haven't given up, though?' Faith asked.

Jack began pacing the verandah. 'They keep trying different things from time to time. I'll be on the back burner for a while and then they seem to get it into their heads to have another go. They've been getting quite inventive recently. Last year an F-111 out of Amberley "accidentally" lost a live 250-kilo bomb on a training mission. Missed the house by half a bee's dick.'

'That must have been pretty scary,' Martin said.

'Scarier for the F-111 jockey and his offsider,' Jack said. 'I took the warhead off a Stinger ground-to-air missile and shot it up his clacker on their second run. They tend to give us a very wide berth now.' He took the walkie-talkie from his pocket. 'But on the plus side, we got us a hole for the swimming pool without having to do too much digging.'

Martin looked over the edge of the verandah into the pool. 'Half a bee's dick is right,' he said.

'And you have absolutely no contact with the organisation now?' Faith asked.

'Nope, but we're hearing some things through backchannels which are pretty disturbing.'

'Backchannels?' Martin asked.

'Insiders, whistle-blowers, whatever,' Jack said. 'There are apparently some other disillusioned people on the inside who want to contact me. Seems like my name's been coming up again, and I don't think it's for Ex-employee of the Month.'

He looked up suddenly. VT was running towards the house carrying something in his arms. 'It's Biggles,' he yelled, 'I think he's been shot!' He took the stairs two at a time, the limp beagle cradled to his chest.

Jack was back from inside the house with a first-aid kit before Martin even realised he had gone. Faith cleared the table and VT gently placed the dog on a thick towel.

'He was crawling back to the house,' VT said. 'I followed a blood trail up the hill and found him.'

Jack cleaned the wound with disinfectant while Faith stroked the dog's head, talking to him in reassuring tones. Biggles looked up at her and licked her hand.

'Small-calibre bullet. Went straight through,' Jack said. 'This is one lucky puppy. Missed all the vital bits, which is a miracle on a dog this size.' He carefully examined every inch of the beagle's body. 'If I haven't overlooked something and there's not too much blood loss, he should make it,' he said as he began expertly bandaging the wound.

'You sure it wasn't shrapnel?' Martin suggested. 'Maybe he tripped one of the landmines or booby traps?'

Jack and VT glanced at each other. 'No way, sport,' Jack said. 'Trust me on that.'

'But even if you and VT know where all the mines are, the dog wouldn't,' Martin argued.

'Martin, I know for a fact it wasn't a mine or booby trap. Biggles would smell them. But that wouldn't make a lot of difference with these particular mines anyway, because of where we planted them.'

'Which is where exactly?'

'Where they'd do the most damage and give us the best protection possible,' Jack smiled. He tapped his temple. 'We planted them in people's heads.'

twenty-five

Biggles was resting in a basket on the verandah, wagging his tail happily as Faith patted him. 'He's looking a lot better,' she said, 'and I think all this tail-wagging is a good sign.'

'Why would anyone want to shoot your dog, Jack?' Martin asked.

'Dunno, mate. Like I said earlier, there's a few people outside the wire who'd like to have a go at me, but plugging Biggles here is a pretty low act.' He knelt down and scratched the dog under his chin. 'Sorry, short-arse, when we find out who did it we'll bite 'em on the ankle, eh?'

The beagle yelped weakly.

'Anyone want to de-stress with a little target practice?' Jack asked, standing up.

'I'm game,' Faith said. 'Could be fun to see exactly where

our tax dollars have gone.'

'I'll stay up here and keep an eye on things,' VT volunteered.

They went down the stairs to the garage, past the campervan and the other vehicles to a small elevator. Two floors down the doors slid open, silently, smoothly.

'Government contract,' Jack said. 'Best of everything, bugger the expense. Hey, it's not like it's their money, right?'

The walls on three sides were lined with metal storage cupboards and rows of Dexion shelving. 'Showpiece for the visiting head cases,' Jack explained. 'We have your guns, we have your ammo, we have your high explosives, both industrial and homemade. Light a cigarette in here and you'll produce a brand new deep-water harbour for the Barrier Reef bare boats.'

Martin and Faith froze.

'Lighten up, guys, it's a joke,' Jack said with a grin. 'It would take a lot more than a match to set this lot off. You'd need a pretty solid wallop.'

The fourth wall was stacked high with sandbags, in front of which stood human-size cut-outs under bright lights. Jack opened the doors on a row of steel cupboards.

'Choose your weapons, ladies and gentlemen. Rifles, pistols, submachine guns. You name it, we've got it. A different death for every day of the week.'

He tossed industrial earmuffs to Martin and Faith and took a weapon down for himself. 'A personal favourite,' he said, 'the Swedish K.' He inserted a magazine and pulled back the cocking lever. 'The 9mm Karl Gustaf Model 45 submachine gun,' he said fondly. 'Thirty-round mag. Very popular with the off-the-books element back in 'Nam.'

'What's the K stand for?' Martin asked.

'Dunno, mate, must be the K in Karl Gustaf.'

'It's Carl with a C,' Faith said. 'The K is for *Kulsprutepistol*, which is Swedish for bullet-spurting pistol.'

Jack's jaw dropped. 'Well, fuck me drunk!' he said.

'I told you,' Martin said.

Faith was nonchalant. 'I've just got one of those memories. I read it somewhere and it stuck.'

'But what were you reading, Faith, and why? That's the question on my mind.' Jack looked at Martin. 'She's scary, mate, even if she's as good in bed as you reckon.'

Faith glared at Martin, who blew her a kiss.

Donning his earmuffs, Jack turned to the targets and lifted his gun. Even with their own earmuffs on, Martin and Faith found the noise deafening. It stopped as quickly as it started. The empty brass casings hit the floor and wisps of acrid smoke were sucked away by ventilators in the ceiling. One of the targets now featured a messy hole in its mid-section.

Jack handed the weapon to Martin. 'Have a go.'

Martin shook his head and put the gun on a bench. 'I've had more than enough of guns, thanks.'

Faith had wandered away and was exploring one of the storage cupboards.

'What about you, Faith?' Jack asked.

She stepped back with a tall wooden bow and a quiver of arrows. 'No, thanks. This is a bit more my style.'

'That's genuine yew,' Jack said. 'None of that fibreglass or carbon-fibre-composite bullshit. Your classic English longbow. Robin Hood to Agincourt. Want me to string it for you?'

Faith expertly hooked her left leg around the bow, pulled down from the top and slipped the string in place.

'Or you can do it,' Jack said.

Faith tugged at the bowstring several times. 'The English actually preferred Spanish yew for their bows, you know. Sometimes Italian.' She fitted an arrow, turned and shot down range, towards a target. The arrow went wide.

Faith looked perplexed. 'Out of practice, I guess. I was in the state junior archery squad in high school.' She shot three more arrows. All misses. 'Dammit, I was better than this when I was twelve!'

She flexed her right shoulder several times, then had a thought. Reaching inside her shirt, she pulled out a soft silicone bag and threw it to Martin. Another pull and the arrow thudded into the groin of the target. 'Well, wadda you know? That Amazon stuff is true,' she said.

'Getting better,' Martin offered.

'It goes where I aim it,' she replied, smiling.

Jack was looking at her dumbfounded.

'Didn't he say anything?' she asked him, indicating Martin.

'Not a word,' Jack said.

Faith shrugged. 'Must be true love, then. That's the only thing that stops a bloke telling all your secrets to his mates.' She walked over and gave Martin a kiss.

He put his arm around her waist. 'Faith is really a truck driver from Geelong named Barry. We're saving up to get him implants and have his dick cut off.'

'I'm shocked, Mr Carter.' Faith put a hand to her forehead, feigning an attack of the vapours. 'Please cancel my home-loan application.'

Jack tossed his earmuffs onto the bench. 'You've sure changed since you used to bang out the blackboard dusters in Miss Johnston's English class, Martin. Let's go upstairs. This is the kind of sobering news that drives a man to drink.'

*

They slept till about four. Martin sat up as Faith came out of the bathroom. She was wearing a light Japanese robe and her hair was slicked back, wet from the shower.

'I gotta tell you, gay men really know how to set up a guest bathroom,' she said, kissing him lightly. 'And I'm glad we passed on lunch.'

'Me too,' he grinned. 'Though I've developed quite an appetite now.'

Faith ducked as he lunged forward. 'Hold that thought,' she laughed and suddenly her robe fell open. Martin stopped and looked at her.

'God, Faith, you are just plain beautiful.'

'You really mean it, don't you?' she said quietly, retying her robe.

'I saw this film once,' Martin said, leaning back on the pillows, 'where all these Prussian military cadets used to duel with sabres, hoping to get a scar on their faces.'

Faith sat on the end of the bed. 'Are you leading me towards dressing in a black bustier and storm-trooper jackboots by any chance, Mr Carter?'

Martin smiled. 'The scar was a badge of honour, a mark of their courage. That's what your scar is, a mark of courage. You had a duel with cancer and you survived.'

Faith looked into his eyes. 'I thought you were an interesting person when I first saw you, Martin Carter, but I guess I really had no idea.' She leaned forward and kissed him tenderly on the lips. 'Now, into that shower, lover boy,' she said.

'What's the panic?' he asked.

'I was watching Jack gathering chillies from the bathroom window. I think those mud crabs have a date with destiny and I for one do not intend to miss it.'

He was just about to step under the shower when he heard her voice through the bathroom doorway.

'You know, Martin, if you ever want to try that thing with the black bustier and the jackboots . . .' And then the hair drier started up.

*

When Martin joined them in the kitchen, Jack and VT were busy chopping and pounding herbs and spices on the large bench. Faith was sitting on the verandah with Biggles, who was wandering about a little unsteadily.

'I offered your services as *sous-chef*, Martin,' she called. 'Confessed my dreadful secret that I don't cook. The boys'll have to start giving you lessons so we don't starve to death.'

'Sounds fair enough,' Martin said. 'What can I do?'

VT held up a lethal-looking chopper. 'The secret to all Asian cooking, Martin, is preparation.'

'And the secret of Australian cooking is lubrication,' Jack shouted. 'I hope you were paying attention when I made those Bloody Marys this morning, 'cos the bar is thataway, sport.'

As he was opening a can of tomato juice, Martin noticed the framed photograph on the wall above the bar. Fuzzy and somewhat faded, the shot was of a group of bare-chested men in camouflage trousers and combat boots holding pistols and M16s. They looked dirty and exhausted, their eyes ringed by dark circles.

'Who are these guys?' he called out.

Jack leaned around the bench top. 'One of the teams I worked with for a while.'

Martin peered closely at the picture. 'Which one are you?'

Jack laughed. 'I know, tell me about it. We'd just spent a month doing tunnels. We were all so rooted our own mothers wouldn't have recognised us. Third from the left.'

Martin studied the picture. He recognised Jack now, but there was also something familiar about the man on the right of the group.

'We're dying of thirst here, Martin!' Jack yelled.

Martin loaded the pitcher and glasses onto a tray and headed to the kitchen for some ice. Faith was sitting up at the counter, watching Jack and VT at work.

Jack grinned at Martin. 'Just explaining to your sheila how we're going to get all our ingredients ready and then relax and have a drink before we start the serious cooking.' Turning to Faith, he held out three large brown hen's eggs. 'VT's got his hands full and we need these beaten. Want to have a go at cracking them into the bowl? Bit of shell won't matter, I can fish it out.'

'I'll give it a whirl,' Faith said. She picked up an egg, held her hand over the bowl and looked at Jack. There was a slight crunch and the yolk and white fell neatly into the bowl. She tossed the empty shell across the kitchen into a bin.

'Well, bugger me,' Jack said. 'Short-order Sal.'

Faith broke the remaining eggs into the bowl the same way. 'I said that I don't cook, not that I can't cook.'

Jack shook his head and VT started laughing. 'When Jack tries one-handed we get egg all over the kitchen,' he said. 'You'd better give him lessons.'

'Drinks,' Martin announced, and they moved out to the verandah.

twenty-six

'The legend of the landmines and booby traps was VT's brilliant idea,' Jack said, sipping his bloody Mary.

'Just my inscrutable Oriental mind at work,' VT smiled.

Jack took his hand and held it. 'It added to the image we were promoting,' he said. 'Best of all, it worked. Before we spread the rumour, we were overrun by fortune hunters looking for the golden gooney bird. We had dickheads with metal detectors from elbow to breakfast.'

Faith sat up straight. 'What the hell's the golden gooney bird?'

'Stuff of dreams, me darlin',' he said, crunching on a celery stick. 'When the Japanese army took Manila in '42 the Philippines gold reserves were missing from the treasury. Tons of gold. Lots of stories went around about what had happened. Everything from it getting dumped in Manila Bay to being smuggled out in American submarines or buried somewhere on Corregidor.'

'Buried treasure. Missing millions,' Faith said with a shiver. 'I love these kind of stories. But why would you have treasure hunters sniffing around your Hills Hoist? We're a long way from Manila.'

'Well, one version of the story had a heavily overloaded Yank gooney bird island-hopping to Australia just one step ahead of the Japs,' Jack explained.

'What's a gooney bird then, apart from a plane, obviously?' Martin asked.

Faith answered. 'American nickname for the C-47 twin-engined military transport, which is a DC-3 in civilian terms, or Dakota to our military. Paratroop transport and glider tug in Europe. Used a lot for parachute supply drops in New Guinea. The diggers on the Kokoda Track called them biscuit bombers.'

'Spot on,' Jack said. 'Anyway, according to legend, one morning this overloaded crate staggered into Port Moresby on one engine. Full of bullet holes and with a dead co-pilot. A ring of military police with tommy guns and fixed bayonets kept everyone well back, apart from the mechanics and refuellers. They patched it up, shanghaied a local bush pilot for the second seat, and it took off late in the afternoon, heading down to Brisbane. It never made it. There were a couple of reports of a plane stooging around this area that night, but nothing was ever confirmed. The plane and whatever it was carrying disappeared without trace.'

'True story?' Faith asked.

'Who knows? No-one ever found anything out there. But with fifty million US in untraceable gold possibly lying about, a whole lot of people wanted to do some looking. So we decided it was either spread the story of our garden full of landmines and booby traps, or open up a Devonshire tearoom.'

Several magpie geese took off noisily from a clump of bushes further down the hill. Biggles sat up in his box. VT stood and stretched casually.

'I'm not sure you have enough coriander, Jack,' he said. 'I'll go and get some more.'

Jack followed him inside, and through the door Martin saw VT pull on a black windcheater and balaclava. He strapped a webbing belt with pistol holster and knife sheath around his waist. The two men kissed briefly and VT disappeared down the stairs.

'Mossies might start biting now that the breeze has dropped,' Jack said when he returned. He lit several citronella candles, then turned out the lights. 'More romantic this way.'

After several minutes, Faith said, 'I can't see a torch out there, Jack.'

'Night-vision goggles,' Jack explained. 'Less disturbing to the nocturnal wildlife.'

They sat in silence for a few minutes, looking out over the hillside.

'Jack,' Faith said at last, 'give me the scoop on the family Starkovsky. That's if you don't mind my asking. Martin told me about the China connection, which I found a bit intriguing.'

'No probs.' Jack settled back. 'It's actually a good story to tell in the dark. My dad was born in Harbin, in Manchuria, in 1918. His old man was an engineer in the Harbin locomotive workshops, where they used to assemble American steam engines for the Chinese Eastern Railway.' His eyes were fixed on a point in the jungle below. 'The railway was actually a Russian enterprise,' he went on, 'with a licence to cross Manchuria down to the coast at Dairen, near Port Arthur. Harbin was the hub for the railway, and pretty much a Russian town. The population exploded after the 1917 revolution, when the town filled up with people pissing off from the communists. Then the Japs annexed Manchuria in '31, and politics and life generally got pretty unpleasant after that. My grandparents decided to move back to Russia in '36 because of all the unrest, and disappeared into the Gulags. Stalin was never all that hot on outsiders and immigrants coming back to the fold. Not a trusting bloke.'

Jack glanced at his watch. 'Anyway, my dad was eighteen then and didn't have memories of any other home, so he decided to skip Russia and head for the international settlement in Shanghai. He was young and fit and he worked for a bit in an all-Russian riot squad they had in the French concession. Pay was pretty scabby, but then he got hired by a Polish-Jewish businessman as a live-in bodyguard. The old bloke was a widower and he took a shine to my dad. He also had a good-looking granddaughter who my dad thought was a bit of all right. Dad liked the old man too, so he stayed on and looked after them both, through World War II and the Japanese occupation. They weren't interned like the Pommy and Yank civilians, but it was still pretty grim.

'After the war, the old man discovered that every single one of his relatives had died in the camps in Europe. Dad reckoned the news killed him. When the communists took over in China and made it pretty plain that foreigners weren't welcome any more, Dad went to Hong Kong with the daughter.'

Jack stopped and checked his watch again, then stood up and reached for a switch on the verandah railing. 'Mind your eyes,' he said, 'it might get a bit glary.'

The whole of the hillside was suddenly lit up as bright as day. Nothing moved. Just before Jack flicked off the floodlights, Martin saw the grenade in his left hand.

'Anyhow,' Jack continued, 'Hong Kong wasn't any picnic in those days, plus it was bursting with refugees from China. When Dad found out that married couples got bumped up the list for emigration, it encouraged him to pop the question to the granddaughter.'

'That doesn't sound too romantic,' Faith said.

Jack laughed. 'I wouldn't worry about that,' he said. 'I reckon my dad and mum had been pretty cosy behind her granddad's back for yonks. Anyway, Iliya Jakob Starkovsky, alias Jack Stark, was born on a ship on the way to Melbourne.'

'Jesus, another bloody boat person,' Faith said.

'I know,' Jack said, shaking his head, 'with all those damn foreigners running around after the war, it's amazing this country turned out as well as it did.'

The lights in the kitchen were suddenly on and VT was standing by the sink with a bunch of coriander. He gave Jack a slight negative movement of the head. Jack slipped the hand grenade into his pocket and stood up.

'All right, boys and girls. We now have coriander, and the mudcrabs are dozing off in the freezer. It's time to fire up the wok and show you how real Singapore chilli crab gets made. And eaten – if you don't finish up with my world-renowned spicy sauce from elbow to breakfast, you're not doing it right.'

In the kitchen Jack handed Martin a bottle opener. 'Because of your sterling work earlier, you are now officially the bartender. Beer's probably the go tonight.'

Martin knelt down and pulled a bottle from the fridge. 'Looks like there's a choice of Tiger and this stuff.' He held up a green bottle.

'It's Tsingtao. Chinese beer. Not a bad drop,' Jack said. 'They took over an old German brewery.'

'Any preference?' Martin asked.

'Nope, just as long as you keep 'em cold and keep 'em coming.' Jack turned to Faith. 'Do you want to organise us some finger bowls?'

'We don't need 'em,' she said. 'Martin and I will just lick each other clean.'

VT deftly caught the bottle of beer as it shot out of Martin's grasp.

*

Next morning Martin rose late. From the bathroom window he could see Faith and VT setting up an archery range below the house. He went to the kitchen to find Jack pouring pineapple juice into a large glass.

'Here you go, digger. I'm making us a couple of cappuccini for when you're done with this.'

They walked out onto the verandah. Faith was slamming arrows into the target.

'Nice butt,' Jack said.

Martin leaned on a verandah post. 'You do, of course, mean the built-up area for archery target practice which is known technically as a butt.'

'No, I meant your girlfriend's arse. But if you're going to get all thing about it, forget it. Cappuccino or duelling pistols?'

Martin laughed. 'Coffee, please. Thought I heard a telephone before.'

'Sorry, did it wake you? It was Max, letting me know my order of canned pilchards is in.'

'Oh, good,' Martin said, 'canned pilchards. I'm getting sick of this five-star crap every meal.'

'Not subtle enough then?' Jack asked.

'Mate, I'm just an ex-bank manager and it sounds like code even to me.'

Jack grinned. 'We'll go for a bit of a drive after coffee.'

Fifteen minutes later, Jack backed the ambulance out into the sunlight and climbed down. 'Half a mo,' he yelled, running back into the garage.

Martin waited in the passenger seat. Jack was back in three minutes with a canvas satchel and the Swedish K, plus a much smaller submachine gun.

'Skorpion,' Jack said. 'Czechoslovakian. Nice little gun.' He handed it to Martin. 'I'll show you how to use it when we get far enough away from the house.'

He started the engine and drove the ambulance over to Faith and VT. 'Just off to the shops, honey,' he called in a falsetto voice.

VT gave him the finger. Faith blew Martin a kiss.

The ride down to the road was very uncomfortable. 'Genuine World War II ambulance suspension,' Jack explained. 'First someone shoots you and then you get to ride in this. You'd probably want to shoot yourself after a couple of miles.'

'So war really is hell?' Martin asked.

'No, mate, it's sheer bloody terror. The hell, quite often, is what comes after.'

They stopped just short of the gate to the road and Jack showed Martin how to cock and fire the Skorpion. Martin didn't much care for it. Jack took some extra magazines from the satchel and put them at Martin's feet.

'You worried Max is going to have words with you about your account?' Martin asked.

'I've only lasted this long because when the little voice inside tells me to be careful I always pay attention,' Jack answered. 'I'm not expecting trouble, but you should always remember the first rule of gunfights.'

'There are rules for gunfights?' Martin asked.

'You bet. Only one that counts, though,' Jack said.

'Which is?'

'Always bring a gun.'

The drive was uneventful, except for a set of tyre tracks running off the road into the jungle.

'Fishermen, maybe?' Martin ventured.

Jack shook his head. 'You'd need a bulldozer once you got more than a hundred and fifty feet in. Nothing but mud, mozzies and mangroves at the other end anyhow.' Jack's eyes were constantly moving, checking the mirrors and the roadside and the track ahead.

'What's the story with Max?' Martin asked after a long period of silence.

'One of the boys,' Jack said. 'SAS. Served in Borneo in the early '60s. Sussed it out after meeting him a couple of times, but he didn't open up till we'd been here about five years.'

'Sussed it how?' Martin asked.

'Dunno really. Something in the eyes, I guess. Plus a couple of scars. The kind that only bullets make. He was invalided out, got a job teaching history, couldn't hack it and went bush. Vietnam vets weren't the first to bail out, not by a long chalk.'

They reached the store in twenty minutes and found Max sweeping the porch. When he saw them he waved, disappeared inside, and came back out carrying a cardboard box. Jack looked around casually but carefully.

Max handed the box through the passenger window to Martin. 'Sorry about the other morning, mate. If I'd known you and the good-looker were mates of Jack here, we could'a rustled you up a couple of egg and bacon rolls.'

'No hard feelings,' Martin said. 'We got some breakfast up the track.'

'He give you some of the tomato-chilli relish?' Max asked.

Martin gave him a thumbs-up.

'Almost better than sex, that relish,' Max said.

'Maxie's always after the recipe,' Jack laughed. Then, with a slight change in his tone, 'Everything we need's in the box?' he asked.

'You bet, mate. Plus a bit extra. Wouldn't like you to forget VT's little treat.'

'So, you going fishing today, Max?' Jack asked.

'Are they biting, you reckon?'

'Could be, Max, could be. Maybe you should shut up shop and take the family out in the boat for a bit,' Jack suggested. 'Leave the tinny tied to the dock just in case.'

Martin looked into the box as they pulled back onto the roadway. 'Does VT like musk sticks?' he asked.

'Hates 'em,' Jack said. 'How many are there?'

'Five,' Martin answered. 'Plus a copy of *Off Road* magazine. And the box of pilchards.'

'Max watches this end of the road for me,' Jack told him.

'And there's going to be trouble?'

'Yep. It'll be five men in a four-wheel drive.'

'That's the five musk sticks and the off-road magazine?' Martin said.

'You got it. Another little code we worked out in case people were hanging about listening.' He drove carefully, watching the road ahead. 'They'll try to stop us first, or at least slow us down. Moving targets are always harder. Keep an eye out for a roadblock. Fallen tree, rocks, stuff like that.'

Martin tightened his grip on the Skorpion. His mouth was suddenly very dry.

'Have a look under the top layer of cans,' Jack said. 'See if there's an envelope for me.'

Martin rummaged through the flat tins. 'It's here, sealed in plastic. Feels like a CD from the size of it.' He stared at the envelope. It was sealed with a sticker of a smiling donut with a snappy bow tie. 'Who's this from?' he asked.

'Someone who's been doing a bit of Internet snooping on my behalf,' Jack said.

'Donuts with Jim?' Martin asked, staring at the envelope in bewilderment.

'Shit!' Jack said suddenly.

Martin's head snapped up. 'What! What is it?' he said, his heart pounding.

'You think you're going to be okay with cocking and firing that Skorpion, mate?' Jack asked.

'I guess, if I really have to,' Martin said. He put the box of pilchards on the floor, grabbed his gun and braced himself.

Jack dropped the ambulance down a gear. 'Keep your eye on me, Martin, and do exactly as I say. It's time to rock and roll!'

twenty-seven

As they rounded the bend, Martin saw a green Range Rover in a ditch. Three men, dressed for fishing, stood in the road waving. Jack slowed and changed down again.

'You'd have to be pretty bloody stupid not to be able to drive a Rangie straight out of a spot like that,' he said. 'Cock your weapon, Martin. Try not to shoot your kneecap off.'

Jack floored the gas pedal and the ambulance slewed slightly as the tyres spun and bit into the gravel, and then it was racing forward. The men were reaching under their fishing vests as Martin yelled over the roar of the engine.

'There's something on the road!'

'Tyre spikes, ignore them,' Jack yelled. 'Fire out the window.'

'What at?' Martin screamed.

'Just shoot, make them keep their heads down. They don't know you're just a bank manager with attitude.'

Martin pointed the muzzle in the general direction of the Range Rover and squeezed the trigger. Nothing.

'Safety's on,' Jack yelled, leaning across to flip the lever. Martin squeezed the trigger again. The cabin was suddenly full of noise and smoke and the clinking of empty shell casings and then they were past.

'What about the tyre spikes?' Martin shouted. 'Nothing happened.'

'Solid rubber tyres!' Jack shouted with a laugh. 'Why do you think the ride's so bad?'

Martin glanced in his side mirror. Two more men had scrambled out from the bush behind them, past the tyre spikes. Red flashes appeared from their hands and something began hammering on the back of the ambulance.

'Don't panic,' Jack yelled. 'We welded steel plate onto the back.'

Martin saw the Range Rover stop to pick up the two men. Something about one of them seemed vaguely familiar. Jack glanced in his mirror.

'We should beat them to the gate. Just.' He fumbled in his haversack and handed Martin a grenade.

'Oh, fuck,' Martin said, looking at it.

'Easy as pie, Martin,' Jack said. 'Just get a firm grip on the body of the grenade, with your fingers over that lever bit. As long as the lever's down, it's safe. Now, use the ring to pull out the split pin. It'll take a serious tug. And don't use your teeth.'

Martin managed to pull the pin even though his hands were shaking.

'They've stopped firing. Put your hand out the window and drop the grenade,' Jack ordered. 'That's the way. Now just open your palm and let her go.'

Martin saw the lever spring off and then the smoking grenade was rolling on the road behind them. There was a thump and in his mirror he saw the Range Rover swerving around a burst of smoke and flame and red dust. Another blast of gunfire and the mirror on Martin's side suddenly disintegrated.

'Maybe you should keep your hands inside now,' Jack suggested. 'We've gained a few seconds, though. I'm going to dump her at the gate. You bail out with the pilchards and head up the hill. Try and keep the ambulance between you and the road. Get behind the first really big tree you can find. The trunk. Leaves don't stop bullets.'

Martin braced himself as they approached the property and Jack slammed on the brakes. The ambulance slid sideways into the gate, knocking it down with a clatter and blocking the entrance. Jack was screaming, 'Out! Out! Out!' and then he dropped a smoking grenade between the seats before leaping clear with the haversack and submachine gun. Martin heard the roar of an approaching vehicle and gunfire and then a thump, louder than the one on the road, just as he was burrowing under what he hoped were bulletproof palm fronds. There was a high-pitched whine from higher up the hill and suddenly the tyres of a trail bike skidded past his head. He heard a funny hollow *doop* sound, followed by an explosion. Then again. There was yelling from the roadway, and the sound of a vehicle revving high and departing. Then it was quiet. Martin rolled over. Faith was standing above him. She had an arrow fitted against the string of her longbow and she was breathing heavily.

'You okay?' she gasped.

He nodded, speechless.

'We came down on the bikes when we heard the shooting along the road,' she said, giving him a hand up.

The burning ambulance completely blocked the gateway. Jack and VT were walking slowly up the hill, arms around each other. VT carried what looked like a short, fat shotgun.

'Grenade launcher,' Jack said as they came up. 'M-79. We outgunned them, so they did the smart thing and pissed off.' He held up a broken arrow with blood on the tip and shaft. 'Good shot, Faith,' he said, looking at the smooth metal point. 'Pity it wasn't a hunting arrow with a nice set of barbs. These target arrows come out way too easy.'

'Everyone's okay then?' VT asked.

They all nodded.

'What's that smell?' Faith said suddenly.

Martin looked down at his trousers.

'Jesus, mate,' Jack said, 'that's a bit grim. I think you've been shot in the pilchards.'

*

They gathered on the verandah. Jack had retrieved the plastic envelope from among the pilchards and was reading the contents. After a while he strolled down to the end of the verandah with VT and they had a long, serious-looking conversation. VT went into the kitchen and came out with two walkie-talkies, giving one to Jack and slipping the other in his pocket. Biggles was anxious to go with him but obeyed the command from Jack to stay. A few minutes later, they heard a trail bike heading away from the house.

'You in big trouble, Jack?' Faith asked.

Jack grinned at her. 'I guess running gunfights on public roads are always a giveaway.'

'Really big trouble then?' Martin asked.

Jack shrugged. 'Like I said, I'm out of the loop, but I had a friend do some research. He hacked into their server and started reading the archived email.'

'Jesus, you can do that?' Martin asked

'You bet,' Jack said. 'No matter what people think, that DELETE button on your computer is like the CLOSE DOORS button on elevators, mostly there to make you feel comfortable. Anyway, the donut boy found what I needed, but then he got the bit between his teeth and hacked his way right into the most secure part of their mainframe. He burned me a CD of some particularly interesting material, but he must have tripped a security program in the process.'

'Could they trace the break-in back to him?' Faith asked.

'Probably not, he's very good at covering his tracks. But since I'm the most likely culprit in a search like this, I'd say I've been sprung.'

He turned and looked over the jungle. 'Guess it might be time to think about folding the tents,' he said.

Just then Jack's mobile rang. He listened to the caller for a long time before speaking.

'Okay, Max. Thanks. That's cool. Listen, mate, you remember that lemon tree I planted out the back of your shop? If you ever want to buy the wife a new frock or take a long trip, dig it up. Besides some of the folding stuff, you'll find my tomato relish recipe. Okay, you take it slow and easy there, mate.'

He pressed END CALL and turned to Martin and Faith. 'The guys in the Range Rover turned up at the jetty. A rubber duckie picked them up and took 'em out to a luxury cruiser that moored in the bay about an hour ago. Max reckons it's just a tad smaller than the *QE2*.' Jack began to pace. 'What am I missing here?' he said, more to himself than the others. He picked up a pair of binoculars and began scanning the area in front of the bungalow.

Faith leaned on the railing beside him. 'It'll be a pity if you have to leave here, Jack,' she said. 'It's so beautiful.'

Martin joined them. 'Although it probably won't be too long before some arsehole like Len Barton moves in and concretes the entire coast anyway,' he said

Jack stopped. 'What do you know about Len Barton?' he asked sharply.

'Not much, other than he's a bit of a racist bastard,' Faith said. 'We picked him up a few days back. He was hitchhiking after his car broke down, so we gave him a lift. Spent the night at his place on the Gold Coast. It was a seriously strange little interlude.'

'Where was the van during the night?' Jack snapped. 'On the street, garaged, where?'

Faith looked at him. 'In his garage, I think. Why?'

'Fuck me dead,' Martin gasped suddenly. Running in to the bar, he grabbed the photo off the wall. 'I knew I recognised this face from somewhere,' he shouted. 'This bloke, it's Albris, Barton's assistant.' He came back out and handed Jack the photo, pointing at the soldier on the far right of the group.

Jack grabbed it from him. 'Fucking Albris!'

'I wouldn't swear to it,' Martin said, 'but I think he might have been one of those guys from the Range Rover.'

'And he's working for Barton! Well, this is not good. Not good,' Jack repeated. 'Barton was the one who originally suggested this whole operation. One of his companies was doing civil construction in Vietnam and he got in real tight with the CIA spooks.'

Jack suddenly stared at Biggles with new understanding. 'And that's why they needed to kill you, pup,' he said quietly. He scooped the dog up and sprinted to the kitchen stairs.

'Move it!' he yelled. 'Everybody downstairs *now*. We may be in some very serious shit!'

Faith and Martin followed at a run. In the garage Jack put the dog down and said, 'Find, Biggles, find.'

Biggles wagged his tail and began sniffing. He made straight for the campervan, circling it twice before sitting down by the back wheel. Jack patted him enthusiastically.

'Good boy! Good boy!'

'We're pretty sure the bikies used the van to run drugs,' Martin said. 'Maybe Biggles can smell some residue?'

'He's not a drug dog, Martin,' Jack said, shaking his head. 'He's a bomb dog – explosives sniffer. Top in his class but he got pensioned off. They built the footpaths too close to his arse.'

Martin looked baffled. Jack was running for the roller door.

'His legs were a bit too short for him to search bigger aircraft effectively,' he yelled back over his shoulder. He punched a button, waited a moment, and then rolled under the slowly rising door, pulling the walkie-talkie from his pocket. He keyed SEND and spoke calmly. 'We got some big problems here, amigo. Crank her up.'

Martin heard a single click, which he guessed was

confirmation, and Jack ran to the back of the van and slid underneath. Martin joined him. Jack searched with his hands and stopped at a square metal plate.

'What's above here?' he asked.

Martin studied the van's underside, trying to get his bearings. 'Toilet, I think. Or maybe the shower.'

Jack grunted. 'Sounds reasonable. Faith,' he yelled, 'we need an electric screwdriver with a Phillips head. Pronto!'

'Travelling,' she replied, and suddenly she was there with them, handing the screwdriver to Jack and pulling in a plastic inspection lamp on a long cable.

'That's my girl,' Jack said.

The light showed that the metal plate was a recent, though well-disguised, addition.

'Hold her in the middle, Martin,' Jack ordered as he attacked the retaining screws. He had the plate off in sixty seconds. 'Well,' he said, 'this looks particularly ugly.'

There were relays and electrical wiring running in all directions up into the body of the campervan.

'Is it a bomb?' Faith asked.

Jack nodded. 'Triggering circuitry for one, anyway. They've probably packed the van's side panels with C4 for a serious wallop.'

'C4?' Martin asked.

'Plastique,' Faith said. 'Plastic explosive, Martin. Military issue originally. Mostly black-market stuff from eastern Europe these days.'

'Biggles would have sniffed this lot out in a second, which is why they plugged him before you arrived. Albris probably did it, it's the kind of thing he'd enjoy.'

'There enough in the van sides to make a serious bang, you reckon?' Martin asked.

Jack looked at the rows of grey and red drums lining the garage walls. 'Yep, more than enough. And I parked the van right where the blast would do the greatest amount of damage. Nice one, Jackie boy.'

'Maybe we could push it outside?' Martin suggested.

'Can't risk it,' Jack said. 'Probably got a delayed-action mercury switch set to kick in after several days without movement. Give her a serious nudge and she blows. That's how I'd do it anyway, and I was trained with Albris.'

'Can you disarm it?' Faith asked.

'Too many wires. Some will be dummies, some will be booby traps. Albris may be a total prick but he knows how to rig a bomb.'

There was a sudden click and a panel lit up.

'I didn't touch anything,' Martin said quickly.

Jack smiled grimly. 'It wasn't you, mate. They've armed it by radio. Probably from that boat Max saw. One of Len's many expensive toys.'

'How long do we have?' Faith asked.

'If I know Len, he'll want to ring me and gloat before he pushes the button.'

Jack's mobile rang.

'Bugger,' he said and slid out from under the van. He scooped up the dog. 'On the bikes! Follow me! Move it!'

Jack dumped Biggles into a milk crate fastened behind a red trail bike and Faith grabbed the one next to it. Starters whirred and Martin climbed on behind Faith. They shot out the door and headed down the hillside, Jack's mobile still ringing.

A couple of k's down the hill, Jack dumped his bike near a large clump of vegetation. Faith followed suit. Jack was running now with Biggles under his arm. Martin and Faith ran too, urged on by Jack yelling back over his shoulder. There was something strange about the thicket of jungle ahead, and Martin could hear a mechanical whining noise.

Jack pulled an axe from some bushes and hacked savagely at a large rope tied to a tree trunk. 'Keep moving!' he yelled, and then the rope gave way and there was a *whoosh*, followed by the rattling noise of ropes moving through pulleys.

Off to his left, Martin saw a massive tree trunk wrapped in cables tumble out of the treetops as the centre of the thicket was torn away. He realised it was a huge green camouflage net and that the falling trunk was a counterweight that had pulled it clear. With the netting gone, Martin could see the helicopter. It was sitting on a concrete slab with its rotor blades slowly turning, and he recognised it as a Huey – from movies on Vietnam. The chopper's matt-green paint was faded and the aircraft looked to be in less than showroom condition.

VT was frantically beckoning to them from the pilot's seat and they scrambled aboard. Jack clambered into the co-pilot's seat, dropped Biggles at his feet, and tugged on a flight helmet. Martin and Faith pulled at lap belts on the bench seat at the rear of the open cargo compartment, their legs awkwardly propped up on a layer of boxes and crates covered by a tarpaulin. The rotor blades were spinning faster now, with a *thwop thwop thwop* sound. Jack indicated several headsets hanging from the roof of the rear cabin. Faith and Martin put them on and could hear Jack and VT talking.

Jack looked back at them. 'Can you hear okay?'

Faith nodded and Martin yelled, 'Loud and clear!'

'No good,' Jack said with a shake of his head. 'You've only got audio back there, no mikes. Now buckle up and hold on.'

Jack pointed upwards with his thumb and VT studied the instrument panel for a moment before nodding. Jack lifted up his mobile and pressed ANSWER. 'Do your worst, Len, you evil fuck!'

Suddenly Martin was aware of a slow, powerful rumble and the helicopter began vibrating wildly. The mountain seemed to be bulging out beneath them and he couldn't make sense of the motion. He was leaning forward in his harness and they were moving, but somehow the chopper appeared to be still firmly on the ground. The rotor blades were making a *thwopa thwopa thwopa* noise, thrashing the air in desperation. He made a 'What's going on?' gesture to Faith. She made a downwards sliding motion and he realised that the helicopter was tobogganing down the hillside, still sitting on its concrete slab.

VT was pulling up on the control column with all his might. A warning horn started blaring in the cockpit. With a reluctant shudder, the aircraft wrenched itself free of the sliding concrete slab. Martin saw earth and rocks and pieces of wood falling all about them and then something smashed hard into the plexiglass window on VT's side. He winced and put his hand to his upper arm. When he took it away his fingers had blood on them.

'You okay, mate?' Jack yelled.

VT nodded. 'Nothing serious!'

Then the helicopter was in clear air. As it banked they saw that the whole top of the mountain was an inferno. The house had disappeared.

'Pity about your cash back there, mate.' Jack's voice was suddenly loud in Martin's ear.

Martin spread his hands and shrugged, squinting as the racing air pulled at his face. Jack rummaged under his seat and came up with two pairs of goggles. Martin found a black crumbly substance on his hands. Jack's voice was in his ear again.

'Sorry, the rubber's a bit perished,' he said, 'but it's the best we can do. They're quite old. Standard issue to pilots on World War II goony birds.'

Faith and Martin looked at Jack blankly.

He grinned and indicated the tarp under their legs. Lifting his feet, Martin rolled back a corner of the canvas to reveal a layer of old wooden packing crates. The faded stencilling on the top of one box read: PROPERTY OF THE TREASURY OF THE PHILIPPINES.

Jack roared with laughter at Martin's expression. Then his smile froze at a loud bang from the engine compartment. The helicopter dipped suddenly. The warning klaxon blared again as VT wrestled with the control column. 'Grab hold of something and hang on tight!' he yelled.

The engine noise turned from a roar to a high-pitched whine and the whole body of the helicopter started to shudder. A series of loud bangs were quickly followed by a rapid loss in altitude. Both Jack and VT were pulling on the twin control columns with all their strength. Martin looked at Faith and mouthed, 'I love you.' She clutched his hand tightly and mouthed, 'I love you too.'

twenty-eight

'Well, this is my idea of heaven,' Faith said as she sipped her pina colada.

Martin looked up from his magazine and smiled. Their sun lounges were shaded by a large, dark-green umbrella, which contrasted nicely with the terracotta tiles on their private terrace. Below the terrace, holiday-makers sunned themselves beside the pool or on the sandy beach. Laughing teenagers cruised a man-made lagoon, pedalling in big, plastic-wheeled aqua bikes.

Biggles, nestled under Faith's lounge, gave a soft, throaty yelp and wagged his tail as Jack and VT walked up the steps from the pool. Both wore swimming trunks and sunglasses, and VT had a thick white bandage around his upper arm. They pulled over a couple of deckchairs and sat down.

'Excellent planning, Jack,' Faith said. 'They blow up your luxurious mountaintop hideaway, so you move to a five-star coastal resort. I have to say I like your style.'

Jack looked up from his drinks menu and grinned. 'I told you it doesn't hurt to be too paranoid in this business. You always have to have a fall-back position.'

'And one with 24-hour room service, no less,' Faith said.

'Bloke who runs the joint owes me a favour or two,' Jack explained. 'He's always got a bed for me and my friends, plus a handy little box of tricks stored away down the back of the left-luggage room. Like I said, it doesn't hurt to be prepared.'

'Having a getaway Huey behind the back shed was a nice bit of planning too,' Martin chuckled.

'Ex-Philippines army,' VT explained. 'We found her hauling coffee in New Guinea and flew her back under the radar a few years ago. It's the only machine to be in if you've got to pull off a manoeuvre like that.'

'I think it might have had as much to do with the pilot as the machine, VT.' Faith raised her glass in a toast.

Jack put his hand on VT's. 'You're right there, Faith, I don't know any other pilot who could have done it.'

When the helicopter engine had started malfunctioning earlier that day, Jack had yelled to VT, 'High or low?'

VT pointed downwards and took the shuddering aircraft towards the surf. Jack turned to Faith and Martin. 'If we go high, Len might pick us up on his radar,' he said through the intercom. 'Which gives the game away. If we go low and the engine packs up altogether, we may not be able to autorotate, which is the only way down without power. But if VT reckons we go low, then it's the right thing to do.'

They headed north with the nose down, almost at wave height, and after several minutes the shuddering turbine suddenly coughed, misfired once and settled into a steady, smooth whine. VT checked the instruments, smiled and gave a thumbs-up.

Twenty minutes later, they were on the ground in a clearing near a white-sand beach. Martin and Faith helped VT pull a large camouflage net over the chopper while Jack made a call on a mobile he took from a pocket on the co-pilot's door. They walked for five minutes to a dirt track where an old, cut-down Land Rover was waiting. The sign on the door featured a palm tree, a golden sun and the words 'St Tropez South'. The driver greeted Jack and VT warmly, and within fifteen minutes Faith was ordering her first pina colada of the day.

'Nice swimsuit, Faith,' Jack said, taking his tequila sunrise from the waiter's tray.

'Why, thank you,' she smiled. 'The resort boutique does an excellent line in '50s styles, which suit me, and being able to sign for things is very handy now that my main squeeze and I are officially skint.'

'Don't worry about it,' Jack said. 'It's all on me.'

'And too bloody right,' Martin chimed in, 'considering what's taking up all the leg room in the Huey.'

'So exactly how did you come across all that lovely gold bullion anyway?' Faith asked.

'It was that bomb from the F-111,' Jack explained, sipping on his cocktail. 'When we started shaping the crater for our swimming pool, we turned up a wing tip. Bloody miracle the contractor who built all the tunnels under the house didn't find her.'

'Those crates looked in pretty good nick for having gone through a plane crash,' Faith said.

'Not uncommon, really. Quite a few aircraft disappeared like that in England during World War II. Apparently if you hit at the right speed, on the right angle, and the ground is soft enough, you can get swallowed up without a trace. It's a bit like punching your fist into a cream sponge. It was the wet season when it happened, and the Met records for that night say it was raining like a bastard. No airborne radar back then, so the poor buggers must have just slammed full tilt into the side of our hill in the dark.'

'And we bought the story about the mythical golden gooney bird along with the legend of the landmines,' Faith said. 'You lie so well I'm surprised no-one's asked you to run for parliament.'

'I'm way out of the government's league,' Jack laughed. 'According to a Defence Department spokesman on TV just now, an unmarked World War II ammo dump in far north

Queensland blew up unexpectedly this morning with no loss of life.'

'No mention of a second-hand chopper fanging its way out of the inferno?' Faith asked. Jack shook his head.

'So we're all dead then?' Martin said.

'Looks that way,' Jack agreed, 'at least as far as Len's concerned.'

'That's the second time this month,' Martin said. 'I'm starting to lose track.'

'Okay then, Jack,' Faith said, 'what's the plan?'

'What makes you think I've got any kind of a plan?' Jack asked casually.

'After lunch, you and VT spent an hour with your heads together. You're definitely organising something, and Martin and I want to help.'

Jack glanced at VT, who nodded. 'Okay,' Jack said, 'it's at least a two-man operation, but someone needs to fly the chopper, so VT is out. This could be dangerous, you understand. It's not really a job for amateurs, but it doesn't seem that I've got much choice.'

Faith raised her glass in a toast. 'Here's to the mission, and to the crew you choose when you don't have any choice. And please, Jack, don't think of Martin and me as just amateurs, think of us as enthusiastic amateurs.'

Jack finished his cocktail in one large gulp.

'What have I done to deserve this?' he said softly.

*

The two couples were sharing the resort's presidential suite. It was the suite President Clinton would have slept in when he visited the Great Barrier Reef, Jack explained, if he hadn't slept somewhere else. There were three double bedrooms running off a huge central living and dining room, and a large balcony overlooking the lagoon and the sea. In the middle of the living room sat a large silver trunk and a suitcase taken out of storage in the left-luggage area. Jack was rummaging through the suitcase and throwing garments onto the dining table.

'Grab what you think fits,' he instructed, 'and go and try it on. You can have any colour you want as long as it's black.'

Five minutes later, Martin, Faith and Jack stood in the living room dressed from head to foot in black. Black windcheaters, black tracksuit pants and black sneakers. Jack looked the other two over carefully.

'Sandshoes fit okay, Faith?' he asked. 'Now, just wear those ski masks rolled up like watchcaps for the moment and make sure you don't lose the gloves. There's a full moon tonight and white hands will stick out like dog's balls.' He glanced across at Biggles, who was sitting near VT. 'Sorry, pup, didn't mean to bring up painful memories.' Biggles wagged his tail.

Jack opened the trunk and revealed an assortment of pistols and submachine guns. He selected several, checked them thoroughly, placed them into a large black sports bag, and closed the trunk. After zipping up the bag, he sat on the trunk and looked at Martin and Faith.

'Now's the time to bail if you think this might get a bit hairy for you,' he said.

They both shook their heads.

'Albris will be wherever Len is,' Jack explained, 'which will be somewhere comfortable. And Albris is the one we have to watch out for.'

'Is Albris really that dangerous, Jack?' Martin asked.

'He's a full-blown psychopath.' Jack stood up and started to pace the room. 'The most dangerous thing about people like Albris is that they expend about ninety-five per cent of their energy making themselves appear perfectly normal. Then they'll kill without hesitation or a second thought.'

'And you two have some kind of private vendetta going on?' Faith asked.

'We trained together and worked together sometimes. Over there. I was better than he was and got promoted faster and he didn't like it.'

'Must be more to it than that,' Faith said.

'We crossed paths in a village up north one day. He had a private army of mercenaries from one of the hill tribes and they had about thirty people bailed up in a ditch. Old men, women and kids.' Jack opened the trunk again and took out a long thin knife in a leather sheath. 'Albris reckoned they were Vietcong and I'm pretty sure if I hadn't turned up he would have blown them all away, and taken a lot of pleasure in doing it. He was seriously pissed off that I pulled rank and spoiled his fun. Seemed to have it in for me after that.' Hitching up his trouser leg, Jack strapped the knife to his calf. 'And Albris really knows how to hold a grudge.'

'Odd choice for a butler on Len's part?' said Martin.

'Perfect choice, really. You can train someone like Albris in all the social graces and then unleash that killer instinct when you need to.'

'Such a lovely world you live in, Jack,' Faith said.

'I'm retired, Faith, remember?' He glanced at VT. 'And true love has made me a better man. Now,' he said, looking back at them, 'if you still want to go through with this, remember what I said. You guys are to hang back and look after the crew. All Len's staff usually hate his guts, so I doubt they'll give us any trouble. If it goes pear-shaped, you jump in Maxie's tinny and POQ. Understood?'

Martin and Faith nodded in agreement.

'And what do we say if we're challenged by anyone?' Martin asked. 'These outfits aren't exactly tropical.'

'We could say we were on the way to the Sydney Film Festival and we got lost,' Faith suggested.

'That could work.' Jack smiled wryly. He took his mobile from his pocket and punched in a number. 'Time to check the state of the pitch with Max,' he said. 'Is Dorothy there?' he asked when the call was answered. 'I'm a friend. What? No, I'm sorry, I must have written it down incorrectly.' He ended the call and the phone rang immediately.

'Maxie,' Jack said, 'as I live and breathe, and believe me

I do . . . Yep, sorry you had to get the willies like that, but we're all just hunky-dory . . . Yep, Biggles too. So how are things hanging?'

Jack listened for a minute, nodded, said, 'Bugger,' softly, then said his goodbyes and hung up. 'Good news and bad news,' he told them. 'Max has been sitting out to sea watching the action with a starlight scope. Albris ran the four goons over to the dock in a rubber duckie and they drove off somewhere. He took the rubber duckie back to the yacht, but not before shooting Maxie's tinny full of holes and sinking it off the end of the dock. He's a careful sod, that Albris. Looks like we've got a problem.'

'Can't Max pick us up and take us out to the yacht?' Martin asked.

VT was pulling on a flight suit. 'Max's cruiser is too big and noisy.'

'VT's right,' Jack said, 'they'd see and hear us coming a mile off. It's a whole lot easier with the goons out of the way, but how the hell do we get out there?'

'You mean you don't have an inflatable boat in the bottom of your trunk?' Faith said. 'I'm surprised.'

A thought struck Martin and he walked across the room and onto the balcony. 'Come and have a look out here,' he called.

The other three joined him. It was after nine and the resort guests had retired to their rooms after a hard day of relaxing in the sun. Martin was looking towards the lagoon.

'If we're borrowing that Land Rover to drive to the bay, then we could easily get a couple of those in the back.'

Jack looked at the lagoon and then at Martin.

'It looks like a pretty calm night out on the water,' Martin added.

Jack tightened the webbing belt around his waist. 'I do believe you're suggesting we head off to a showdown with Arthur Leonard Barton and his psychopathic sidekick in a couple of plastic pedal boats.'

'The two on the end are mostly black,' Martin said, warming to his theme. 'They'd be even harder to spot than Max's silver tinny.'

'Well.' Jack scratched his head. 'It's a plan. And it makes about as much sense as anything I can think of. Probably more. I guess we should give it a whirl.'

'Bags I get to steer ours,' Faith said.

twenty-nine

Arthur Leonard Barton jabbed at his sticky date pudding with a fork. Too damn chewy. He realised it had been a mistake not bringing the chef from home with him on this trip.

At that same moment Albris realised his own mistake – standing with his back to the dining-room door. The cold metal of a pistol muzzle pressing into the base of his skull made the hairs on his neck stand up.

Len looked up from his pudding as Albris raised his hands. 'You are a dick, Albris,' he said. 'I warned you. No bodies, no bits, no confirmed kill. You should have kept looking till you had an answer either way.' He put down his fork. 'Shit for fucking brains,' he said slowly.

A muscle fluttered under Albris's left eye. 'That's why face to face is better,' he said through clenched teeth. 'Face to face, you always know for sure.'

'Only if you win,' Jack said. 'And you stuffed it up out on the road, big-time. Outgunned by a bank manager. Jesus!'

An increase in the pressure on his neck forced Albris towards the centre of the cabin. Jack followed him in, keeping the pistol aimed carefully at the back of the bodyguard's head. Len wiped his mouth with his napkin.

'You'll need armour-piercing bullets if you intend shooting him in the head, Jack,' he said.

'Ah, I've missed the warm regard you have for your loyal staff, Len.' Jack indicated the table with the tip of his pistol. 'Sit down at the table, Albris, like a good boy. With both hands around that ice bucket.'

Albris sat. Jack kept the pistol aimed at his head. 'If you do anything even the least bit odd,' he said, 'I will shoot you. And that's not a threat, it's a promise.'

Walking behind Albris, he removed the Glock automatic from under his jacket. Martin and Faith stepped over the door sill into the cabin, Martin carrying the Skorpion.

'You should remember Martin and Faith, Len,' Jack said. 'You all had dinner together recently, I believe.' He handed the Glock to Faith. 'Pity you sent the four stooges back to the mainland, Len. Deck security was a little light on.' He motioned for Len to get up.

'Couple of them were injured, so I sent them to see a quack,' Len explained calmly as he stood up, his hands raised. 'I'm a compassionate man, Jack, your opinion notwithstanding.'

Jack expertly patted him down for weapons and then motioned for him to sit.

'I guess you must have been bawling your eyes out when you triggered the explosives in our van, then,' Faith said.

'It's just business, girlie,' shrugged Len. 'I needed a delivery vehicle. Yours was the only one going to the right place with any real chance of being allowed in. Jack here was getting way past his use-by date and starting to smell. Publicly.'

'So you kept the cops off our backs and our names out of the papers? To give us a free run?' Martin said.

Len smiled pleasantly. 'I will admit to being in a position to call in favours at all levels of government and across the media.' He reached for his tobacco pouch and started to roll a cigarette. 'That body swap in the four-wheel drive was good. We thought you'd carked it there for a minute. Had the forensics guys in a tizz. Me too. Then Albris got it sorted and you resurfaced, picked up that campervan, which was ideal for our purposes, and everything was back on track.' He licked the cigarette paper and sealed it.

'Bad luck for us, I guess,' Faith said. 'We wind up being collateral damage.'

'You have to see it from Len's point of view,' Jack said. 'He's got a nice little operation going, collecting intelligence for the government and on the government. Add that to his business empire and you've got a very powerful individual.

Anyone who threatens that is expendable. It's not personal. Right, Len?'

Len took a long drag on his cigarette. 'Exactly, Jack,' he smiled.

'I guess one thing in your favour, Len,' Faith said, 'is you do some of your own dirty work. That hitchhiker act of yours was very good.'

'Knew you wouldn't be able to resist stopping for an old coot like me, darlin',' he said. 'Besides, Albris kept screwing it up. Years of training and he still has trouble with the concept of gentle persuasion.'

'Looks good in a suit, though,' Faith said. 'And impeccable manners.'

'He's quite a conundrum, our Albris. Great around the house but goes bloody psycho when I let him out.'

'Once had a cat named Leroy who was a bit like that,' Faith said. 'Having him neutered solved most of the problems.'

'Fuck you, bitch!' Albris snarled. He swung in his seat, taking his hands from the ice bucket.

'Come on, children, let's not fight,' Jack said. 'Martin, is that Skorpion on full auto?'

Martin glanced down at the fire selector and nodded.

'Okay,' Jack said, 'the next time Albris takes his hands away from that ice bucket, pull the trigger and hold it down till the magazine's empty.'

Albris glared at Jack and returned his hands to the ice bucket.

Jack smiled sweetly. 'And by the by, Len, I should warn you I've seen Martin in action. Sitting that close to Albris, it'll be your turn to become collateral damage. No offence meant, Martin, but you do tend to spray it about a bit.'

Faith had been moving about the cabin, inspecting the fittings. 'This is a lovely boat, Len. Nothing but the best. Even the blonde in the school uniform in your stateroom. Very top-shelf.'

'Told you, love,' Len said, 'the better half's in Paris shopping. The girl okay?'

'She's fine. Conveniently for us, she had a very nice set of fur-covered handcuffs in her purse.'

'Okay, Jack,' Len said, 'let's get down to tintacks. What do you want?'

'I just want a long, quiet life, Len. And your boat.'

'Or what?'

'Well, for starters, that girl in your bedroom looks about fifteen. Do her mum and dad know she's in the bedroom of a sleazy old billionaire on a school night? Wouldn't look too good in the Sunday tabloids.'

'Oh, grow up, Jack,' Len snapped. 'People trying to get on my good side are always sending their teenage daughters over in the family Bentley to butter me up. When you're as fucking rich and powerful as I am, mud doesn't stick. And don't forget, I *am* the Sunday tabloids.'

Jack walked over to Len and whispered in his ear. Len frowned.

'You are an A-grade prick, Stark,' he snarled.

'Worse than that, mate, I'm an A-grade prick with a CD full of photographic evidence.'

Len looked at him coldly. 'What do you want, exactly?' he asked.

'I told you, the boat and a quiet life for me and my friends.'

'Why the boat? You can have airline tickets to anywhere in the world.'

Jack shrugged. 'I feel like an ocean cruise. Besides, we've got a ton of luggage and you've got lots of other boats.'

Len seemed to be considering this. 'Do I get the photographs then?'

Jack smiled. 'Well, that would make me a bigger dick than Albris here, wouldn't it?' He pulled a sheaf of folded documents from his back pocket. 'And here's a bit of luck, Len,' he said cheerily. 'We found the ship's papers in your office safe. And I thought the whole point of a safe was you kept the door closed.'

Jack slid the papers across the table to Len. 'You sign the transfer of title and we motor away.'

Len leaned back in his chair and folded his hands behind his head. 'Contracts made under duress are easily nullified.'

Jack tossed a pen on the table. 'Don't dick me around, Len. You cross me, and one click of a mouse plasters your personal life all over the web. And you know how efficient that is, you've used it. Like you've used me.'

Len held Jack's gaze as he leaned forward and picked up

the pen. He paused for a moment, then signed the papers and threw them back across the table.

'Want to be a witness, Albris?' Jack asked. 'Faith here can show you how to make an X.'

'I should have killed you when I had the chance,' Albris snarled.

'Jesus, mate, be fair,' Jack said. 'Every time you had the chance, you didn't have the balls. Or the nous.' He folded the documents and put them in his pocket. 'And there's something that puzzles me, Len. You knew you had the bomb in place after Martin and Faith arrived, so why didn't you just flick the switch right then? You'd have heard the bang down on the Gold Coast.'

Len took the last drag on his cigarette and exhaled slowly. 'I wanted to cruise up and have a front-row seat, Jack. I just love a good pyrotechnics display.'

'Especially if I'm standing right in the middle of it,' Jack said.

'Let's just say that was a bit of a bonus.' Len stubbed out his cigarette. 'Or would have been if things had worked out.'

'Fair enough, but in that case, what was all that high-testosterone bullshit out on the road about?'

'I'm afraid the ambush thing was all Albris's doing, Jack, and strictly against my orders. Stupid bloody idea. He doesn't understand it should never be personal.'

'That's always been his problem, Len. He likes to see the look in his victims' eyes.'

After a long silence, Faith walked over to Len. 'There was an old couple in a campervan like ours,' she said. 'We gave them our mobile and I swapped number plates. That didn't cause them any serious trouble, did it?'

Albris looked uncomfortable. Len shook his head. 'They're okay,' he said. 'They had a bit of a run-in with Albris after he tracked you to the pub. One of his boys crashed the party and got a description of your van and the rego number. Took him a while to get back to the chopper with the details. Found it hard to tear himself away from the roast lamb, apparently.'

'And?' Faith asked.

'Albris was pretty pissed off when he eventually spotted that blue hair from the chopper and realised you'd done a switcheroo. He pulled them over to find out what was what, but the old girl gave him better than she got. Told you my generation was pretty tough, girlie.'

'Don't call me girlie,' Faith said. 'And don't put yourself in the same class as Cliff and Hazel. They're way out of your league.'

Len looked around the cabin. 'By the way, where's your bumboy, Jack?'

'He's hovering around somewhere, Len. Don't fret about it.' Jack glanced at his watch. 'I think we need to get moving. All ashore that's going ashore. The crew voted to stay on with us to the first port of call. They also voted you the meanest bastard of all time.'

'You really should try being nicer to the people who

prepare your food, Len,' Martin said. 'You wouldn't believe some of the things they've been putting in your soup.'

'Time to go, gentlemen,' Faith announced, 'and trust me, I'm using the term very loosely. Do you want to get the poppet up on deck, Martin?'

He nodded. Faith held up three life jackets. 'We need to hang onto that rubber duckie, so I'm afraid you're going to have to put these on.'

Arthur Leonard Barton turned white.

'It's not as bad as all that, Len,' Jack said. 'The weather's just perfect for a little cruise in a pedal boat.'

'They're two-seaters,' Faith said. 'You might want to draw straws to see who gets stuck with Albris.'

*

The two bobbing pedal craft were long behind them when Jack cut the throttles and the huge boat slowed, then stopped. He began flicking switches on the bridge console. Suddenly the rear deck was flooded with light.

'Gotcha,' he murmured. 'Martin, you wanna go topside and check if the helipad is lit up?'

'So that's what that is,' Martin said. 'I thought this tub had its own tennis court.'

'Could be a squeeze for the Huey, but VT will put her down if she can be put down. No swell, which is good. We'll just let her drift.'

Jack was hunting through drawers and cupboards. He

pulled out a large pistol and some thick, waxed cardboard tubes. Up on deck he cocked the pistol and fired it into the night sky. There was a trail of smoke and then the blinding light of a flare, which began falling in a slow arc back to the water.

A few minutes later, they heard the *thwok thwok thwok* of the Huey flying towards the flare. Jack lit a wick on the end of one of the cardboard tubes and orange smoke began to billow from it. He handed it to Faith.

'Go to the lower deck, you two. Keep the smoke visible so he can judge the wind direction. And keep your heads down.'

Martin watched as VT guided the huge helicopter down onto what seemed an impossibly small space. It took three attempts, but finally Jack made a throat-cutting gesture and VT shut down the engine. Faith and Martin clambered back up to the top deck.

'This is why we left the crew locked up,' Jack said. 'We want to get the gold off and stowed before the sun comes up. And then we need to lose the chopper.'

VT rolled back the tarp from the Huey's cargo and handed Martin a black garbage bag. 'Surprise!' he said. 'There's a couple more in here.' It was the cash from the bank.

Martin and Faith were stunned. 'But I thought it went up with the van?' Faith said.

Martin plunged his hand into the bag and pulled out a fistful of notes. 'Apparently not!'

VT laughed and pulled out the other two bags and tossed them to Martin.

'VT found them when he gave the van a quick once-over when you arrived.' Jack explained. 'Not that we don't trust old school chums who drop in, but you can probably see now that paranoia sometimes has its place. Piss-weak hiding spot. Albris was a lot better with that fucking bomb.'

It took almost four hours to shift the gold to a deck locker, which had originally held two inflatable pontoons, intended to be attached to a helicopter's landing skids to make the aircraft amphibious. VT decided he could jury-rig them to the Huey, to allow him to put it down on the water so they could ditch it. A couple of well-aimed shots into the pontoons would deflate them, and the helicopter would sink without a trace.

'It's risky, but better than a low-level hover and then jumping out,' VT said.

Jack nodded in agreement. 'That's how I knew he was out after Saigon fell. Saw him offloading people onto a carrier deck and then flying his Huey over the side. It was live on TV. Held my breath until he bobbed up after the chopper went under.'

Just after dawn, with the floats fitted, VT took the Huey up and tentatively settled it on the ocean about a hundred metres from the boat. Jack was circling in the rubber duckie. Just as the rotors stopped moving, the left-hand pontoon broke away and the helicopter tilted over to one side.

'Shit!' Faith said, watching through binoculars from the bridge.

VT leapt clear and began to swim towards the rubber duckie. Martin, standing on the rear deck, saw Jack stand up suddenly and begin firing his pistol in the direction of the swimming man.

'What's going on?' he yelled up to Faith.

'It's a shark!' she yelled.

There was a flurry, a white shape twisting, and then blood in the water as VT scrambled into the inflatable boat. The two men hugged. The rubber duckie circled the blood-stained patch of water and Jack leaned over the side. Several minutes later, the boat was scudding back towards them, bouncing over the waves. Faith tied the line off and steadied the craft as a soaking VT came back on board. A slick grey triangle lay in the bottom of the boat at Jack's feet.

'Don't normally hold with eating shark fin because they driftnet 'em. Got this one fair and square, though.'

They manoeuvred the huge fin onto the deck. Jack was smiling broadly. 'Len's chef is Cantonese. We can probably work out what to do with this between us.'

'You think Len and the others would have been okay?' Martin asked.

'They'll be fine. I had Max keeping an eye on them with a starlight scope from his cruiser until we were long gone. He was going to pick them up just before dawn.'

VT pointed. The Huey was half submerged. Suddenly the second pontoon came away and the helicopter went under. They stood silently for a few minutes.

Faith was the first to speak. 'Breakfast, I think. And then we need a plan.'

'I agree about breakfast,' Jack said, 'but we've got fifty million bucks. Why do we need a plan?'

'Fifty-one,' Martin said.

'Sorry, mate. Our gold is US dollar value. You've only got the South Pacific peso. We may have to put you two deadbeats on the oars.'

'Give them a big enough boat and they always turn,' Faith said in mock disgust.

'However, we do have a slight liquidity problem, Martin,' Jack went on, 'so I suggest we swap half a million of your cash for one of our million gold.'

'Sounds great to me,' Martin grinned, 'but I think one of us is getting screwed.'

Jack adopted a serious tone. 'We need someone on deck at all times to keep an eye on the crew and the gold, so any screwing will need to be done to a schedule.'

'Right,' Faith said. 'Jack, the galley. VT, deck watch. Martin, you'll be coming with me. How's that for scheduling?'

The three men looked at her. Six eyebrows raised.

'What can I say? Piracy on the high seas sharpens my appetite.'

thirty

Macau, the oldest European settlement in Asia, was colonised in the sixteenth century by the Portuguese. Situated on the Chinese coast near the Pearl River estuary, it reverted to Chinese rule in 1999. Now the once-sleepy enclave was sleepy no longer. The pre-handover construction boom saw the completion of an international airport and bridges linking the outlying islands of Taipa and Coloane, and Macau was now a tourist destination on a par with Hong Kong. The arrival of four Australians by boat, even if it was a very large boat, made little impression.

The four newcomers lived on the boat and quickly settled into a casual lifestyle of exploring the markets and back streets and sampling the local cuisine, with its unique blending of Portuguese, Indian, Malay, African and Chinese influences. On several evenings each week they could be found in restaurants like the Litoral, A Lorcha or Solmar, dining on African chicken, chilli-garlic prawns, grilled Portuguese sausage, and red bean, pork and vegetable stew. One of the foursome always ended the meal chatting in the kitchen with the chefs.

Several months later, they bought the Pousada do Estoril, a rundown, two-storey, six-bedroom hotel with a tiny bar and a small dining room. Located off Avenida Almeida Ribeiro, the hotel was part of old Macau. All the original interior fittings were carefully removed and stored and the building was quickly demolished.

The locals waited for the next high-rise to appear. It didn't. A car park was excavated and then the original Pousada do Estoril reappeared. Three storeys now. The original art deco bar, a beautiful dining room with eight tables for two and one table for four, a state-of-the-art kitchen, four magnificently appointed guest rooms, two private residences on the third floor and an exquisite rooftop garden. Elegantly framed black-and-white photographs decorated the walls. The pictures documented a unique journey by campervan up the east coast of Australia.

The bar and restaurant opened as 'Jack's'. The bar was too small for the cool crowd, so they left it alone. The restaurant had one sitting per evening, five evenings a week. Bookings and confirmations were made only by email. There was no written menu. The food was sublime. Jack's kitchen brigade was the best. The waiters were attentive yet almost invisible. The barman mixed a sensational classic Manhattan and refused all orders for 'silly, fluffy cocktails'. The guest rooms were always taken, even though they were never advertised and had an unlisted phone number. Within a year, the hotel and restaurant had blended seamlessly into the Macau scene.

Only one untoward incident occurred, the accidental death of a drunken tourist who apparently tripped outside the building very early one Sunday morning. The fall to the pavement snapped his neck and fractured his jaw. Eyewitness reports that the man had been attempting to scale the building and had fallen from near the top were quickly discounted by local police. A report of an empty shoulder holster was also amended: the item was actually a security pouch for travel documents and credit cards.

The police took a statement from a guest in the hotel, a gentleman who was visiting Macau with his family. Since he was a police officer in Australia, his version of events was accepted, as a professional courtesy, by local detectives. According to his statement, unable to sleep he had been on the rooftop terrace in the early hours of the morning and had witnessed the entire incident. Senior Sergeant Colin Curtis was pleased with the quick resolution of the investigation since it allowed him to continue with a very pleasant family holiday. The only downside was that he was unable to join his children parasailing as he had coincidentally broken his right hand on the night of the incident.

After two weeks in cold storage, the unclaimed body was finally identified by representatives of the Australian consulate. The dead man, Albris Smith, a 53-year-old former public servant, was from Runaway Bay on the Gold Coast and had been on a Magic of the Far East package tour. Returned to Australia for burial, his casket was briefly delayed at Sydney airport by the arrival of overseas dignitaries and media heavyweights attending the state funeral of Arthur Leonard Barton.

The eulogy was delivered by the prime minister, who praised Barton's achievements and selfless dedication to his country and community over many years. It was a tragedy, therefore, that he had died alone in a senseless, single-vehicle road accident on the Sunshine Coast. Rumour had it that he had selflessly spent the afternoon entertaining two underprivileged teenage girls at the Wet and Wicked theme park, and later aboard his recently acquired luxury motor cruiser. Eyewitness reports of a second vehicle's involvement in the fatal car crash were quickly discounted by police and investigators from a special agency within the government.

Elsewhere on the Sunshine Coast that week, old diggers at the annual Rats of Tobruk reunion warmly welcomed the participation of a former enemy, a visiting one-time Afrika Corps NCO who held the Iron Cross and also possessed a wonderful singing voice. Thus the veterans were able to sing 'Lili Marlene' in English and also enjoy it in the original German.

In a spirit of camaraderie the president of the veterans' group persuaded the local car-rental firm to waive the insurance excess on some minor panel damage to their guest's vehicle when he returned it at the end of his stay. Former *Unteroffizier* Rollo Kleindorf, Panzer Grenadiers, was most appreciative.

Within days of the funeral, Barton's business empire was absorbed into the holdings of a major US-based international media conglomerate, and the non-media assets were rapidly sold off.

The prime minister expressed an opinion that the move to overseas ownership and control of Barton's newspaper and television interests was something his government could live with and he was re-elected shortly afterward for another four-year term.

*

On a balmy Saturday evening the roof garden at the Pousada do Estoril was set for a dinner party for four. Jack was fussing over the barbecue. VT relaxed on a chaise longue with a dry Martini and several auction catalogues from dealers specialising in early Chinese cloisonné ware. Biggles was snoozing at his side. Martin leaned on the edge of the balcony, sipping a gin and tonic.

Faith was due back from Hong Kong, where she had

been for several weeks, the first of which was spent in a private hospital recommended by her reconstructive plastic surgeon. Martin looked down at the vibrant street life. This was certainly a long way from Burrinjuruk.

Jack joined him at the balcony rail. 'Hope she's on time, mate,' he said, 'the coals are about ready and those ribs are marinated to within seconds of perfection.'

The two men looked out over the bustling night traffic of the city. Taxis and private cars, horns blaring, competed with motorbikes, scooters and pedicabs for space on the narrow streets. 'Not exactly the kind of retirement you were expecting, eh Marty?'

'You can say that again.' Martin shook his head. 'It's like a dream, except the dream part is the first fifty years and the real bit is the last twelve months.'

Jack swigged on his beer. 'I can relate to that. It's true love, Martin. That's what makes it real.'

'Becoming a romantic in your old age, Jack?' Martin teased.

'Nah, just a pissed old poof barbecuing ribs on his romantic rooftop hideaway in the mysterious East.'

'Barbecuing ribs for the love of your life, Jack, that's got to be something special.'

Jack looked over at VT. 'He is pretty cute, isn't he? I guess I was always a sucker for Asians – and don't you say a fuckin' word, Martin Carter, and take that smirk off your face. You've been spending way too much time with Faith and her dirty mind and she's corrupted the finest blackboard monitor class 3C ever had.'

'I wasn't going to say a word.'

'Yeah, right.' Jack took another pull on his beer. 'You know, you're looking good, mate. And I mean that in a strictly non-gay way. Lost the gut, got a bit of muscle tone going, touch of a tan.'

'Cholesterol's normal too,' Martin said, 'and I'm off the blood-pressure drugs. Armed robbery, sudden death and crazy librarians are obviously good for my health.'

'Some prescription all right, that woman,' Jack chuckled. 'You've been missing her quite a bit, eh mate?'

'Too right,' Martin sighed. 'Phone calls aren't the same, but it's how she wanted it.'

Faith had insisted on spending the time alone in Hong Kong. She wanted to come back to him with no bruises and no bandaging.

'You know, you two make quite a couple,' Jack said. 'The boys in the kitchen always talk about how you hold hands when you go out walking.'

Martin laughed. 'I'm still scared she might run away.'

Jack raised his beer in a toast. 'Beware of your belonging,' he said.

Martin joined him in the toast. 'Beware of your belonging indeed,' he smiled.

'So how's the *Belle Chance* coming along?' Jack asked.

The *Belle Chance* was a 42-foot, Cheoy Lee-built clipper

that was being restored in Macau's best boatyard. 'Going well,' Martin answered. 'Another few weeks for the rigging and sails, some sea trials, and then we take off.'

'Me and VT will miss you both,' Jack said, moving over to the barbecue. 'It's not going to be the same.'

Martin joined him and the two men inspected the coals. 'It's not like it's forever, mate. We'll just keep going till we're sick of sailing, or sick of each other.'

Jack poked at the coals with the tongs. 'I can see you getting sick of sailing, but I won't leave a lamp in the window for the other. Anyway, just remember, your apartment is here whenever you want it.'

'I know,' Martin said. 'Thanks, mate.'

'You two can go home if you want to, you know,' Jack said. 'Those new passports I got you are the real thing. Me and whoever's running the government now have agreed to let sleeping dogs lie. You'd call it a gentleman's agreement, I suppose. Not that either side really qualifies.'

'We might go back one day,' said Martin, 'but right now I'm liking things just as they are.' He settled into a chair and propped his feet up on the railing.

Jack grabbed a couple of beers from the bar fridge and handed one to Martin. 'Nice for you having Colin around for a couple of weeks, despite that early-morning unpleasantness.'

Martin twisted the cap off his beer. 'His family seemed to have a good time,' he said, 'thanks to you and VT showing them round.'

'We aim to please,' Jack said. 'And Col really reckons the powers that be back home made a million-dollar bank heist and a dead bikie just disappear?'

'Seems like it. He says it's like it never happened. The bank staff and security guards got extremely generous compensation packages, and the Albury wallopers accidentally shredded every single one of their files.'

'Politics and money, mate,' Jack said, shaking his head. 'And they reckon war is a dirty business.'

Martin stopped drinking mid-swig. 'Oh, and I just got an email from Col – the ex buzzed off with one of her sleazebag truckie boyfriends, who eventually dumped her and the kids at some low-rent back-of-Bourke roadhouse. She and the girl are waitressing and the boy's a kitchenhand. And it's in a satellite blackspot – no access to broadband.'

'And they tell ya good things don't happen to bad people,' Jack laughed. They clinked bottles and Martin glanced at his watch. 'So tonight's the big unveiling, eh?' Jack asked. 'I bet they look terrific.'

'You do realise you're talking about the breasts of the woman I love,' Martin said with mock outrage.

'Oh, come on, Martin,' Jack laughed, 'we all love her. You love her, I love her, VT loves her and Biggles loves her. And we're all gay. Except for you.'

'Biggles is gay?' Martin choked on his beer.

'Camp as a row of tents,' Jack said. 'Raging.'

'I don't believe it!'

'Think about it, mate. Ever see him hump her leg?'

Martin stared at Jack. 'Jesus,' he said, 'what a world.'

Biggles had woken up at the mention of his name. He wandered over to the two men and poked his nose out between the balcony rails. He gave a low growl, then yelped.

'Hello, here's trouble,' Jack said, leaning over the balcony.

Martin scrambled out of his chair and leapt to the railing. His heart was pounding.

On the street below, Faith had just stepped out of a cab and was paying the driver. Her hair was shorter and blonder and she was wearing an elegant black slip of a dress with a red cropped jacket. She looked fantastic. Martin gave a wolf whistle. Faith looked up and laughed.

He smiled right down to his socks. That was the package he loved. That face. That laugh. That woman.

'Piss weak, Martin,' Jack scoffed. 'Here's how you do it.' He brought his fingers to his lips, gave a long, loud slow whistle, then leaned over the edge and yelled, 'Hey gorgeous, show us ya tits!'

Faith smiled sweetly and opened her jacket, flashing the low-cut top of her dress.

Martin stared. 'Crikey,' he said softly.

Jack stared. 'Struth, Martin, I may have to rethink this whole being-gay thing.'

Biggles barked and wagged his tail.